Infected

Alan Janney

@alanjanney
ChaseTheOutlaw@gmail.com

Second Edition
Printed in USA

Cover by MS Corley
Artwork by Anne Pierson
978-0-9962293-4-0 (print)
978-0-9962293-3-3 (ebook)

Sparkle Press

For my family

Prologue

Los Angeles Times. May 1st. 2018.
"A Night With Natalie North." By Teresa Triplett

He warned us.

The Outlaw told us that we would see more…creatures like him soon, but we weren't receptive. He expressed the danger to Los Angeles, but we laughed him off. The man in the mask was stepping outside of his innocuous narrative, or so we thought, and the citizenry didn't appreciate the intrusion. Wasn't his fifteen minutes of fame enough?

We were mistaken. Los Angeles is *still* staggering. We have paid the price for our folly, for our arrogance. However, even in retrospect, how could we have possibly been prepared? I've watched the videos countless times and I still cannot believe what I'm seeing. Who *are* these people? And why can't we find them?

And speaking of missing persons, what has become of the masked man himself? We all watched him die, completely incinerated. Didn't we? Or did we all collectively hallucinate that awful night?

I first heard the rumors a week ago, and then the grainy photographs began circulating. Whispers in the dark that our hero hadn't succumbed to mortality just yet. Perhaps we are not abandoned after all.

The one person who might know for sure agreed to talk with me but either cannot or will not comment on the Outlaw. Natalie North has just finished her spring semester and is packing for Vancouver to shoot a movie. Her agent and manager has purchased her a condo in New York City, in case Los Angeles is no longer safe when filming wraps in August.

We sit down for coffee and she doesn't mince words.

"The Outlaw has been incredibly decent to me, and he might be Los Angeles's best hope for peace, if he's alive. Even if I knew anything about his life, his death, or his whereabouts, why would I betray him to the media?"

She is not mad. She is simply matter-of-fact.

I don't have an answer for her, other than a selfish one; I would sleep better at night if I knew he was still alive.

(continued on page 3A)

Infected
Die Like Supernovas

"There were giants on the earth in those days…Those were the mighty men, who were of old, men of renown."
Genesis 6:3-4.

"Sir Launcelot took another spear and unhorsed sixteen more of the King of North Galys' knights, and with his next, unhorsed another twelve; and in each case with such violence that none of the knights ever fully recovered."
– Sir Thomas Malory, The Tale of Sir Lancelot

Chapter One

Tuesday, January 1. 2018

"This is a bad idea," I said.

"You've said that before," Katie Lopez beamed at me.

"It still is."

"You're cute when you're jealous," she said and she touched me on the nose with her finger. I sat on the bed in her small, pink and perfumed room, watching her get ready for her date. I hated the outfit she'd picked; it was far too small and tight. But she just laughed when I suggested she wear sweatpants and a hoodie. Her finger turned my whole face hot and tingly.

"I'm not jealous," I protested. Again.

"Yes you are," she said, arms raised to fasten her silver necklace. "And I like it."

"I'm worried. Big difference."

"You're jealous but you're really not allowed to be. You have a girlfriend. Remember? The prettiest girl in school?" she reminded me pointedly. "And I have a date with a gorgeous Patrick Henry Dragon."

She was right about two things. One, I did have a girlfriend. I honestly kept forgetting that over the weekends. Her name is Hannah Walker and although she's high school royalty she's also very committed to her school work and cheerleading, even over the weekends. We'd never even been out on a real date. And the second thing Katie was right about, I *was* jealous.

In fact, I'm in love with her.

I had been for years. I fully admitted this to myself for the first time a few months ago, when she almost died. She'd been kidnapped in October and the police couldn't find her for over twenty-four hours. Thankfully she'd been rescued unharmed but that day was the worst of my life. Katie is my childhood best friend and I don't want to live in a world without her. I really like Hannah, my girlfriend, especially when I was around her. She's overwhelming. But Katie is a way of life for me, as important as oxygen.

"You can not, you *can not* go on a date with a Patrick Henry Dragon. We're Hidden Spring Eagles. The Dragons are our rivals," I said.

"I know! It's forbidden love, which is romantic," she grinned, and she began doing something to her face in the mirror with a makeup brush. She'd been growing increasingly pretty as she transitioned out of childhood. Did she know that? I was positive she didn't care; she only cared about being our school's next valedictorian.

"It's not romantic. And it's certainly not love! Ugh. The Dragons are scum," I said and took another bite of a chocolate bar. Katie kept her room permanently stocked with chocolate for me. I'd been bingeing on the stuff recently. She lived in an apartment down the street from my family's townhouse.

"Tank is not scum," Katie admonished me. "He's too perfect."

"Tank *is* scum. Trust me. He's a big fat dumb scumbag."

"Chase," Katie snapped. "I've been waiting to go on this date for over two months. It's January. He asked me out in October!"

"November," I corrected her. November 1st. I'd never forget that day. That awful awful day.

"Whatever! Mamá has had me barricaded in here for two months, like I'm in the witness protection program or something. I've been anticipating tonight for sixty days, Chase. So please try and not ruin it for me?"

What could I say? Nothing. I *wanted* to say so many things but *could* say none of them. What I wanted to tell her most of all?

The guy she was going out with tonight was the very big fat scumbag that had kidnapped her two months ago. She just didn't know it. And I couldn't tell her.

I secretly tailed her car downtown. Her mother was driving her to Tank's apartment in the city, and I trailed five cars back in my trusty old Toyota. Her mother, a sweet Latina lady, drove five miles under the limit so I had no problem following through the thick Los Angeles traffic. Katie would kill me if she knew.

In the stylish northeastern section of the cavernous city, not far from Echo Park, her burgundy sedan disentangled itself from the snarl and eased to a stop next to a familiar brick building. I parked illegally a block away and watched through the stop-light traffic. I was intimately familiar with that five-story apartment building. I'd never been in it, but I'd been on top of it. Weird, but true.

A massive young man emerged from the building's grand double-door entrance. It was Tank Ware. The best high school football player on the planet. Junior at Patrick Henry High. Athletic freak. Absurdly handsome. Mind-bogglingly wealthy. A latino, like Katie. Local thug. Slum lord. My nemesis. And Katie's kidnapper. Despite Katie's kidnapping being videotaped by TWO helicopters, including one flown by the police, Tank had miraculously escaped. No one knew his real identity, not even Katie.

Well, one person knew. Me. But I couldn't tell her.

I had four reasons. One, Katie already suspected I'd developed a crush on her and so she'd just assume I was lying due to jealousy. Two, everyone else would assume I was lying to get revenge on Tank, whose team had defeated mine in our recent football championship. Three, I worried what Tank might do to Katie if I 'snitched' on him. Four, and of conclusive importance, I couldn't prove a thing.

As always, Tank was wearing white gloves. One day I'd figure out why. He opened the sedan's passenger door and extended his gloved hand to Katie, but only because I didn't have laser beam eyesight and couldn't vaporize him on the spot. Blushing beautifully, Katie accepted the offered hand and stepped out of the car. Katie's mother climbed out of the driver side and walked around to be greeted by the handsome couple who had emerged from the apartment building. The two ladies hugged and then the grown-ups chatted amiably. Katie was smiling up at the young man and bouncing on her toes in excitement.

I wanted to die. But instead I pulled out a mask.

I hadn't worn the mask in two months, not since I fought Tank and found Katie. I wore it to hide my face, obviously, but it had turned into something else, something ridiculous and out of control. Cameras had filmed me while wearing the mask and national interest had been piqued. I'd been given a nickname, and now suddenly the whole world was after me. But no one knew the real identity of the Outlaw. No one except Tank, which made my blood boil.

So now he and I lived in an uneasy truce, a cold war that threatened to boil over any day.

I found a hidden corner and scrambled up the wall, my fingers and shoes grabbing surfaces that barely existed. This new trait of mine was still unnerving. I flung myself over the parapet and ran to Tank's five-story apartment building, reaching the roof via a pristine fire escape staircase. Everything was familiar. I'd been here several times visiting Natalie North, an actress that claimed to be in a romantic relationship with the Outlaw. She wasn't exactly wrong about that. But she wasn't right either. The Outlaw was just me in a ski mask, not some cool superhero. A case of mistaken identity. Or superimposed identity. Or…something weird.

I felt exposed on the roof, because this building was only five stories high and it was surrounded by taller towers. Millions of windows stared at me from above. Was I being watched?

I glared at the penthouse door. It stared back. What was I doing here? What *could* I do? It's a free country. Katie can date whoever she wants. If I bust down the door and interrupt their date, Tank would unmask me. I'd be humiliated. But…was I just supposed to sit by quietly and let it happen? Let her date her own kidnapper? I stalked back and forth, fuming.

Then, the unthinkable happened. Without warning, a bag was dumped over my head and synched at the neck. Simultaneously my hands and ankles were bound from behind. It happened so quickly, so neatly and so professionally that I was immobilized before I could move a muscle. I cried out, disoriented and confused and angry, and I was lifted off the ground. What was *happening*?! I couldn't think, couldn't process. The unseen world beyond the bag swayed and jumped. I got the impression of movement, of speed, of air and power. I kicked and bucked furiously but the hands holding me just clamped down harder. My screams got no farther than the hot bag around my face. I pulled and strained desperately at the binds around my wrists to no effect. It was useless. I could do nothing to prevent the interminable journey.

Someone laughed. A voice said, "He's mad," and then I was dropped onto the ground. With a final distressed roar, I snapped my wrists free and tore off the bag.

I was in the clouds! Or at least it appeared that way for a shaky, woozy instant. I tried to stand but the sudden change in altitude made me lightheaded. Plus my feet were still bound. I glared at my surroundings, wide-eyed. I was on top of a skyscraper, sitting on a helipad. What. The. Heck.

"Take it easy, kid," someone said. "If you fall off then I did all this work for nothing." A man was crouched on the asphalt three feet away. He reached down with a gloved hand and picked up the bindings I'd just broken. He grinned around a cigarette burning between his sharp white teeth. "Looks like I nabbed the right guy. Those were police grade plasticuffs you just snapped, hero."

My first instinct was to hit him. Hard. I was trembling, afraid and angry, and my stomach was boiling with adrenaline. But something about the man gave me pause. He appeared...formidable. He was built solidly and gave off the impression of dangerous energy. "Who are you?" I asked warily.

"That depends," he said and he snapped the plastic cuffs around my ankles with a quick knife thrust. He collected the bag and the two broken cuffs and walked to a black satchel near the iron staircase. He was wearing a black shirt and black cargo pants with a pistol holster clipped to his belt. His features were hard, the lines around his eyes were deep, and he was completely bald. He shoved the bag and the cuffs into the satchel, and he sat down crisscross on the helipad.

We were on top of the US Bank Tower, the tallest tower in the city. The colorful array of light panels gave it away, providing me with just enough ambient light to examine my captor. The air up here was cooler and the wind sang through the antennas.

"That depends on what?" I asked.

"Who I am depends on whether or not you're insane yet," he said simply. "I know that doesn't make much sense. Not yet."

"You got that right. Do you know who I am?"

"Partially. I know you like to call yourself the Outlaw," he grinned around his cigarette again. I touched my face; my mask was still on. "Seems a little...stupid, you ask me. But your mild-mannered alter ego? I have a few educated guesses."

"You were waiting for me on top of that building."

"Right you are." He held out a box of cigarettes. "You smoke?"

"No," I scoffed. "People still do that?"

"Smoking won't kill you," he smiled darkly. "Not you."

"Tell me who you are," I demanded and I stood up. I was frustrated and feeling punchy.

"Soon, kid. I promise. First," he said and he blew smoke into the atmosphere. "Let me take a few guesses about you."

"Make it quick or I'm leaving."

"The door is behind me and I won't stop you. First guess, mate. You're suffering from headaches," he said and held up one black gloved finger.

"So? It's been a stressful few months."

"Two," he said. Another finger. "You're having stomach pains too."

"This is ridiculous."

"Three," he continued, unimpressed with my surliness. "You're eighteen or nineteen. Fourth, you're experiencing intermittent superhuman speed bursts. You cannot predict or control these episodes. Am I correct?"

....whoa...I was speechless.

He kept going, "Fifth, you're having similar episodes with superhuman strength. Yes? You can run faster, jump higher, or you may be able to climb, or dig, or swim, or throw, or go without sleeping, or think faster, or even seem to make time stand still. Most of those true?"

Neither of us spoke for a long time. His gloved hand, all fingers extended, was like a slap in the face. He'd been right, five for five. Eventually he dropped his hand; he knew he was right. The whole world had incorrect guesses about me. This guy…knew everything.

"Who *are* you?" I asked. "How do you know this stuff?"

"That's easy," he puffed. "I know because I can do those things too."

Chapter Two
Tuesday, January 2. 2018

His words landed like bombs.

"Hold on," I said. "You're...you can do things? Like me? Like climb walls?"

"I can," he nodded. "But I can do them a lot better. You'll keep developing, over time."

"You've seen the news," I guessed. "Most people believe what they saw was just camera tricks or a hoax."

"We both know that's not true," he said gruffly. "Where do you think your abilities come from, mate? How can you suddenly jump rooftops? Or do whatever the hell else you can do? Do you ever wonder?" he asked.

"Sure."

"Did you think you're the only one on the planet? That can do these things?" he asked, pointed white teeth flashing. His voice was gravelly. He had a faint accent, but I couldn't place it. Australian? It wasn't very noticeable, like it'd been worn away.

"I don't know," I shrugged. I couldn't focus. It was like trying to concentrate during a tornado, I was so disoriented. "Wow, this is...this is incredible. How many people like me...like us...are there?"

"Not many."

"Where are they?"

"We're scattered, here and there. We don't all live in a commune, or something like that," he chuckled around the extinguished stub in his mouth. "I'm the guy that greets the new recruits. And I have four pieces of information for you."

"Okay."

"Four things you need to know," he said again.

"Got it. Four."

"It's a good news, bad news thing," he said while fishing another cigarette from his pocket. "Two good, two bad."

"Give me the bad news first," I suggested.

"The first thing you need to know is good," he said. He lit the cigarette and spewed fresh blue smoke. "You're not an alien."

"Oh…okay. Whew? I guess?"

"You haven't been bitten by a radioactive spider. Nothing stupid like that. The changes you're undergoing are easily explained. You don't have super powers. Nothing so glamorous. Simply put, you're sick."

"I'm sick?"

"You have a virus, to be exact. Same as me. Same as the rest of us with this unique condition. We call ourselves the Infected."

"The Infected? You said it was a virus, not an infection," I pointed out.

"I didn't pick the name. But you're right, that's always bothered me too."

"And you've determined I have this virus?"

"Unless I miss my guess." He pulled the black satchel to him and from it he retrieved a zippered portfolio. He tossed the portfolio onto the helipad and indicated I should open it. Inside were dozens of x-rays and MRIs. The pictures had circles drawn on them, but even with those clues I still didn't know what I was looking at. "We don't know much about the virus. Minimal research has been done. We Infected don't want to be lab rats, so we're a pretty secretive crew."

"What's this circled between the lungs?" I held up a x-ray.

"The thymus. It usually atrophies during adolescence. However the virus stimulates the thymus and keeps it active for the rest of your life, which causes growth abnormalities. The x-ray in your right hand is *mine*. The x-ray in your left is a normal adult's. See the difference? Same with the MRI pictures. The virus also stimulates the adrenal glands, the testes, the frontal cortex, and lots of other crap I can't remember. The virus is stimulated by fight or flight episodes. These hyper-aggressive states accelerate the virus's symptoms."

"All these medical documents mean nothing to me. What exactly does the virus do to your body?"

"I don't know why I even keep those records," he sighed. "No one understands them."

"Sorry."

"What does the virus do? It causes massive physiological changes. Those of us that survive will have a greater volume of adrenaline in our veins, more serotonin, more epinephrin, better circulation, faster mental processes, a higher quantity and quality of quick twitch muscle, greater bone density, better immune system, rapid healing abilities, significantly heightened hand-eye coordination, hyper-accurate senses, great strength…that kind of thing."

"Whoa…"

"Now you see why it's a secret. Pharmaceutical companies would spend millions of dollars tracking us down and slicing us up to bottle the virus. Governments would try to weaponize us. Our lives would be over."

"Aren't you stronger and faster than pharmaceutical companies?"

"Sure, kid. To be honest, we could topple a small government. But a small group of us against the might of the American military? Get real."

"So you can't fly? Or shoot laser beams out of your eyes?"

"Don't be an ass, kid," he growled. "You have a disease that causes your body to overproduce parts of itself. You're not Superman. It's your body, just sped up and strengthened."

"Wait…you just said…*those of us that survive*. What does that mean?"

"That's the second thing you need to know," he said with a grim expression. "The virus is powerful. The body isn't made to endure the changes it's manufacturing. It almost always over-loads your system and your brain just…turns off."

"Turns off?"

"That's the nasty part of the virus. It's almost always fatal. I'm sorry."

"Fatal," I repeated. I felt like someone had poured ice water down my back.

"Those headaches and stomachaches you've been having? That's the virus. And they're going to get worse. That's why there aren't many Infected alive. The virus kills everyone who gets it, basically."

I didn't say anything. I remembered standing outside Katie's apartment and dry heaving in her shrubs because of stress and headaches. He gave me time to digest the news. How much madness could the brain absorb? I had to be near the limit.

Fatal. I could be dead before my senior year. Before summer. No more Dad. No more...Katie. I wanted to laugh it off, but too many things he said rang true. Fatal. Fatal. The concept was still abstract, like it didn't affect me. Fatal. I couldn't digest it. I numbly walked to the edge of the helipad. The US Bank Tower was tall. I didn't know exactly how tall, but it was over 70 floors. The enormous lights below us cast our conversation into surreal shades of neon. I stared over the city, a blanket of glowing crystals sweeping to the ocean. Behind me the lights stretched to the Angeles National Forest mountains.

"I've done the math. One kid in ten million gets infected. Ninety percent of those kids die when they *start* puberty. Nine-ty per-cent. The virus is too strong," he said and exhaled a cloud of smoke. "We call it the Hyper Human Virus, for lack of a better term. You have to be a freak to survive it."

"And if you do, you're superhuman," I mused.

"Those that survive puberty, which apparently you did, almost always die at the end of adolescence. For you, mate, that's right now. Something to do with the development of the frontal cortex. I'm not a doctor and so I'm probably remembering the wrong terms."

"So...you're saying that statistically my brain is just going to turn off soon."

"Or you'll go insane. That happens a lot too."

I barked a laugh and said, "Speaking of insanity...this is the most over-the-top, ludicrous, outrageous, ridiculous thing I've ever heard! Can you prove any of this crap?"

"Don't believe me?"

"Your story would be more believable if you had evidence. Other than your incomprehensible medical records."

"That's what they all say," he sighed, and he reached into his pocket. "Ye of little faith." He pulled out a handful of quarters and tossed one to me. "Bend it."

"Bend it?"

"Bend it," he repeated.

"It's a quarter. It's hard. I can't. You bend it," I said and threw it back. He caught it and immediately folded the coin over on itself, pressing it neatly in half. Then he did it again, using only two fingers, and he tossed it back. The bent edges were warm. Impossible! "Fine. You're strong. I'm impressed with your strength. Wow. Yay for you. That all you got?"

"Watch," he said and he started juggling the quarters. He had at least ten. His hands were a blur, although he appeared to exert no effort. "So, this virus. It affects different bodies in different ways. I'm strong, but not as strong as some. I'm quick, but not as quick as the others. But I do have heightened hand-eye coordination. And you've forgotten one thing. How'd you get up here?"

"I don't know. I had a bag over my face," I shot at him.

"I carried you," he said. "And we didn't use an elevator. Or the stairs. Explain that." He caught all the quarters in one hand and began flexing his fist. "We went up the old fashioned way. We climbed." He squeezed and his arm trembled and then he threw me a small ball of hot metal. The quarters had all been fused into one solid piece.

"That's incredible," I breathed.

"I have the disease, I survived, and now I can do that," he said quietly. "You might be able to survive too. There's a trick to it. That's the third thing you need to know."

"Okay," I said, numb, staring into the ball of quarters. "Tell me the trick."

"Starting to believe me?" he grinned without humor, another cigarette now dead in his teeth.

"I don't know. Probably," I said and rubbed my eyes. "Maybe."

"If you can get through the crucial late adolescence period, then your mind and body will be almost in-de-structible. The changes hit me hard close to my nineteenth birthday. The pain came in waves for a few months, and then it stopped. Everyone says the same."

"The pain?"

"Growing pains from hell," he nodded.

"Tell me how you did it."

"Like I said, there's a trick. At lease we're pretty sure. It's hard to do, and even if you can manage it you still might die," he shook his head as if re-experiencing the ordeal.

"Tell me."

"Here it is, kid. Number three. The good news. The hope. During this whole thing, your brain will be vulnerable. Your brain is crucial. The only shot you got is relaxing. Calm down. Sleep. Find peace and rest and avoid all stress. Your brain and your psyche are very fragile and tender, and any stressors you put on either will snap them. Imagine your brain as a partially torn tendon. If you try to exert the tendon it'll simply snap. The tendon must be fully healed before you put any significant weight on it," he said, pointing at the patella tendon in my knee. "Just like your brain. You will snap it in half by exerting it before it's healed."

"That sounds easy," I chuckled in relief. "I just won't put any weight on it. On my brain and psyche, I mean."

"Ain't so simple, kid. Two problems. One, the pain you'll be in will not allow you to relax. Two, your body will be pumping so much adrenaline through your veins that you won't be able to sit still. Your systems will be super charged. You'll explode if you try to sit still. In other words, to survive you must be relaxed and at peace, but the virus won't allow that. It hurts and irresistibly demands action. You crave action. Thus, your Outlaw gig."

"My Outlaw gig?"

"You think it's mere coincidence that you started this nationally celebrated charade at the precise time the symptoms started? No way, kid. It's no accident. The virus was driving you into the night, to the top of towers. We Infected die young like supernovas. We burn up fast and bright."

"That makes a lot of sense," I admitted. It all fit. And at the same time, this was madness.

"Also, stay away from alcohol or anything else that messes with your brain."

"So…this trick is good news. Which means there is more bad news," I remembered.

"Right. The fourth thing you need to know."

"Great," I said dryly. "Can't wait to hear how this gets worse."

He lazily but efficiently withdrew a revolver from the holster strapped to his thigh. He pointed it at my forehead and thumbed back the hammer, and the weapon made a heavy clicking sound. My breath caught.

"I'm not going to kill you," he said evenly. "But I came here tonight prepared to. My mission was to determine if you were insane yet. If you were…bang. I'd put one in your temple and be on my way."

"What makes you think I'd let you shoot me?" I asked with much more stability and bravado in my voice than I felt. I wanted to squirm away from the GIGANTIC barrel of his gun.

"Kid," he laughed around the extinguished stub in his mouth. "I know you're fast. But you're still getting used to your own body. Me? I've had mine a long time. But I can tell you're not crazy. You are lucid and logical and rational. So I'm here to educate you. Take a good look at this gun. I want you to realize how serious I am. How serious the Infected are."

"Okay."

"The fourth thing is this. If you start to go insane, you will be executed."

"Executing the new recruits doesn't seem very collegial," I growled.

He lowered the hammer and holstered his revolver. I enjoyed a deep sigh of relief. "My job isn't to be friendly. My job is to evaluate the newbies and then either educate or execute them."

"Why would I go insane?"

"The virus is causing powerful changes in your body. Usually you'll simply fall dead, likely from an aneurysm. OBE. Overcome by events. That's where your headaches are coming from," he said, pointing at me with his dead cigarette. "The virus is too strong. Bam, dead. Easy. No messy cleanup. However sometimes the result is that the brain breaks but doesn't stop. Thus, insanity. If that occurs, we can't wait for the aneurysm. We finish them off before the virus gets around to it."

"Why do you finish them off?"

"Imagine the nightmare scenario if we didn't. If you're sick and some of your symptoms are insanity and freakish strength, then you're going to hurt a lot of people. And draw attention."

"So you enforce the secrecy," I nodded. That made sense. Morbid sense.

"Right."

"How do you find the new recruits?"

He chuckled without humor and said, "A person developing superhuman abilities while simultaneously losing their mind isn't hard to find. If you know what to look for," he said pointedly.

"Like the Outlaw," I realized.

"Like the Outlaw," he agreed. "At least you've been smart enough to cover up your insanity with a mask."

"How many times a year do you do this?"

"Christ, you ask a lot of questions. A couple times a year, on average" he said.

"How many Infected are there total?"

"If you survive, you'll bring the total number up to ten."

"That's it?" I cried.

"That I know of. Might be others in hiding."

"And you're the boss?"

He frowned and shook his head. "We don't have a boss. I just meet the new recruits. That's my job. Now you're someone else's problem."

"Unless I go insane," I reminded him. "Then you'll come kill me."

"No. Not me. I just handle the initial encounter. But I will tell you this, kid. We are a secretive group. We don't like attention. And you dressing up like a superhero and jumping around on roof tops? That draws attention."

"So?"

"Like you said, we enforce the secrecy." He made a gun with his thumb and finger. "Pow." He dropped his thumb and shot me.

"You're threatening to kill me if I keep acting like the Outlaw," I realized with a snarl.

"Not me kid," he spread his arms out wide, palms up, grinning. "Not my job."

"Whose job is it?"

"It's the Shooter's job," he said.

"The Shooter?!"

"Yeah, I know. Not a great name. But, it fits this particular individual."

"Ridiculous," I snapped. "You're here to tell me that I'm going to die in a few months. And if I keep attracting attention, someone named the Shooter will come shoot me even sooner than that?"

"Not *will* come. *Has* come. The Shooter's plane landed last week."

"This is the most bizarre thing I've ever heard," I almost yelled. "So what's your name? The Revolver? The Killer of Crazy Infected Newbies?"

"My name's Carter."

"Your name sucks," I grumbled.

"Sorry, mate."

"So I've only got a few months left," I sighed, trying to keep my anger in check and keep the facts straight. "Unless I find a way to relax. And quit gallivanting around as the Outlaw."

"Bingo. No more televised roof jumping."

"What about you? Can you jump over buildings from the street?" I asked. "I jumped up two stories a few months ago."

"I got you up here, didn't I? But I'm getting old now. My knees aren't the same as they were. I could probably *throw* you over a building."

"How old are you? Now that you've survived, how long will you live?" I asked.

"I plan on being here a while. And let's just say I'm older than your great grandparents. I'm aging slowly."

"How can I climb walls?"

"Simple. You're stronger, including your fingers. Inhumanly nimble with unreal dexterity. Your finger tips and feet can take advantage of ledges you can barely see. It's not magic."

His phone rang. I could see it light up in one of his pants pockets. He unzipped the pocket and retrieved the vibrating device.

"Yes? …things are fine. …I think the costume is stupid too. …Right." He hung up.

"The Shooter?"

"Yep," he said and he flicked the dead butt over the edge of the helipad into the Los Angeles night.

"Is the Shooter watching us?"

"Nah. You're nothing I can't handle. Aren't you hot in that thing?" he asked, indicating my mask.

"It's permeable," I replied in a fog. "So what happens now?"

"You die."

"Listen to me," I snapped, pointing my finger at him. "I'm not going anywhere. Understand? I'm not afraid. Not of you, not of your Shooter, and not of your virus. I'll do what I need to do to beat it, if it's even legit. I've overcome bigger obstacles than this. I'm going to live a long time. Get used to it," I said from some unknown reservoir of confidence and surety.

"I like your arrogance, kid. Survive and we'll talk further. I'll stick around, and check on you now and then. Sometimes I just go home but…you're an interesting case. I'm curious to see how this plays out. I want to see if the virus or the Shooter kills you first." He stood up and shrugged into his backpack. "Before I go…" he said and he pulled out a newspaper. It was a copy of a football profile written back in the fall. A portion of the article was written about me. The rest was written about Tank. "This is you, isn't it?" he asked, pointing at the picture of me. "I thought you might be Tank, but despite the mask I can tell that you're not him. You're Chase Jackson."

"That's my mild-mannered alter ego," I replied.

"Oh. One final piece of advice. Don't go to a doctor for help. They draw blood. And your blood is a very important and very valuable secret. Shooter will kill you instantly if you try. Hopefully we'll meet again," he smiled grimly. Then he scooped out another handful of quarters and bounced them in his hand, measuring them, organizing them. "Good luck to you," he said and he hurled the quarters at my feet. I flinched away, expecting the coins to ricochet and scatter in every direction. But they didn't. To my astonishment, all the coins were neatly imbedded halfway through the rock hard surface.

Unreal. He'd buried the quarters into the asphalt.

I glanced up…but he was gone. I spun around, searching the roof. Nothing. He'd vanished.

"Show off," I scowled.

The date was over. I perched like a guardian angel on top of Tank's roof, exhausted from the long trip back from the tower. Tank and his parents waved goodbye to Katie and her mother. I needed to send Tank a message. A strong one. He was tormenting me by going on this date, and I wanted to hit him back, to let him know I wasn't going anywhere. I didn't want to hurt him or his family. I only wanted to convince him to leave me and Katie alone.

So I threw the metal ball of quarters through his window, like a pitcher throwing a fastball. The glass pane shattered and things smashed inside. When Tank returned upstairs he'd find a nasty surprise waiting. As the crash was still echoing off the surrounding cathedral of windows I fled the scene and decided Carter might be right. About everything.

Which meant I was in trouble.

Chapter Three
Wednesday, January 2. 2018

Wednesday. The first day of the rest of my life. I had two goals.

Stay alive.

Stop Tank from hurting Katie.

Simple. I could do that.

Second semester began today at Hidden Spring High. Our school is in an affluent section of Glendale, a wealthy suburb of the Greater Los Angeles Area. Our school is new and polished, with state-of-the-art equipment ready in every room. Despite the amenities, we still have the same problems other schools have; loneliness, depression, anger, peer pressure, all that fun stuff.

I had Pre-Calc first period, Spanish Three second, Advanced Strength and Conditioning third, and Chemistry fourth. My girlfriend Hannah and I shared no classes this semester, but Katie and I had Spanish Three together. This would be interesting.

My relationship with Hannah Walker was complicated. We hardly ever saw each other. She was a cheerleader and fully immersed in the basketball season. In fact, the pace of her life had recently increased because she had to prepare for the upcoming spring cheerleading dance competition. Plus, she was an extremely driven student. She stayed at the library long into the evenings, re-writing notes, reading through her text books, and practicing for tests. Her desire to get into the top Universities absolutely and entirely trumped her romantic life.

Despite being almost a nerd about her grades, she completely ruled the school, though that hobby didn't interest her much. Due to her good-looks, her family's prosperity, and her position as the cheerleading captain, she was already at the top of the social food-chain without much effort. But winning high school popularity contests didn't figure into preparations for her future. She exercised her fame just enough to maintain her reign over the social scene, and that did not include unnecessary dates with her boyfriend.

It was a strange arrangement between Hannah and I, but it worked. I guess. The pros outweighed the cons, as she liked to point out. The primary benefit was that it left me ample time for Katie, for whom I'd leave Hannah in a second.

My life is weird.

Hannah met me in the school's parking lot on Tuesday, our first day back after New Year's break. She kissed me and ran her hands through my hair and warmly asked about my weekend. This was a weekly performance she believed necessary to secure my loyalty.

"Have a good day, quarterback," she cooed and she strutted off to her first class. I didn't move. People began flowing around me in the hallway. *Quarterback.* That's right! She was primarily interested in me because I was the quarterback of our football team, but I was never going to play football again. I was either going to die any day, like Carter predicted, or I'd survive and have to give up the sport. I couldn't play against other kids when I had a tremendous advantage. Right?

In fact! The disease explained my success last season. I played FAR too well and nobody could postulate how a rookie like me had achieved so much. I could throw a football forever and outrun the whole team. Holy moly, this explained so much. I'd been cheating! *Was* it cheating? Did a disease that made you faster and stronger before killing you count as cheating?

The bell rang. I was late to class.

"How was your date with Tank?" I asked as Katie and I dropped our backpacks and sat next to each other in Spanish class. I tried and failed not to stare. Her cheekbones and her dark eyes and her perfect skin and her brown hair and her quick infectious smile were becoming harder to ignore.

"Are you listening to me?" she frowned, interrupting my thoughts.

"What? Sorry. Go ahead."

"I said, are you sure you want to hear about it?"

"Of course," I said.

"It was magical!"

"Never mind," I groaned. "I don't want to hear about it."

"Too bad. You asked. His parents are super nice, and they are crazy rich. I mean, wow. And Tank is very sweet and kind."

"Tank is a stupid name," I grumbled.

"No it's not, shut up. He cooked us dinner. Can you believe that?! He cooked for me. Some sort of chicken in raspberry sauce. And Mami liked him too. And it was so nice to get out of the house!"

"What'd you talk about?"

"I don't know," she shrugged. "Not a lot. It was a short date. His parents wanted to know how I've been since the abduction."

Katie had vaulted into a temporary celebrity after being rescued by the Outlaw. The police and the media had interviewed her for a couple weeks straight, and she'd even been featured in a small article inside People magazine. Her story didn't have much staying power because she didn't remember a single detail.

"We'll be able to talk longer on our next date," she said.

"Your *next* date?" I asked, sitting up straighter.

"He asked me out again," she beamed.

"Did you say 'Yes'?" I shouted in alarm.

"Of course! He's so nice, and oh so fine."

"I think he's ugly," I said.

"Of course you do. You're jealous."

"Oh shut up," I sighed, and class started.

Going out again?! What did I expect? That Tank would accidentally let it slip that he was the one that kidnapped her? This was a nightmare. I couldn't concentrate the rest of class.

At lunch, we sat with Cory and Lee, our two best friends. Cory is a quiet giant and plays football on the offensive line. He's black, wants to be a chef and primarily listens to classical music. Lee is a little Asian genius that tutors me in math. Like most days, he was dressed in an Outlaw shirt. Lee is also an inventor, and had tried for weeks to get the Outlaw's attention on Craigslist so the masked vigilante could experiment with one of his weapons. When Katie had been kidnapped I'd pulled on my mask and gone to visit Lee as the Outlaw. I'd used his electroshock device to help rescue Katie, and Lee had been talking about it ever since. If he ever found out that I was the Outlaw he'd be crushed.

Despite our protests Katie regaled us with details about her date with Tank. Cory, Lee and I felt like the parents in Romeo and Juliet, trying to stop this forbidden love.

"I still don't think Tank's the Outlaw," Lee frowned. "I don't care what those conspiracy websites say, dude. No way. Tank is not the Outlaw." As always, Lee kept his eyes fixed on the news channel broadcasting from the television suspended on the wall behind us.

"Yeah, he's absolutely not," I agreed. Much of the world had forgotten the Outlaw in the two months since his disappearance, but not Lee. He steered our conversation back to him about once a lunch. Rumors were rampant online about the Outlaw's alter ego, and one of the debated possibilities was Tank Ware.

"Did you ask Tank if he was the Outlaw?" Lee asked Katie.

"No," she said slowly, uncertainly.

"But...?"

"But he mentioned the Outlaw several times," she admitted. "When we were alone."

"He did?" I said, surprised and angered. "What'd he say? What do you mean alone?"

"He thinks I should know who the Outlaw is," she said. She appeared uncomfortable and hesitant, and she played with her lunch. "He wanted to know if I'd heard the rumors about him being the Outlaw."

I said, "He wishes. His giant bulbous nose would never fit into that tight mask. Did he knock over anything with his huge nose?"

"His nose is perfect. But I don't know what to believe. I've never met the Outlaw, you know."

That's true. Katie had never met the Outlaw. Maybe she should. Hmmmm. That could be hot. I started sweating.

"I met him," Lee said for the thousandth time. "And Tank is no Outlaw, yo. You know what I'm going to do?"

"You're going to text the Outlaw," Cory said, speaking for the first time. "S'what you always say."

"Yeah, I'm going to text the Outlaw," Lee nodded.

Katie smiled and said, "You've texted him a hundred times. He never responds."

"Yeah, but I'm going to tell him about Tank pretending," Lee scowled. "He's gotta know. He's gotta whip some ass."

I kept quiet. I had two cell phones. One was for personal use. The other was for Outlaw business, and Lee had been texting the Outlaw phone incessantly since I'd called him on it in October. I hadn't responded. I didn't know what to say.

"Besides," I said. "The Outlaw is gone. No one has seen him in two months. I bet we never see him again."

"No way, dude," Lee shook his head. "No way. He's coming back."

"The riots are getting worse," Katie observed, watching the television. A new controversial law had ignited minority unrest in Los Angeles, and the violence was escalating. Thousands broke curfew every night. The jails were completely full. Racial tensions had erupted into fights at schools everywhere recently, including ours. The law was aimed at illegal immigrants and it was incredibly harsh. Most citizens couldn't believe the bill had been signed into law, and sympathized with the latino community's outrage, but laws were laws. The local congressmen and women did not appear interested in overturning it so far.

"Yeah," Cory sighed philosophically. "And the Sniper isn't helping."

"What Sniper?" I asked.

"Someone is running around downtown, nailing people with wax bullets, yo," Lee chimed in. "No one has seen him. Or them. He's either hiding in a car or shooting them from a long distance."

"Wax bullets," I mused. "Do they hurt?"

"Yes, but not bad. Non-lethal. Scares the bejesus out of the victims," Lee laughed. "This guy is just causing trouble. Sounds kind of fun."

Katie scolded him, "Lee, that's an awful thing to say."

"See for yourself," Lee said and he slid me his phone. A grainy security video played, obviously of a gas station. After a few seconds one of the pumpers jerked, spun in a circle, and collapsed. The other customers stared curiously before ducking behind cars. "See, man? Nobody seriously hurt. People just freak out, act like they're dying."

"So weird," I said, and then I stood up. "Be right back."

Our cafeteria had to be the only one on the planet with floor to ceiling windows on every wall. The floor sparkled with all the sunlight streaming in. I walked across the raucous lunchroom to see my girlfriend. She sat at a power table with the most popular girls in school, chatting and eating carrot sticks and drinking bottled water. My journey attracted attention, especially from Andy Babington, Hannah's ex-boyfriend.

"Hey babe," I said, arriving at her table. A thousand big eyes with long lashes turned to scrutinize me.

"Hello boyfriend," Hannah Walker smiled at me.

"How were your classes?"

"Good," she said. She smiled again. I smiled too. So did everyone at the table. She waited. I waited. And I thought desperately of something else to say. "How were yours?" she asked.

"Oh, good!" I said. "Yeah, good."

"Good!"

"Yeah," I said. I shoved my hands into my pockets. "Good."

She smiled again. Me too. I was blanking on every other word in the dictionary. I stood there, paralyzed and perspiring.

"I'll see you later?" she asked, effectively dismissing me.

"Sure. Definitely. See you," I said awkwardly, pathetically, and slunk back to my table. That was awful. Girls are so confusing. I'm probably the worst boyfriend in the world, but she didn't make it easy on me either.

Lee said, "That was ugly, bro."

"Crash and burn," Cory rumbled.

"Yeah crash and burn, bro."

I mumbled, "Thanks guys."

"Really really bad," Katie said through a beautiful smile. "Just painful to watch. Go do it again. Otra vez."

"Shut up."

"Anyway. How's your father?" she asked, changing subjects. My father was still recovering from a car accident. He used to be a police detective but he'd been unable to do his job for almost a year.

"Getting better," I said. "He finished physical therapy."

"That's great news. Good for him!" she gushed. "I didn't know physical therapy was over. You never tell me anything anymore, not since we stopped sleeping together."

"What?" Lee demanded.

"What?" I asked her, turning red.

"Not like that," Katie said, blushing too. "Back when you used to sleep on my floor. When that creep was texting me and you persisted on bunking in my room."

"Oh," I laughed. "Right. Yeah. Then." I wished I could tell her the creep texting her was really Tank. That would change everything. But I couldn't. Oooooooh the secrets, the awful secrets.

"So your dad really is feeling better?" she pressed.

"Yeah, he's good."

I was good too. Really good. The warnings from Carter felt faraway, almost imaginary, like a dream. I went to sleep early that night, my covers and pillow were perfect and cool from a faint January chill. My dad had fallen asleep in his chair facing the television. The house was quiet. The doors were locked. My girlfriend had texted me a picture of her smiling, telling me she was sorry about being awkward at lunch. I had no headaches. Nothing hurt. Life was bliss.

For that one night.

Chapter Four
Thursday, January 3. 2018

"Chase Jackson?"

I turned to see who called my name; a girl I didn't recognize was approaching. She was wearing football pads, which was such an anomaly that I forgot to respond.

We stood on our school's green practice field under a cloudless deep blue sky. School campuses are a hubbub of athletic practices after classes end. From my vantage point I could see the cross-country team jogging, the cheerleaders tumbling, a few wrestlers stretching outside the gym, and the junior varsity soccer team huddled around their head coach. The varsity football team was with me, drilling. Football season was over but we still practiced our craft several days a week, those of the team that weren't playing other sports.

For the moment I was alone with a hopper full of footballs. Except for the new girl. I'd been staring at the footballs warily, wondering if I truly was sick, remembering a practice in August when I'd nearly thrown a football clear out of the stadium, and idly calculating how far I could throw one now, when she'd shown up. She was attractive but not in a cute way. She might be the most fit and athletic girl I'd ever seen. She looked hard but friendly. Her brown hair was cut short, barely reaching her chin.

"You're wearing football pads," I observed intelligently. I'm so smart.

"So are you. I'm Samantha Gear," she introduced herself and shook my hand. "You can quit checking me out. I'm trying out for Varsity kicker next year."

"I don't understand," I floundered.

"Are you Chase Jackson? Or the village idiot?"

"Maybe…both?"

"I'm a kicker. I'm good," she said slowly, patiently, like I was dense. Which I was. "I'll kick field goals. For the football team."

"But you're a girl," I observed less intelligently.

"I'm good at that, too."

"Can girls play football? I mean, are they eligible?"

"Girls kick for teams all over the country. It even happens in college now," she explained with a touch of defiance. I didn't blame her. "Rumor is you're a good quarterback, and I wanted to introduce myself."

"*Lucky* quarterback, more like it," Andy Babington laughed, walking up beside us. Andy was the starting quarterback last season until he broke his hand. He is tall, blond, strong and attractive. We were not on the best terms. He was practicing with us, honing his throwing motion, because he was throwing for college scouts soon to earn a scholarship. "Right, big guy?" he asked and smacked me on the back. "So. A girl kicker. Hah."

"More like a kicker that's also a girl, and also getting a little exasperated with stupid boys. Who are you?" she studied him with mild disapproval, which made me like her more. She crossed her arms and glanced between us. Andy stiffened.

"I'm the starting quarterback for the Hidden Spring Eagles," he shot at her. "When my hand's not broken."

"Never heard of you. And real men keep playing, even with broken bones. I read that Chase played with fractured ribs and busted organs."

"We already have a kicker next year. Thanks for playing. You're dismissed," he sneered.

"I just watched your boy kick," she bit off the words. "And that's what he is. A boy. I can kick farther in my sleep."

"Yeah right," Andy laughed, hands on hips. "Who are you anyway? A nobody."

"I just moved here from Oklahoma, where I own the state record for long distance field goal. And if you weren't so fat I could kick *you* through the uprights," she said, and then she grabbed my jersey. "Follow me, Chase."

I let her draw me away from a fuming Babington. I obediently followed because she was fascinating. Who has that kind of guts? That kind of confidence?

"I thought you were bigger than this," she said, scanning me from shoes to hair. She appeared disappointed. "You look taller and broader in the pictures."

"I get that a lot."

"Time for you and your coach to watch me kick," she said. "And you could have backed me up, you know. With what's-his-name, the second string quarterback," she said, and she backhanded me in the gut. Hard.

"I don't even know you," I grunted, rubbing my stomach. "And I already forgot your name."

"But you think I'm hot."

"Uh…" I stammered.

"It's okay. I'm used to it. Besides, I'm in your math class. We met in pre-calc yesterday."

"We did?"

"Yes," she rolled her eyes. "Now introduce me to your coach."

She pulled me towards Coach Garrett, a tall, ramrod straight man under a baseball cap and sunglasses.

"Coach," I said as she shoved me from behind. "I'd like you to meet someone."

"I'm Samantha Gear," she interrupted me and shook his hand. "My former football coach called you yesterday, I hope?"

"Yeah, yeah," Garrett said. "That's right. The girl kicker with the state record."

"That's me," she confirmed. "I'd like permission to work out with your team."

"Well this is a first," he grinned, chomping on his gum.

"Not really. Happens all the time. Babington is already trying to get rid of me, but Chase Jackson wants to see me kick. See if I'm any good," she said, lying smoothly.

Before I could deny this, Coach said, "Knock yourself out. Field goal unit is warming up."

"Great!" She jogged on to the field.

Coach Garrett and I stood silently as she introduced herself to the long-snapper, the holder and our current kicker. I didn't even know our kicker's name. Embarrassing. I need to get better with names, apparently. The four of them kept stretching; the three guys did their best not to stare at her but they failed. Coach Todd Keith, our offensive coordinator, walked up to watch the recent developments.

"I'll be damned," Garrett said.

"Can she kick?" Coach Todd Keith asked.

"Guess we'll find out," Coach Garrett said.

I said, "She's like a whirlwind."

"She's got moxie, I'll give her that."

"What's moxie?"

"Stones, Ballerina," he said, referring to me by my hated nickname. "Sand. Guts. She's got guts. This is going to be trouble," he said, gum smacking. "A lot of damn trouble. But she's the best looking thing I've ever seen in pads. Eh, Chase?"

"Are you allowed to say that, Coach?"

"Just make sure you keep your hands off her," he ordered.

"Coach, I..."

"I'll never forgive you if you blow it with that cheerleader," he barked. "Hands off."

"Yeah, definitely, no sweat," I said. "Hands off." Assistant Coach Todd Keith laughed.

Our kicker lined up and kicked a forty-yard field goal, which was pretty good in high school. He stood aside, nodding his head smugly, confident in his superiority.

Then Samantha Gear kicked. Her lines were long, her posture straight, her muscles hard, her motion fluid, and her form perfect. She drilled the ball. Absolutely destroyed it. I'd never seen a ball kicked that hard. She made a forty-yard field goal that would have been good from over fifty, a length very

very few teenagers can reach.

"I'll be damned," Garrett grinned again. "Got ourselves a new kicker."

Just then, the outdoor public-address speakers blared to life.

"**Students and staff. We've just been ordered by the Sheriff to execute a campus lockdown. If you are near the building, come inside immediately and you'll be escorted to the nearest classroom. If you are closer to the parking lots and you have your keys, please get into your vehicle and drive home immediately. If you see anyone you don't know, do not approach them. This is not a drill. The police will be arriving soon. I repeat, we've just been ordered by the Sheriff…**"

The announcement continued. Schools are scary places recently, with campus shootings happening more frequently, and this was as terrifying an announcement as I could imagine. We were much closer to the parking lots than the school structures, so all the coaches began bawling out orders, urging us to our cars. Kids sprinted off the fields, confused but convinced.

Katie! Where was she??

But…she had no extracurricular activities today. She's already home. Thank goodness.

What about Hannah? I glared through the rushing mob of athletes until I spotted her across the field, gathering her bags. She wasn't moving fast enough. I sprinted to her, weaving through the other kids, with a sack of footballs bouncing over my shoulder.

"Hannah, we have to go," I yelled.

"I'm coming, I'm coming," she replied. "I'm sure this is just precautionary." I hefted the bags she'd been struggling with and turned towards our cars.

That's when they arrived.

A heaving sea of humanity climbed over the ivy fence on the border of our school's practice fields. Hundreds and hundreds of men. They were scrambling up the chain link fence and the vines and landing on our grass. Those who had already made it over were sprinting towards us, towards the school. It was a haunting, freaky sight.

"Ugh. Who are they?" Hannah asked with disdain.

"I don't know. Let's go," I said with more urgency, and we started jogging towards the car. "This is obviously not precautionary."

The gangs of people behind us were shouting in Spanish. I risked a glance backwards. All the attackers looked hispanic. So this was a protest, one of the recent racial riots.

"*Vete a casa! No habrá problemas! Ir a casa o vamos a hacerte daño!*"

"Jackson, you okay?" someone shouted. It was Samantha Gear, jogging alongside us.

"Who's she?" Hannah inquired. For the moment, I ignored her.

"Do you know what they're saying?" I asked Samantha.

"They're yelling that we need to leave or they'll hurt us. Telling us to go home," she replied.

"Good idea. Get out of here, kicker," I shouted, leading Hannah into the parking lot. Samantha vanished among the luxury cars. Hannah and I found her car and loaded the bags.

"Get in?" Hannah asked me, lowering into the drivers seat. Jeez she was gorgeous. She'd never starve; she could sell a hundred cars a day just by climbing into them.

"No, that's okay," I said, monitoring the crowd of latinos still on the fields. We were safe now. There would be no violence. The protestors weren't attacking students or coming into the parking lot. They were just overturning trashcans and spray painting messages on the grass and the walls. The men had a message that they wanted to reach national attention, and rioting on a rich campus was a sure-fire way to do it. In a minute or so they'd disperse before the authorities arrived. "Take off. Text me when you get home safely."

"I will. Thanks boyfriend!" she called, gunning the engine and joining the congestion jockeying for the exit.

I walked away, a little shaky from the adrenaline rush. Los Angeles was getting more and more dangerous and the violence was spreading. A recent Dodgers game had been postponed for safety reasons. This protest wasn't mean spirited or overly savage, but how long could that last?

I was angry. Angry and jumpy. I probably shouldn't have been but the sudden riotous onslaught had startled me and now I was mad. These guys were only trying to make a political statement that could improve the living conditions of their children...but I was still pissed. I didn't want to hurt anyone, just cause a little trouble.

I dropped the black mesh football bag and grabbed one of the the balls. The bulk of intruders was about fifty yards away, swarming and spray painting one of the fields. After a moment's inspection I spied one of the leaders. He was issuing orders and laughing.

"Okay, my friend," I said. "Pride goes before the fall."

I spun the ball in my hands and pathways began to materialize in the air. I could almost literally see the angles I should throw if I wanted to hit him hard or hit him soft, hit him in the head or in the stomach.

I could do anything with this football.

He turned to stalk towards a thicket of spray painters near the bleachers and I spotted my moment. I set and loosed a tight spiral that went whistling across the parking lot and straight into his foot as he was striding. I'd thrown hard. The collision caused him to miss his footfall and he fell, landing sharply with a cry.

Beautiful! Glorious! Hah! I was so far away that he never even looked in my direction.

He rose in a rush, furiously casting about for the cause of humiliation. His friends were laughing at him. He tried to storm off but another football streaked in, again disrupting his stride, and again he collapsed. He was outraged!

Well, that was fun. But perhaps I shouldn't be a bully. Time for me to go. I left the fuming man on the ground behind.

I spotted my car from a distance. It was...it looked...it was on fire! What?! Smoke was pouring out of the cracked windows, and the chairs smoldered. As I approached, the interior fabric reached a terminal heat and caught fire all at once. The rear view mirror was dripping. The texture of the paint and the glass was changing, distorting. There was a guttural cough under the vehicle and then a louder hot crash as the gas tank exploded. My old faithful beat-up Toyota was toast.

I laid in bed that night monitoring the news, exhausted from talking with police and my insurance agent. The police declared arson. No one had seen a thing. I could postulate one culprit, but I certainly wouldn't tell the cop that Tank Ware had done it in retaliation for me throwing a ball of quarters through his window. The insurance adjuster would send me a tiny tiny check soon for a replacement car, but it wouldn't be enough. My father had glared from his lazy-boy, like it was all my fault.

My bank account still had some money from a generous gift I'd received last year, and I was about to open my account online to check the balance when the news coverage of our school attack came on the television. The Sheriff officially labeled it a protest against the recent sanctions passed in congress. No one had been hurt and only six were arrested, the vandals with spray paint cans. Then another news story caught my eye and I sat up in bed.

A smiling news anchor I didn't recognize said, "And perhaps our most important news story this evening, or at least the juiciest…we have an Outlaw sighting! You probably know the Outlaw has been missing in action for months, not seen since the dramatic rooftop showdown with the mystery villain that kidnapped teenager Katie Lopez. The internet has produced hundreds of Outlaw copy-cat photos, but none were substantiated as authentic. However, two nights ago that all changed. The infamous Outlaw made an appearance on top of his favorite haunt, the rooftop of a condominium building that houses famous movie starlet Natalie North."

"This would be newsworthy enough, but the story only grows more outlandish. We know about this Outlaw sighting because apparently dozens of amateur photojournalists installed cameras zeroed in on that particular rooftop, all eager to capture the masked man in action. As you can see in this raw footage, the Outlaw leaps into the screen and stops in front of the rooftop door, perhaps waiting for Natalie North? We don't know yet. But then, the bizarre happens. The Outlaw is attacked!"

I sat up straighter, riveted to the screen. Holy moly! This was actual real footage!

"On the bottom of your screen you'll see two individuals sneak up behind the Outlaw and capture him! A bag is forced over his head, and his hands and feet are bound. Watch as the Outlaw is hoisted up and carried off, and the whole attack happens in a matter of seconds."

I stared, spellbound, as the screen replayed the incident over and over. The camera wasn't very close, obviously situated in one of the office windows surrounding the building. Carter could move so fast! And who was that dark figure helping him? The Shooter?

"However, the story still isn't over. With all the cameras that exist in our world today, we should be able to get another glimpse of where the Outlaw was taken, but no other footage exists. In fact, most of the footage that existed of this incident has inexplicably vanished. Let me repeat, the video that you just saw is the only remaining video of the capture. All of the other data has been erased. Here is our correspondent Joe Walsh with more."

The camera switched to a man in glasses sitting at a computer. He said, "Forty-eight hours ago, the digital community witnessed a computer hack like nothing the world has ever seen, and it all centers on this character, the Outlaw. All known footage of Tuesday's Outlaw incident has simply vanished. I mean, the video data has been erased. Wiped clean. Personal computers, servers, data warehouses, cellphones...all gone. It's the most impressive virus ever documented. Someone, some unnamed mysterious computer genius has apparently built a program that crawls across the entire internet and all the hard-drives and also all the intranets, and does it incredibly fast. What does the program do? That's what the most brilliant minds on the planet are working on right now. But this is the only plausible explanation we can come up with for how all of the video and all of the data on all of the computers were hit at the same time. Or at least, all hit within minutes of each other. This virus found every piece of video from Tuesday night's Outlaw appearance...and permanently deleted it."

"You may be wondering," the man continued, adjusting his spectacles, "how this one video remains. How did Channel Four news get a copy of it, when all other copies were destroyed? Well, the answer is simple. This video wasn't stored digitally. In other words, it wasn't stored on a computer. Our video was shot with an out-of-date camcorder and stored on a physical cartridge not connected to the internet. Brilliant, right? However when the journalist tried to email us his video, the email was intercepted and deleted! This super virus is scanning millions of emails every minute! One of our tech guys drove to the journalist's house and physically retrieved the cartridge containing the video that you just viewed.

"So the real question is, why this Outlaw incident? Why would this computer hacker, or group of hackers more likely, choose to reveal their existence with this stunt? What, exactly, is being hidden?"

"And where is the Outlaw? And is he safe?" the news anchor returned to the screen and kept talking. Just then, one of my phones buzzed.

I had two phones. Or rather, Chase Jackson had one phone. And the Outlaw had another phone. The Outlaw's phone was pink. Long story but it used to belong to movie starlet Natalie North. In fact, Natalie North was texting the Outlaw right now.

>> Oh no!!!!! Are you okay? Are you hurt? I just saw the news!

I smiled. Only one girl knew this was the Outlaw's number, and she cared about me. That was nice.

I'm fine. Nothing I couldn't handle. Thanks for asking.
>> I'm so glad! I was very worried.
>> Were you coming to visit me? =)
No. Was on a business trip. Kind of.
>> >=(
>> Who were those people anyway?

I'm not exactly sure, I replied, and rubbed my forehead. My brain was starting to hurt. **We didn't exchange business cards.**

>> I haven't seen you in two months! Where have you been?

Before I could reply, another message arrived on the Outlaw's phone from a different number. It was from Tank, who bizarrely enough had texted with the Outlaw previously.

>> ...Hope you're not dead, pajamas...
>> ...I've been looking forward to doing that job myself...

I grimaced against the pain building in my skull and typed, **Still here, ugly. Not going anywhere.**

>> ...Next time I'mma strap you into your car before I ignite it.

I hurled the phone across the room. Of course it was Tank! I HATED that guy. I retrieved the device and was pounding out a reply when he texted again.

>> ...you throw a rock into my living room? I destroy your piece of junk car. Payback. And the Latino girl will suffer for it...

Katie! Outraged, I started to reply but then I...I couldn't breathe. I had no oxygen. I was suffocating! I sucked in air to no effect. I tried again. Nothing. My lungs refused to respond. Sweat broke out all over my body. The walls, the very walls of my room, started to collapse on me. The ceiling began lowering. My head cracked and pain spilled in. I gasped and only swallowed agony. I needed oxygen! Peering out through clenched eyes I realized I was wallowing on the floor.

It was a panic attack. It was the virus! Carter was right. I'm dying!

Calmdowncalmdowncalmdowncalmdown!

I did my best not to writhe and shake, but it was impossible. He'd said that my brain was tender and could snap. Seems like tonight's news was enough. No air. Like a plastic bag was over my head.

RelaxrelaxrelaxrelaxrelaxrelaxyougottarelaxChase!!

I was dying and it was taking forever.

Katie...

Finally, right before the blackness and stars consumed me, I found a trickle of air. I sucked as hard as I could but it wasn't enough. I heaved in air but found only a mouthful. Again and again and again and again I pulled in insufficient air, barely staying conscious...still alive...shallow breath, shallow breath...still awake...shallow breath, shallow breath...Katie...still alive, shallow breath, deeper breath, deeper breath...lights coming back on...maybe I'll survive this...

Sweet oxygen. My lungs began to re-inflate. I didn't dare move though. I'd never open my eyes again. The pain had been awful. I found a shirt with my hand and pulled it under my head blindly, and then I collapsed into sleep with the television on, unsure if I'd wake up.

Chapter Five
Friday, January 4. 2018

"It's gotta be PuckDaddy," Lee said, sliding into the adjacent chair. My first class, Pre-Calc, hadn't started yet, which was good because I hadn't fully woken up; I'd spent the previous night tossing and turning and groaning on my floor. Lee is a math whiz and had already taken all the math classes our school offered, and so he helped tutor students like me for additional credits. He was wearing an Outlaw shirt.

"Lee," I said blearily. "I don't know what you're talking about. So shut up."

"PuckDaddy, baby! You've heard of him, I know you have, bro. Everyone has."

"Go away. I hate you."

"Can't believe you don't know who PuckDaddy is, dude," Lee shook his head.

"What about PuckDaddy?" Samantha Gear asked. She dropped into the chair next to me, opposite Lee. I'd forgotten she was in this class. I'd probably be seeing more of her, considering that Coach Garrett had unofficially dubbed her our new kicker.

"Who are you?" Lee asked suspiciously.

"I'm pretty. Do you really care what my name is, little man?"

"No," Lee admitted. "And I'm not little. Do you really know who PuckDaddy is?"

She shrugged, "Of course. Well. I mean, I'm familiar with the moniker. I didn't think many people were. Isn't he a big secret?"

"Pretty girls like you aren't supposed to know about guys like PuckDaddy," Lee stated, trying to digest this strange turn of events.

"I'm full of surprises. Want to sit on my lap?"

"...................what?" Lee asked finally after working his mouth silently for a long time. Samantha had green eyes that she could turn on like tractor beams. Lee appeared helpless; his face was turning summersaults. "Yes?"

"Come on over here, little man," she coaxed, leaning back in her chair. "And whisper about PuckDaddy in my ear."

I said, "Both of you either shut up, or tell me what on earth you're talking about." This was like watching a dorky version of Beauty and the Beast.

"PuckDaddy is one of the baddest dudes on the planet," Lee started.

"He's a computer hacker," Samantha interjected.

"Hey. Hot new girl. I'm telling it. He's not just a computer hacker. He's a digital god, dude, a networking wizard. He's been a myth in hackerdom for years, just lurking in the Deepnet. Dude makes most programmers look like crackers instead of hackers," Lee gushed in adoration.

"He might not even exist," Samantha said. "Most think he's a rumor."

Lee demanded, "Okay. Seriously. How do you know this stuff?" She just arched an eyebrow at him and smiled. "Anyways. After the Outlaw incident, hackerdom is buzzing, bro. Straight churning. He exists! PuckDaddy revealed himself by pulling off the biggest stunt the programming world has ever seen. Erasing all those videos is basically impossible. Has to be him."

"Are you a programmer?" Samantha asked him.

"No way, baby," he grinned and pointed at himself with his thumbs. "I'm applied sciences. An inventor."

"PuckDaddy is the one who erased the Outlaw videos," I said, pulling on my lip. "Why would he do that?" I already had a guess. PuckDaddy worked with Carter! Carter said the Infected hated publicity and so PuckDaddy was cleaning up the evidence? It made sense. If this guy actually even existed.

"Nobody knows," Lee said.

Samantha said again, "He might not even be real. He's a legend."

"He exists," Lee burst in excitement. "And he's connected with the Outlaw! And the Outlaw is back, baby!"

"Shhhhhhh!!!" We got shushed by several of our classmates, frantically doing homework before class started.

"The Outlaw is gone," I stated.

"He is?" Samantha asked. "Are you sure? How do you know?"

"He was kidnapped. He's gone for good," I said and I meant it. After last night's debacle on my floor, I wanted nothing to do with the mask anymore. I just wanted to survive the next few months.

"Nope," Lee grinned. "He's back! I told you."

"What about the kidnapping video?"

"Natalie North tweeted last night, dude. She said the Outlaw is okay. She's like the only person who would know. He probably just whipped their asses and then made out with Natalie."

"Ugh," I groaned. "Natalie." Natalie and her twitter account.

"Ugh," Katie groaned. "Why is it always Natalie North?"

"Cause she's super fly, dude," Lee said and bit into his sandwich. Katie was staring at the television over our lunch table. The station was re-broadcasting the Outlaw news. Around us the cafeteria roared; kids letting off steam.

"I know this," she glared at Lee. "I met her. Remember? She visited me in the hospital. But why does the Outlaw only visit her? And never me?"

"The Outlaw wasn't visiting Natalie," I said instinctively. But I couldn't finish the sentence. I couldn't tell her the Outlaw had been keeping an eye on her date with Tank. Stupid stupid Tank.

"Yes he was," Katie sighed. "And then some stupid computer nerd stole all the photos of him. The first good photos we've had in months."

"PuckDaddy," Lee said with a seriously offended disposition, "is NOT a computer nerd."

"Yeah, don't even talk like that," Cory said sagely, chewing on homemade chicken salad. "Could be listening."

"PuckDaddy," Katie considered. "His name is like a cross between Sean Combs and Midsummer Night's Dream."

"What?" Lee said blankly.

"Shakespeare," she said, searching for signs of intelligence in our eyes. "You three are illiterate."

"Maybe the Outlaw *will* come visit you," I told Katie. The idea was exciting!

"No way, man," Lee said. "He never leaves the city. He's a city dweller. Besides, the Outlaw is probably tracking down the Sniper."

"What Sniper?" I asked.

"Dude. You forget *everything*. The LA Sniper! Remember? Wax bullets?"

I scoffed, "The Outlaw doesn't care about the Sniper."

"Sure he does! The Sniper got three more last night!"

"Three more what?" I asked.

"Victims. Duh."

I laughed and said, "I'm sure the Outlaw has more important things going on than stopping a practical joker. This guy is just scaring people. The victims are all okay, right? Just bruised."

"You don't know the Outlaw like I do!" Lee shouted. "Remember, bro. I met him! And trust me. He's going to get the Sniper. And he doesn't leave the city. He can't visit Katie."

I rolled my eyes. "It's not like he's *trapped* there. He can go where ever he wants."

"Besides," Cory reminded Katie. "You have Tank now."

Lee said, "Barf."

"I don't *have* Tank," Katie perked up, smiling. "But we are going out again. Soon."

Lee said, "Barf."

"Nooooooo," I groaned. "Not again. One date was enough."

"Oh my boys," she said, smile widening. "My jealous boys."

"Ugh. Just thinking about you dating him gives me a headache," I said, rubbing my forehead.

"Speaking of headaches," Cory rumbled. "You need a ride home?"

"Yes," I sighed. "I don't know what I'm going to do about a permanent ride yet."

My girlfriend ambushed me after school. She was waiting for me at the exit, bouncing on her toes with a million-kilowatt smile in place. Most of my fellow students slowed down just so they could look at her.

"Hi quarterback!" she sang.

"Hi Hannah," I smiled back. "This is a nice surprise."

"That's not the real surprise," she said and she grabbed my hand. She pulled me out of the school doors and into the sunlight. "The real surprise is that my father is here!"

"Oh," I said, blinking into the sun. "That is...a...surprise."

"He's in the parking lot. Come on!"

Hannah's father looked like money. He was wearing a gorgeous suit, had a thick head of gorgeous silver hair, and generally gave off Presidential vibes. I bet his stylish glasses cost more than my car. Or at least more than the insurance agent told me my car was worth after it blew up.

"Good afternoon, Chase," he said and politely accepted my handshake.

"Nice to meet you, Mr. Walker."

"Pleasure's mine. I enjoyed watching you play football last season. You're a credit to this fine high school. I helped build that field, you know."

"I...did not know," I stammered. "Thank you?"

"Don't thank me *yet*," he smiled benevolently. "Hannah tells me that you helped protect her from the Hispanics during the riot."

"The Hispanics? Oh, the protest, right."

"Call it what you like, son. This place was crawling with spics, and I am grateful that you took care of my only child."

"Well," I shrugged. "I guess that's what boyfriends do." *Spics??*

"Only good boyfriends," Hannah said, still tightly holding my left hand.

I could never predict when she'd pour on the affection and when she'd act distant. Were all girlfriends this complicated?

"I helped pass that law, you understand," Mr. Walker said. "I'm an advisor to the *senator*, and it's about time someone notable, someone of *prestige*, took a stand on the influx of hispanics into our once great city. The Hispanics were rioting because of that law, because they're afraid of justice."

"Oh yeah?" I said. I knew nothing about politics or laws. But I had a feeling I disagreed with him.

"But I'll discontinue this tangent before I begin to preach," he smiled. "Hannah is giving me the warning look."

"Thank you, Daddy," Hannah said.

"The spics destroyed your car," he said. "Hannah informed me, and then I read the report in the newspaper."

"That was a good car," I nodded. "I will miss it."

"Well, let me see what I can do to help," he said. "I'm a financial consultant to many of our nation's *finest* automobile manufacturers, including Mission Motorcycles. You have heard of them?"

"I don't know much about any cars. Or motorcycles," I admitted.

"Well, it just so happens, they owed me a favor and agreed to give me a short-term loan on one of their new electric bikes," he said. And it was then that I realized we were standing beside a gleaming black, silver, and orange motorcycle. I hadn't noticed before because our school parking lot always looks like a luxury car showcase, and I'd grown numb to the opulence. A sleek black helmet hung from each handle. Mr. Walker placed his palm on the seat and said, "This bike is yours. Until you get a new car."

"Wow," I breathed. A motorcycle!!

"Isn't it sexy?" Hannah smiled. "It looks like it's from the future."

"It does," I agreed. "I'm almost afraid to touch it, like it'll fly off. But sir, there's no way…"

"Please don't be so ungrateful as to refuse, son. That's low class, and that's not the Walkers. You are in *elite* company. Dating my daughter has advantages, as I'm sure she's told you. You just keep performing on the football field."

"Oh...right," I said.

"I'm gratified I can help," Mr. Walker said and shook my hand again. "I'm expecting big things from you. Don't let me down. It's electric, so you'll need to charge it at night. Fill out the paperwork in the storage compartment and return them signed to Hannah tomorrow. If you wreck it, I'll have you drowned off Long Beach. I wish I could stay, but I'm late for a meeting with the Board of *Supervisors*. Hannah, tell your mother I'll be out late," he said and got into the back seat of a black sedan that whisked him away.

I texted Cory, **I don't need a ride home. I'm all good.**

We were flying! At least that's what it felt like. The bike gave the impression of riding a strong blast of air. It was fully electric and very quiet, other than a high-pitched whine when I really started picking up speed. Hannah's arms tightened around my torso when I opened up the throttle on the highway.

I could still feel the wind on my skin that night when Tank texted me. Or, texted the Outlaw. I was scanning my Twitter feed, reading updates about two more high-velocity wax bullet shooting victims. The Sniper was getting more creative. Tonight he shot someone inside a restaurant through the front door, and he always hit them in the same place: the right shoulder. Every time, dozens of victims, either the front or the back of the right shoulder, pow! The Sniper's streak was very impressive.

One tweet caught my eye. NBC News tweeted that their military consultant confirmed these strikes were obviously the work of a professionally trained military shooter.

Trained shooter...

Whoa! Of course! How had this not occurred to me before? Carter told me the Infected Shooter's plane landed a few weeks ago, right before these shootings started. I'd been so dense, not putting the clues together. The LA Sniper *was* the Infected Shooter! Like Carter, he probably hung out on rooftops. He'd spot a victim, shoot them, and then disappear. The Infected weren't supposed to draw attention to themselves; how was the Shooter allowed to do this and I couldn't even wear a mask? He must be bored or something, playing these pranks, just wasting time until...

Until it was time to kill me.

The back of my neck turned icy. The professionally trained sniper NBC News had referred to was here for me. Maybe I should start wearing armor. That's when Tank texted the Outlaw.

>>...Got another big date coming up, pajamas. And she's going to pay for your sins. I'm going to seduce her, confuse her, use her, and abuse her. All for you.

I saw red. I trembled with rage. I couldn't make my hands work. Deep inside my skull another headache rumbled.

>>...And then? And then I'm coming for you.

>>...I haven't decided if I'm going to drown you, cut you into pieces, beat you to death, or blow a hole through you with a shotgun while I make my date watch.

Great. Now two people are going to shoot me. That settles it.

I texted Lee. But I didn't text him from Chase Jackson's phone. I texted him from the Outlaw's phone, like I had once before.

Kid. I need help. I need a bullet-proof vest. Can you get me one?

The reply was instantaneous.

>>YES!!!! THE OUTLAW IS BACK BABY!!! I can get you a ballistic vest, no problem!!

I grinned, picturing Lee's face tomorrow at school. I decided to have some fun. But you can't tell anyone. Total secret.

>>YEAH YEAH SURE!! How soon do you need the vest? And what will it be used for?

I need the vest ASAP. I'm going after the LA Sniper.

>>I KNEW IT!!! WOOOOOOOOOOHAAAAAA!!!

That might give me some protection from the Shooter and Tank. But it wouldn't protect Katie.

Maybe it's time she met the Outlaw.

Chapter Six
Saturday night, January 7. 2018

In the past few months, I'd jumped off a five-story building, been shot at, played in a championship football game, been kidnapped, chased by a pit bull, and participated in several fistfights, including battling a maniac on top of a building while helicopters fired warning shots at us.

But I had never been more scared than I was now, standing outside Katie's door. She lived on the bottom floor of an apartment complex, and the rear sliding glass door opened directly into her bedroom. I could see movement through her curtains. The California January night was cool and quiet but I was on fire, pulse racing. I'd spent a significant portion of the last few years in her bedroom, talking, watching TV, doing homework, playing on our phones, laughing, secretly adoring her. She was perfect.

I took a deep breath and put on my disguise: the ski mask, and the bandana tied Rambo style. I didn't know what else to do. Katie didn't know Tank was her kidnapper. Katie didn't know her date was planning on hurting her, both emotionally and physically. And I couldn't tell her. Even if I could, she wouldn't believe me.

I was in love with her. I couldn't just *watch* her get hurt.

I'd debated calling her from the Outlaw's phone, but that number was getting passed around too much. Natalie, Tank and Lee all had it; that was more than enough.

Before I could chicken out, I unscrewed the light bulb in the outdoor sconce and knocked on her door.

"Here we go," I sucked in. A flurry of movement, the filmy curtain pushed aside, and a beautiful smiling face appeared. I loved that face. She screwed up her eyes, peering through the glass as her hand futilely worked the light switch. Then…recognition. She gasped. I held a finger to my mask to silently shush her. She nodded her head, said, "Okay okay okay, oh gosh, okay okay, oh my gosh," and then the curtain fell back into place. I couldn't hear her but I could read her lips.

"This is a terrible idea. This is stupid. But…kind of awesome," I said to myself. Chill bumps covered my whole body. I couldn't wait until she came outside. I winced against the pounding in my head.

She came back, brown eyes still wide, and held up her hand. "Give me two minutes," she said, and then vanished. Back again in five seconds, "Okay? Is that okay?" I nodded. Her voice was almost entirely muted by the glass. "Oh my gosh, okay!"

When she finally did come out, my breath caught. I'd never seen this outfit before. She wore a cute little white tank top that…wow. She better NOT wear that shirt for Tank. Her hair had been brushed and she smelled intoxicating. Time itself stopped and held us frozen. I wasn't sure I could move.

Even though I *was* the Outlaw, I was also intensely jealous of him, that Katie would dress like this when he visited. I kind of hated myself. And I wasn't real happy with *her* either. Why did she never wear this around Chase Jackson?

I backed beyond the tall evergreen shrubs into deeper night, drawing her after me.

"Is it really you?" she asked, her voice a tremulous whisper.

I nodded. I reeeeally didn't want her to recognize me. I was able to creditably disguise my voice, with help from the mask. To aid in the deception, I'd drawn a few designs on my neck with a black sharpie that peeked above the collar of my shirt, like tattoo camouflage. The more differences I could manufacture between the Outlaw and Chase Jackson the better.

"Are you...are you mad at me? You look like you're angry with me," she said. I was about to reply but a fresh wave of pain hit my brain and took my breath away. I shook my head, trying to loosen the tendrils of discomfort. Whenever my pulse started to race, my headache worsened. "Then why are you here?"

"I'm here for you," I said. I can make my voice *really* deep. Sometimes when I wear the Outlaw suit, I sound larger and I feel larger too. "I haven't seen you since that night."

"The night on the rooftop," she nodded and hugged herself. "Thank you for finding me."

A thousand responses ran through my head. You're welcome. My pleasure. Anything for you. Any time. Don't mention it. Let's make out. None of them seemed to measure up to the Outlaw's required gravitas. So I said nothing. I'm a genius.

"I'm glad you came," she smiled. "I've been hoping you would."

Again, another bout of agony. This time my knees buckled. Carter was right...the headaches were going to kill me.

"Are you okay?" Katie cried, reaching out a hand to steady me as I lowered to the ground. This was not going well. The Outlaw isn't supposed to fall over.

Then she touched me. My neck. As if by magic the pain lifted. She placed her hand on my shoulder and her skin touched mine and every muscle in my body relaxed. Muscles I didn't know I possessed unclenched and my head cleared.

"Yes," I said, marveling at her. "I'm fine."

"You don't appear fine," she said, examining me in concern. "I mean, you do. You're gorgeous. But...you look unwell." She'd never seen the Outlaw's face but he was gorgeous? I hated that guy. "I saw the kidnapping video," she said and she lowered to her knees beside me. "Did they hurt you?"

"Yes," I lied, thankful for the excuse. "But they won't anymore."

"Who are they?"

"It doesn't matter. That's not why I'm here. I want to warn you," I said.

"Warn me? About what?"

"The guy that kidnapped you is still out there."

She nodded.

I continued, "Have any memories surfaced about his identity?"

"No," she shook her head, looking spooked. "I wish I did. Do you expect him to try again?"

"I do," I said. "I don't want to frighten you, but it's important."

"Why me?" she asked, and to my astonishment she wrapped her hands around my arm and rested her head on my shoulder. "I'm scared."

"It's because I returned your phone a few months ago, in September. The thief is obsessed with me now, and he considers you a link."

"You remember returning my phone?" she perked up. "I presumed you forgot all about it."

"I remember."

"Why *did* you return my phone?" she asked, her smoldering eyes practically melting my mask away. "And why did you rescue me? How did you know where to find me? The police asked me that about a hundred times."

"It's a secret."

"Pretty please tell me?" She looked up at me through her lashes, which was a super effective strategy.

"I'll tell you one day. If I can. Until then…keep safe. Don't go out with anyone you don't know. Stay with your friends and family," I said. *And don't go out with Tank!!!*

She nodded and said, "Okay."

She was no longer touching my skin and my headache was returning. Experimentally I took one of her hands and pressed it against the exposed skin between my glove and my sleeve. As our bodies touched directly I experienced the same calming effect. The pain drifted away.

"What are you doing?" she laughed softly.

"Sorry," I said. "I…don't touch people often."

She examined me for a long time and I was glad it was dark and I had a mask to hide behind. My face was burning in embarrassment.

"Take off your gloves," she said, tilting her head to the side. "And you can touch me with your hands." I wanted to do that so bad I was trembling. But that could lead to disaster. I said nothing. She touched my neck with her fingers. "How old are you?"

"Not much older than you."

"Perfect," she cooed. I recognized that voice. She used it to tease me sometimes when we were alone. I took her hand in my glove and held it. "You don't have to be lonely. Not with me."

"Lonely?"

"Isn't it lonely being you?" she asked. We were completely hidden from the rest of the world. Just us.

"A little," I said. "But aren't we all a little lonely?"

"All us superheroes?" she smiled.

"There are no superheroes," I told her. "Just us regular people. And I think we're all lonely."

"You're a hero to me, you know," she said, and she played with my hair. "I don't remember that night. But I'm still grateful."

"Do you have friends?" I asked cautiously. This was dangerous territory. I wanted her to talk about Chase Jackson.

"How much do you know about me? When I imagine you, you're always keeping track of me from a distance," she laughed. "Which is a little far fetched, I know."

"You're not...entirely wrong. I know a little."

"I knew it!" she grinned.

"It's a very innocent crush. That's all."

"My crush on you isn't so innocent," she said and she nuzzled her nose playfully into my mask. I ground my teeth and fought down the robust urge to rip the mask off. "But to answer your question. I have friends, mostly boys, and they kinda suck. No offense, but boys don't make great friends. I need a friend that I won't fall in love with, and vise versa. I need a good friend that's a girl."

Fall in love with??!

"Like Natalie North? I adore her. Can you get me her number? I met her once."

"I know."

"You know I met her? How?" she asked.

Whoops! How *would* the Outlaw know that? "Because…Natalie told me."

"Oh. Right. She's very nice."

"She is," I agreed, nodding. "The real Natalie is as nice as her media persona."

"Is that why you like her? You both wear masks?"

"That's why she likes me. Very perceptive of you," I said. "She thinks we have that in common."

"Are you two still…you know…dating?" she asked and she nudged me with her shoulder. "It's a very romantic story."

"No," I said. "I haven't seen her in months."

"Aw," Katie said. "I bet she misses you!"

"The Outlaw doesn't really exist," I sighed. "It's just a mask."

"No. That's not true. The Outlaw is bigger than that. I know you're probably a real person under there but to the world, to the rest of us, to me…you're very real. We need you."

"I just cause more problems than I solve," I grunted. "By a long shot. That's why I've been gone."

"Are you married in real life?" she asked.

"No," I laughed, careful to alter my voice. I forget how mysterious the Outlaw persona is. My best friend just asked if I was married. Surreal. "Remember? We're about the same age."

"Good," she smiled.

"What about you? You must have a boyfriend."

"No," she said, pursing her lips. "My situation is…complicated."

"How so?"

"Just typical high school boyfriend girlfriend stuff," she shrugged and the strap to her tank top slid off her shoulder. Focus! "Want to hear something interesting?"

"Sure," I said, but it was nearly time for me to go. I'd been here too long, taking too many chances.

"Do you know the guy that gave you the taser? Last year?"

"Yes," I said slowly, sorting through my web of lies and connections. "How did you know about the taser?"

"He told me. His name is Lee and he's my friend!"

"The guy from Craigslist is your friend?" I asked, faking surprise.

"Isn't that a wild coincidence?"

"That's bizarre. His device really helped. It completely incapacitated Ta...that guy on the roof."

"Were you injured in that fight?" she asked me.

"Yes," I nodded emphatically. "Badly. That guy is awful. He's huge. And mean. That's why I want you to stay safe. Here. In Glendale. Away from the city."

"So you *can* get hurt," she mused. "Does that mean you don't have real super powers? Like, really really no super powers?"

I chuckled and said, "Really really, there's no such thing as super powers. But...I am abnormal. I'm weird in ways I'm still learning about."

"Like what?"

"That's a secret too."

"Are you friends with PuckDaddy?" Katie asked.

"Why do you ask that?"

"Because he was erasing all the video of you. Right? Wasn't he helping you out?"

"Not exactly," I shook my head. "It's all hard to explain."

"Were you scared that night? When you were kidnapped and PuckDaddy erased the evidence?"

"Yes," I said. "Very. A lot of the Outlaw stuff is scary."

"So PuckDaddy is a bad guy?"

"My life is...complex. I don't know if he's a bad guy. But he's not a friend. I don't have any real friends. At least the Outlaw doesn't."

"I'm your friend," she smiled.

"Thank you," I smiled back. But she couldn't see that. "I need to go. Remember why I came here," I said and I stood up. "Stay away from people you don't know well."

"Before you go," she said and she help up her phone. "Can I take a picture of you? Or just look at you in the light? I can barely see you."

"No," I snapped. I snatched her phone and tossed it into the grass near her bedroom door.

"Hey!" she laughed.

"No pictures."

"Why are you so bashful with the media?" she teased me. "The world loves this stuff."

"It's best not to take ourselves too seriously," I said. "Especially me. I won't be around for long."

"Why not?"

"I need a favor. It's important. Don't tell anyone I was here. No one. Okay? Not even the guy from Craigslist," I said, doing my best to impart severity.

"Okay. But then I want a favor too."

"What?" I asked warily.

"Promise me you'll come back to visit soon. When you can stay longer. This has been the best ten minutes of my life! I know I'm still a teenager and you're a grownup…but…this is nice, right? We can be friends. I feel like we're a great fit." She smiled so big my heart almost burst.

"I promise that…I will come back if I can," I said and then I vanished, leaving her in the dark. I was long gone in a matter of seconds but even across the distance I could hear her sigh.

⸺

Chase Jackson's phone was vibrating when I returned home. I had a text from Katie Lopez.

>>CHASE!!! I miss you SO much!! I have so many things to tell you but I can't!!! AUGH!!! Please come visit SOON!!

Girls are so weird.

But that. Was. The best thing. Ever!

I was going back soon. A promise is a promise! Woooooooo!

Chapter Seven
Saturday, January 14. 2018

A week. A week went by and I was stewing.

No word from Carter. No clues about PuckDaddy. Silence from Tank. Natalie hadn't texted. My girlfriend was affectionate but distant. Katie and I kept revolving around each other in a weird, tense, unspoken, hot relationship. She never mentioned the Outlaw visit. My Dad was feeling good. I went to bed early each night and I hadn't suffered any more migraines.

All the nothingness that kept happening was driving me crazy. I was boiling over. In the past I always preferred quiet Saturday nights. Tonight I was doing jumping jacks. I was wired. I'd already attended a boring party with Cory and came home. He persisted in going to bed at a hideously early hour. Now I had nothing to do. But I could probably dig up something reckless, if I wanted. Which I did.

I was contemplating throwing pebbles at my girlfriend's window or, even better, throwing bricks at Tank's but thankfully the Outlaw's phone beeped. It was Lee.

>> **Outlaw!! Your vest is ready!**
I'm on the way.
Boom!

The motorcycle tore silently across the suburbs on a high-pitched cushion of air. So much speed, so little sound. It's touchpad display glowed cheerfully. I parked a few blocks away and ran to Lee's backyard.

He was waiting, trembling, delirious with excitement. It was just me under the mask. Calm down, Lee. You're making me feel guilty.

"Outlaw! You're here, dude!" he quietly shouted at me.

"What do you have for me?" I growled, even quieter.

"Here." He handed me a heavy gorgeous black vest.

"It's NorthFace?"

"Nothing but the best for you, dude."

"NorthFace makes bulletproof vests?" I asked, examining the thick vest. It was a work of art that glistened with zippers and buckles.

"Basically I bought the nicest ski vest I could find and then modified it. This is made out of bombproof ballistic nylon. I sewed in flexible kevlar plates, but kept all the pockets. I figured, Mr. Outlaw, that this could be like your Bat Belt."

I chuckled, staring at the vest in wonder. I loved it.

"It's an avalanche-proof vest, but I took out that airbag. I can put it back in if you want."

"No. That's okay," I replied.

"I sewed in some elastic around the edges, so it'll stretch a little bit, for when…you know, when you…get bigger?"

"When I get bigger?"

"Right, dude? I've seen the video analysis," he said, unsure of himself, his voice quavering a bit.

"What analysis?" I asked.

"I mean…sorry. It's just, that, on the videos it looks like you get bigger. Taller. …don't you? Sorry, dude. I thought…"

"It's fine. Forget it."

"I feel dumb now, dude. Is it supposed to be a secret? Ahhh. My bad, you know?"

"Lee," I said quietly. "This vest is perfect. How much do I owe you?"

To my surprise, he looked deeply offended. "Dude. I made this for you.

Actually I made two vests. Now we both have one."

"You need a ballistic vest?" I smiled through the mask.

"I figure," he stammered a little awkwardly. "I figure that if I keep helping you, I might get shot at too. You know, dude...like we're....like we're partners?"

"Partners," I grinned.

"You think Natalie North will like the vest?"

"Maybe I should go ask her."

Back at the motorcycle, I stuffed my black shirt into the storage compartment and zipped on the vest. Perfect fit. Bet I looked super fly too.

I wasn't interested in Natalie North romantically. My life was outlandish enough. But her opinion mattered to me. She was really the Outlaw's only friend.

I took Highway Two to Interstate Five, pushing the bike close to 100 mph. Tonight I was the Outlaw, and the Outlaw soared. I flew down Natalie's off ramp near Chinatown, found my favorite hidden parking spot, and climbed up the wall. I didn't analyze this superhuman feat; just went straight up and over.

Are you home? I texted her.

Two minutes later, **>> No, but I will be soon. Why?**

Coming to visit.

>> It's about time! =) See you soon.

Her rooftop was monitored. I knew that now. The Outlaw had hoodwinked thousands of people into believing he actually existed, and so they set up cameras to spy on him. Instead of climbing to her roof I hid in the shadows below, on top of the adjacent structure. I crouched down to wait. The ambient city noise filtered up to me and I smiled, enjoying it from above.

Five minutes later my phone beeped. A new text message. From an unknown number.

>>Hey moron what r u doin

What on earth? Only three people knew the Outlaw's phone number, and I didn't recognize these digits. Had to be a mistake.

>>Thats right Im talking 2 u

Wrong number, I replied.

>>im savin ur life dummy get the heck out of there

Could this person really be trying to communicate with *me*? The Outlaw?

>>u think carter was messin around with u? Shooter gonna burn ur ass

Whoa! I jumped up. Whoa whoa *whoa*!! Shooter? Carter? **Who is this???**

>> y r u wearing ur bike helmet instead of the mask?

You can see me? I asked, glancing around, completely freaked out.

>>im everywhere. now move

Who are you????

Just then, Natalie texted me. **>> I'm coming up the elevator right now!**

Come to the roof, then walk down the fire escape, I told her.

>>get out of there now idiot, the stranger texted me again. >>b4 natalie north gets there

Talk to you later, I replied.

>>wait!!! listen, stoopid!

>>i don't know y im even bothering but...

>>turn your helmet speaker on

>>pair the helmet's bluetooth with your phone

>>trust me

I sighed but did as he asked. The stranger spooked me too much to ignore. I paired the bluetooth headset with my phone, so all calls would be routed to my helmet.

Natalie North came hurrying down the stairs. There were several reasons why she made over five million dollars per movie, and one of them was her appearance. She was so pretty it hurt.

"Hi stranger," she smiled.

"Hello Natalie," I said.

"Whoa. Your costume is different." She hugged me and then stayed there.

"I'm sorry I didn't text you for two months. That's not how a good friend acts."

"Let us be clear about one thing, Outlaw," she said into my vest. "I will not fall for you again. I am over you. Well, truthfully, I'm as fascinated by you as the rest of the world, and I'm very covetous of my position as girlfriend of the superhero. But I've...matured in my understanding of our relationship."

"I understand," I said, even though I did not. At all.

"Just kidding, let's make out."

I laughed. That was funny. And made my heart skip a beat. But no. I had Katie. No! I mean, I had a girlfriend. Not Katie. I couldn't stop *thinking* about Katie, though. At this moment I couldn't even remember my girlfriend's name.

"I was out on the town," she said. "My publicist states that for the sake of my image and media presence I need to go out, pretend to be a *bon vivant*, frolic merrily and hang out with guys and let the whole world take photographs."

"Makes sense," I said.

"No it doesn't. Nothing about my life makes sense. I even brought a boy home with me, just so magazines can gossip," she said and looked up at me. "I wish you'd take off the helmet, so I can see your face. Or at least your eyes."

I flipped up the helmet visor so she could see my eyes and said, "You brought a boy home?"

"He's only a close friend. He's gay, actually. But the tabloids don't know," she said and stepped back to examine at me. "Why the costume change?"

"Do you like it?" I said and I held out my arms to the side.

"Very much. It's quite dashing. You have nice arms. But..."

"But what?"

"I remember you being bigger than this," she said, with a confused grin. "I vividly recall feeling minuscule when I sat in your lap."

"I believe," I said slowly, carefully, thoughtfully, "that I might be able to...increase in size?"

"Wow!" she laughed and clapped her hands. "Really?"

"That would explain why my shoes have split in the past. And why I look bigger in some pictures," I said, thinking out loud. "But it might only happen when my heart rate speeds up? Or my adrenaline is pumping? I'm not sure. I haven't figured this out yet."

"Like the Incredible Hulk?" she asked. "So you really have super powers?"

"No," I said. "No super powers."

"Then how on earth could you increase in size, silly?"

"I'm not positive that I can. But I might. And it's from a disease."

"A disease?" she asked, concern wrinkling her forehead. "What kind?"

"I don't know the technical name," I said. "I don't know much about it at all. I know it's rare. As it takes over my body, it activates certain organs and does weird stuff and makes me stronger and quicker." The truth just kept pouring out of me. I hadn't planned on sharing my secrets, but the control I could exercise over my body was...diminished, at the moment. I was able to mask my voice to a dark growl, but it was hard. I had too much energy!

"Sounds similar to the movie *Phenomenon*," she said, her eyes raised to the sky in thought.

"I haven't seen that one."

"Great film. John Travolta has a brain tumor that engages more and more of his brain as it grows. The tumor makes him much more intelligent."

"Yeah," I agreed. "It does sound similar."

"Except he dies at the end."

"Yeah, me too!"

"That's not funny."

"I'm not joking," I said. "Almost always fatal."

"No," she said, her hands going to her mouth. "Please be joking."

"Very high mortality rate."

"No no no no," she said again.

"But. I plan on beating it."

"Have you been to the doctor?" She took one of my hands between both of hers.

"No. It's extremely rare and most people just die from it and nobody knows why."

"Have you told anyone? Does anyone know?"

"You're the first," I admitted.

"Gosh. You must feel so alone, all the time. I forgot how much we have in common."

The phone rang. In my helmet. It startled me so badly that I jumped. It must be the guy who'd been texting me.

"Hang on," I told Natalie and then I answered the device in my helmet.

"What?" I growled.

The speaker's helmet crackled to life and a male voice said, "Greetings idiot."

"What do you want?"

"Oh nothing. Just to tell the mighty Outlaw that he's about to be arrested."

"Explain," I demanded and I turned in a circle, scanning the area.

Natalie North noticed the change in my demeanor and whispered, "What's going on?"

The voice said, "The FBI has been monitoring your girlfriend's building, genius. They have arrived and are on the way up."

"Oh jeez," I groaned.

"What?" Natalie asked again.

I told her, "We're about to have company."

"Don't take off yet, dummy," the voice in my head said. "I want to hear what the Feds have to say."

"They're here to arrest me," I shouted into the helmet. "I have to leave now."

"Who is here?" Natalie asked. She was glancing around in alarm.

"Listen idiot," he said in my ear. "You need to trust me. They are too well organized right now. They'd track you straight to your house. I'm working on it. Talk to them and don't run until I give the signal."

"Who *are* you?"

"I'm Infected, baby. Just like you. Except I'm awesome," he said and I could hear a smile in his voice. Infected! Another one! He was helping me? "And I'm about to save your life. You big dumb idiot. Now go up to your girlfriend's roof. We need to draw all the feds up there."

I hesitated.

"*Trust* me," he said.

"Come on." I grabbed Natalie's hand and ran up the circular fire escape. I drug her the entire three flights. No sooner had we arrived than hidden flood lights snapped on and lit up the night. Pow! The sudden brilliance was obviously meant to be disorienting, and the spectacle was effective. The penthouse door crashed open and men in black poured out. They held flashlights with one hand and were resting their other hand on the pistol in their holster. Shouts, orders, noise! Natalie and I were quickly surrounded.

Chapter Eight
Saturday, January 14. 2018

"This had better work," I whispered.

"I agree," the voice in the helmet said. "Otherwise the Shooter has to smoke you right here, right now."

"Are you watching this?"

"Of course, stupid. It's totally sweet."

Natalie was pissed. She was red in the face and yelling at the agents, who appeared stern but maybe a little unnerved by the force of her fury. She *was* Natalie North, after all.

"You know what?" she snapped and whipped out her phone. "I'm recording this. We'll see how the media judges this intrusion."

"No cameras," one of the agents ordered and three of them descended upon her, grabbing at her phone.

My blood was pumping. My headache was increasing, but I didn't care. I was going to tomahawk throw each of these agents off the roof. They couldn't touch me! I *owned* the night! I could feel the vest growing tighter.

"Hey, whoa, everyone calm down!" a new voice said, and a man who looked like Captain America without the mask rushed onto the roof. He started hauling the agents away, which might have saved their lives. And mine. "Give her back the phone," he commanded. Natalie's phone was returned and she leveled her icy glare at him. "I assure you, Ms. North, there is no need to record this. For starters," he said and then lifted his hands up to the surrounding skyscrapers. "I imagine this is already being recorded by hundreds of cameras. Your friend here has made sure of that. And second, this is completely legal. There is a warrant out for his arrest."

"You're here to arrest him?" Natalie lashed out.

"I'm Special Agent in Charge, Isaac Anderson, ma'am. Los Angeles Federal Bureau of Investigation," he said and he handed over his credentials for her to scrutinize. "And all I want to do is talk."

"Give me your number," I growled. "And I'll call you from a pay phone. We can talk all night."

"I'd prefer to talk in person," he said, and then to his credit he backed away. His hands were up, as if in surrender. "No pressure, no arrests. Just exchanging information."

"Let Natalie go," I said. "I don't like her being here with all these goons."

"That's an excellent idea," he agreed.

"I'm not going anywhere," she told him, and at that moment we were more afraid of her than the pistols.

"Okay, that's fine. We can do it that way," he said calmly. Despite myself, I liked this guy. He was a cool customer. "In fact, if you will promise to give me a few minutes of your time, I'll send these guys back downstairs."

"Good," Natalie said. "Get rid of them."

"Lame," the voice in my head whispered. "He's playing a game. He's got all the exits covered. He thinks you can't get away, so it's really a lame gesture he's making. Keep him talking."

"I'll stay," I told Isaac Anderson. "I've got nowhere to be. I was taking the night off from fighting crime, anyway."

Special Agent in Charge Isaac Anderson cracked a smile and said, "Okay, gentlemen. You heard the man. Wait downstairs."

The agents in their tactical pants and flashlights and pistols and shiny black jackets all began egressing down the staircase. So far this was going exactly as Anderson had planned it.

"Full disclosure, guys," Anderson told us when we were alone. He indicated the brilliant spotlights. "We're still being recorded. Everything you say and do is being caught on camera. Okay?"

"What do you want?" Natalie asked. "He hasn't done anything wrong."

"I'm afraid I disagree with you, Ms. North," he said politely. "He's unlawfully broken and entered, resisted arrest twice, disturbed the peace, assaulted…a lot of people, and impeded an investigation. Plus, the whole…self-appointed law enforcement…masked enterprise thing is illegal. I'm probably forgetting some other laws he's broken."

"He did those things for noble reasons," she shot back. She was still standing between me and Isaac Anderson with her arms crossed. "He's a good person."

"That's exactly what I'm here to find out," he said.

"I count ten guys total," a whisper in my ear told me. "Did you park in the alley near the Italian joint? There's a Fed near there, too."

"What should I call you?" Anderson asked me. "I feel a little silly calling you Outlaw."

"Stupid question, Anderson," I replied, growling. I did not want my voice analyzed.

"Should we all sit down?" he asked.

"No," I said.

"No," Natalie said.

"I've been tracking you for a while now," he chuckled. "I couldn't decide if I was happy or sad that you disappeared for those two months." He waited for a response but neither of us said anything. He cleared his throat and continued, "Do you realize what an untenable position I'm in? The world wants you to be a real superhero and I'm supposed to arrest you."

"I wouldn't try, if I were you," I said.

"Right. I don't want to use force. Nobody wants that. It'd be best for everyone if you and I cooperated."

I shook my head and said, "I'm not feeling very cooperative, Anderson."

"That's a good line," the voice in my head snickered.

"You and the federal government *are* going to have a conversation. I'm here tonight on its behalf. Consider me a temporary peace offering. The L.A.P.D. needs to ask you some questions, and so do several federal agencies. The best way for that to happen would be us riding together to my office," he said.

"Not going to happen," I replied. "Ask your questions here."

"We need to know your identity. We need to discuss your involvement in the Katie Lopez kidnapping. We need to discuss the charges against you, including your illegal vigilante escapades. The cyber division wants to know about the recent internet hack. And we need to talk about you…physically," he finished uneasily.

"What does that mean?" Natalie asked.

"Ms. North, we have video of the Outlaw doing strange things. On the recordings, it looks humanly impossible. Is it a hoax? Does he have weaponized special equipment? Or is it something else? We need to know what's going on."

The voice in my ear crackled, "You ready to jump off the roof?"

"What??" I whispered.

"We're almost set up. Is your motorcycle in that alley?" the ear piece asked.

"Yes," I hissed.

"Perfect. Stand by."

"So?" Anderson was asking. "Can we go peacefully to my office and have this conversation? You have my word, which is being recorded, that I will not arrest you if you comply."

I shook my head and said, "Negative."

"The other option, I'm afraid, is less pleasant," he said, and his handsome trustworthy face turned hard. "We will arrest you. This building is surrounded. There are no exists. You will be taken by force to a holding cell in the U.S. Marshal's office."

"Just about ready," the whisper said.

"There's a third option," I told Anderson slowly.

"I'm all ears," Anderson said. "Anything to avoid violence."

"I'm going to leave," I said, my heart about to pound out of my chest. "You give your number to Natalie. I'll call you sometime and answer whatever I can."

"I cannot allow you to leave," Anderson said.

"Wrong, Anderson. You cannot stop me."

"Oh, this is going to be good," the voice giggled in my ear. "Jump down to the lower roof in the direction from which you came. Ready when you are, Outlaw."

"Let's do it. I'll see you around, FBI," I said.

"Wait…" he warned.

A lot of things happened at once. Even though my headset had warned me, the chaos was staggering. The banks of bright lights began to shatter one at a time, like fireworks exploding, crashing sideways. Natalie screamed as the world erupted. Special Agent in Charge Isaac Anderson's phone started ringing. Car horns everywhere began to bawl; judging by the cacophony, alarms were going off by the hundreds. And then the electricity to our city block was cut. We plunged into darkness as every light around us extinguished. Frenzied honking below. The spectacular sequence was high-definition movie-quality impressive.

"Jump, idiot," the voice said in my ear. "Get to your bike."

I ran to the edge of the roof, mustered up my resolve, and jumped. I *really* jumped. I launched myself far, far up into the sky. Way too high! I yelped in shock as the buildings fell away. I whirled my arms in the atmosphere, helpless, arcing at an inhuman height.

"Hey," my helmet said. "Where'd you go?"

For a second, the cosmos was quiet. Dark buildings crowded below, silhouetted by the silent blazing city. How high was I? Seven stories? Eight? Nine? I began the descent. The night whistled against my face shield as I plummeted. The rooftops rose up in a fierce rush.

"Ohshootshootshoot!" I ground my teeth and crashed into the roof. Feet first. Miraculously upright. Still alive. I was…okay! Unbroken and alert on the second-story commercial structure next to Natalie's apartment building. The roof tiles had buckled but held. "…wow. *That* was awesome."

"At your bike yet?"

"No," I said and I accelerated across the roofs. I could move like lightning when I wanted. A familiar euphoric sensation was overtaking me. Being Infected was the best! "Getting close."

"Carter's going to kill me. Not sure you're worth this," he said.

I jumped again, fell two stories, and landed in the dark alley beside my bike. A lady nearby shrieked.

"Power's coming on," he warned and towers of light began humming back to life. The world resurfaced.

"Okay," I panted. "I'm on the bike."

"Move. Head south."

"Which way is south?"

"Oh god you're dumb. Turn right."

I hit the throttle and tore off into the street. The bike responded by popping a wheelie and nearly ripping out of my hands. I clung on and navigated frantically through the traffic. Cars with honking alarms lined the streets.

"Here they come. Turn left at the light."

Two black Chevy Tahoes roared around the corner, nearly colliding with me, lights blazing and sirens screaming.

"I'm being chased!"

"Of course you are! This is wicked awesome! Turn right and head for the Second Street Tunnel."

"The tunnel? You sure??"

"Trust me. Those are the only two cars they had ready. It'll be another minute before the rest of their squad is rolling. You'll be long gone by then. Head straight down Second Street."

I gunned it, weaving and slicing through the thicket.

"We might get cut off," he said. "So in the tunnel, slow down and let them get right behind you. Then power slide into a U-turn and come back out. They won't be able to follow. Tunnel is too small. I hope. There it is!"

I plunged into the shiny underpass, doggedly pursued by the two wailing Feds. The enclosed space exploded with the FBI's unbearable lights, and the squawking hurt my ears through the helmet.

Stalled traffic ahead. I charged at it and then got off the gas. In the side mirror I watched the FBI narrow my lead. Closer. Closer. Almost touching my rear wheel.

I yanked on the brake, gunned the engine and spun away. My rear tire laid down a thick coat of rubber while the bike twirled into the opposite lane, aiming back down the tunnel, facing the FBI's trucks. It happened too fast and they crashed, trying to follow. They collided and plowed into the wall together. I was already gone before they could reverse.

I took a deep breath and held it. By the time I released the air I was four blocks away and home free.

"Nice work!"

"Woohoo!" I cried.

"I can't keep up with you on the monitors," the helmet said. "Do you feel invincible? Indestructible? Are you driving like a maniac?"

"Absolutely," I howled. "Wooooooo! That was awesome!" I felt high, almost light-headed with delirium.

"That's the virus talking, and it's going to kill you, stupid. Slow down. Go the speed limit."

"Why?"

"Because you're not Batman, dumbass!" the speaker rattled. "What the hell is wrong with you? You're a kid. You don't want anyone to know where you live. You left the FBI behind, so slow down, don't draw more attention to yourself, and get out of there. Stay south on Alameda, get on Interstate 10 and go home."

I obeyed. The chaos quickly faded in the side mirrors. I drove through resplendent sections of the city unaware of the recent power outage. None of these cars had alarms honking. My blood pressure slowly returned to normal. Soon I vacated the heart of the city and headed north.

The high wore off. My body crashed. I felt drained. I was both starving and sick to my stomach.

"Thanks for the help," I said, groggily.

"Shut up. Go home and sleep before you throw up or your head explodes."

"So you really are Infected," I marveled, fighting the desire to race around the cars ahead. They looked like they were moving in slow motion.

"Duh."

"What's your name?" I asked.

"PuckDaddy."

The line went dead.

Chapter Nine
Tuesday, January 17. 2018

I didn't get out of bed Sunday. Everything ached: my bones, my head, my stomach, all of me. The light was a torment. Finally, around dinner time, I roused and ate everything in the house, and then I slept again. My father was worried about me for the first time in months. I even skipped school Monday.

I didn't text PuckDaddy. He didn't text me. The Shooter didn't show up to waste me. Carter didn't swing by and kill me himself, even after Saturday night's hijinks. I'd acted foolishly, thoughtlessly, irrationally. My emotions and adrenaline had usurped my sanity, like I'd been drunk. I *must* guard against that in the future.

Monday night, Natalie texted me.

>>Captain FBI is not very happy with you.

I smiled and replied, **I like him.**

>>He gave me his number.

Why??

Are you're going to date an FBI agent???

>>Maybe. He's kinda hott. But the number is for you. He wants you to call him.

Oh. Right, I texted. I shouldn't be jealous. I'm not allowed to be jealous. I have a girlfriend. And I was in love with Katie, besides that. Wow, my life's messed up. Just thinking about the girls churned my stomach. **You guys would be a handsome couple.**

>>How'd you do all that?

Do all what?

>>Make the lights erupt, extinguish the electricity, ignite the car horns, all that?

It's a secret, I typed. And it was, even from me. I had no idea how PuckDaddy did it.

>>He was extremely startled. And impressed. You should have seen his face.

>>I witnessed your jump. So did Captain FBI.

>>It was high.

>>Impossibly high.

>>He knows you're not normal now. He also knows about your disease. He has an audio recording of our conversation.

Uh oh. I'm dead. Carter was going to kill me.

The next morning at school Samantha Gear lowered into the seat next to me. I hadn't seen in her in a few days and I forgot how striking the kicker was; her body looked like a cage-fighter's or a triathlete's. She was attractive, but in an intimidating way. Lee dropped into the seat next to her.

"See, dude," he cackled, giving her his phone. "I told you."

Samantha sighed, exasperated, "Told me what, handsome?"

"See for yourself," he indicated the phone.

"I'm tired, Lee. I'm going to break your phone if this is a joke. What am I looking at?" she asked.

"The Outlaw, dude. Of course."

I half choked on the chocolate granola bar I was eating, and I said, "What??"

"The Outlaw, Chase. I told you!"

Samantha screwed up her eyes at the screen and said, "I don't see anything." I peered over her shoulder. Sure enough, there I was. I wanted to throttle Lee. He'd taken a photograph of me Saturday night behind his house. "The picture's too dark. And I just see someone wearing a helmet."

"That's him!" he blurted out.

"No it's not. That's you, wearing a helmet," she said and tossed him the phone back. "I hate you."

"Chase, tell her," he said miserably.

I asked, "Tell her what? She's right. The Outlaw doesn't wear a helmet."

"Yes he does! Didn't you see the film of him talking to the FBI? He was wearing the same helmet, dude, with the vest I made him."

"Ah crap," I groaned. "I forgot about that FBI thing."

Lee frowned, "How could you forget? It's all over the news, bro."

"You made him a vest?" Samantha asked Lee, pulling out her homework. Homework! I'd forgotten to do mine. Now I was two days behind. Dang it. "You sew?"

"Heck yeah I did," Lee crowed. "A ballistic vest."

"Ballistic?" Samantha asked. "Why?"

Lee grinned delightedly. "He's going after the LA Sniper. Wants to be able to survive a gun shot."

"Oh he is? The Sniper?" Samantha laughed. A rich, husky, contagious sound. "That's hilarious!"

"I agree," I said. "He's not going after the Sniper. Just wants to be safe, is my guess."

"He going hunting," Lee nodded sagely. "He told me so."

Katie touched me in Spanish 3. She was laughing at a joke and innocently pushed my arm. The instant her hand touched me, I melted. All of my worries, all of my stress, the distant throb in the front part of my brain were all lost in the warmth of her flesh. Like magic.

For the rest of the class, and into lunch, I kept taking her hand or finding ways to touch her. She alternated between confused, annoyed, and pleased with my insistent attention. I told her the truth, that it made me feel better. She smiled and wrinkled her nose. But I didn't take my hand off. And I felt great!

Lee and Cory thought the touching was weird. Even Samantha Gear did, who had started sitting with us. I could sense Katie was unsure of the new seating arrangement, even though she was nothing but nice and accepting of the kicker. As an experiment, I walked over to Hannah Walker and placed my hands on her neck and said hello. She beamed, and although Hannah caused butterflies to take flight in my stomach, she did not take away my headache. I glided back to my table, but Katie wouldn't let me touch her anymore. Girls are weird.

"Hey. Where's my sandwich?" I asked, sitting back down.

Katie told me, "Cory ate it."

"Cory!" I shouted at the giant.

"You snooze," he said, his mouth full of food.

"Don't eat my food! I'm really hungry."

"Here," Katie said and she slid me her apple. "I'm not going to eat it."

"This sandwich is really good," Cory said appraisingly, examining the remaining portion in his big fist.

"I know," I grumbled. "I put extra jelly on it."

Samantha asked, "Aren't you a cook, Cory?" The big guy nodded and she said, "Cook for me."

"What?" Lee asked, bolting upright. He shot looks at both of them.

"Yeah," Samantha continued, using her green laser beam eyes on Cory. "Invite me over tonight and cook for me."

Cory looked a little confused and a little scared and a little intrigued. "You wanna come over tonight?" he asked, gulping his food. She nodded slowly. "Why?"

"I like big guys," she shrugged. "And I like food."

Lee interjected, "You want to come over to *my* house? I'll order take out."

"You missed your chance," she answered. "Now I only have eyes for Cory."

"Why?" Cory asked again.

"Cory," Katie scolded him. "You're a good-looking guy. Don't act surprised when girls like you."

"Exactly," Samantha smoldered. "Invite me over. It's perfect. You're handsome and I'm pretty."

"You are pretty," Katie agreed, unscrewing her juice. "I'd kill for those eyes."

"Oh shut up," Samantha poked her. "You're so hot it makes me want to bite you. I would literally shoot Lee in the head if I could have your skin."

"I think," Lee said, "that our relationship has taken an unfortunate turn. Now shut up everyone. I want to watch the television."

"Ugh. More Outlaw headlines?" Samantha asked. She'd brought slices of chicken, two bananas, a carrot, and two chocolate bars for lunch. Not even Cory would dare touch her food. She's intense. But I liked her. "I'm so tired of those. You're obsessed, little man."

"No, no. The FBI thing is old news, dude. This is about the big rumble last night."

Katie asked, "What big rumble?"

"Do you never check twitter? Or watch television?" Lee demanded, seriously affronted.

"No," Katie said, and her cheeks colored a little. "Not last night."

"Why?" Cory asked, still chewing on my sandwich. "What happened last night?"

Katie answered, "I had a date."

"Oh my goooooooosh," I groaned. "With Tank?"

"Yes."

"Noooooooooo."

Katie asked, "What's wrong with you? Why do you keep rubbing your head? Do you have a headache?"

"I'm fine," I muttered. "Just hold my hand."

"No."

"Why didn't you tell me you had a date?"

"Because it happened so last minute," she replied. "I hadn't heard from him in over a week, and I assumed he wasn't going to text me again. But then he just called me out of the blue, said he was out front in his car, and we went to dinner."

"I hate it. Hate hate hate it."

"I've seen pictures of Tank Ware," Samantha grinned. "That's one big kid. Muscles on muscles, probably benches twice his weight. Attractive, too."

"I think so!"

"No he's not," I growled.

"Did you have a good time?"

"Yes," Katie said, hesitating a little, as if she wasn't sure. Her eyes darted my way for a fraction of a second.

"That means you didn't!" I hooted triumphantly. "I can tell! Wooohoo!"

"No, I did," Katie retorted. "He and I are…very different."

"You're perfect, he's the devil, duh," I pointed out.

"It was fine. We laughed a lot. But he acted a little abnormal. Like he had a hard time concentrating. It's just bizarre, you know? He hadn't contacted me in almost two weeks and then he shows up like everything is okay? I'm just not sure I trust him."

"Good," I said. "You shouldn't."

"Boys are strange," Samantha Gear said, nibbling on her chocolate. "Guys are still by and large in a Cro Magnon phase of maturity. I bet Tank wanted to make out too."

"Yes," Katie admitted, scanning me for a reaction. My face didn't even twitch. Fortunately she couldn't tell I accidentally crushed one of the table's metal legs; I clenched my fist and the metal pinched and melted like butter.

"And?" Samantha pressed.

"And I didn't. He wanted to come to my bedroom, but I said no. Maybe next time," she shrugged.

"No. Not maybe next time! That guy is scum and doesn't deserve to live in the same state as you," I practically shouted.

Samantha murmured, "*Someone's* jealous."

"Protective. Worried. Not jealous. There's a difference. And shut up."

Samantha sniffed and said, "Don't you have a girlfriend?"

I frowned. "Yeah? So?"

"Why don't you sit with her? I've seen her. She's the hottest girl in school. Maybe in the whole city."

"Second hottest," I corrected her instinctively.

"Who is first?"

"Katie."

"Aw!" Katie smiled.

"My relationship with Hannah is complicated," I explained. "So complicated I can't figure it out."

"She can't be happy about you sitting here with this Latina goddess," Samantha indicated Katie, who blushed in pleasure.

I said, "I'm not sure Hannah has emotions, actually. She's like a robot. Think of our relationship like a really well balanced math equation."

Samantha shook her head and said, "Your life is weird, Chase."

"I agree," I sighed. "But I don't know how to fix it."

Lee interrupted us and said, "You guys are missing all the good stuff."

"What good stuff?"

"The war!" he chirped and pointed at the screen. There was aerial footage of a large-scale riot, or protest, or something. I couldn't tell. Rivers of people were surging into each other. Cars were overturned. Cops with riot gear were forced back. The helicopter was taking fire from somewhere. Bodies fell off houses. The injured and the dead were left behind as waves of combatants receded to crash again somewhere else.

"Where is it?" I asked.

"South LA," Lee said. "Near Compton. And Carson. I read last night that each side had ten thousand guys going at it, bro. Twenty thousand total."

Katie asked, "Going at it? What does that mean?"

"A giant fight. Punching, knives, guns. You know, man, a war."

"Why?" I asked. "Is it about the immigration law?"

"No one knows," Lee intoned, staring rapturously at the screen. He lived for media drama. "Even the people involved don't know. In fact, I read that the Bloods and Crips and MS-13 members were all fighting among themselves, too."

"What is happening to Los Angeles?" Katie asked. "It's scary."

"The Police had to send everyone they had. Filled the streets with tear gas to break it up. Lasted from seven until four this morning, dude."

Dozens were dead, according to the banner at the bottom of the screen. *Dozens*?! Many claimed to have been hit with wax bullets, presumably by the LA Sniper. Or, the Infected Shooter, as I thought of him. The news channel began to show pictures of wanted individuals, suspected in beginning the fray.

I lost interest after a handful scrolled by but then one of the mugshots caught my eye.

"Hey. I know that guy," I blurted out.

"How?" Samantha asked me.

"Oh, well...," I said. His name was Guns. Or at least that was his nickname. I'd seen him hanging out with Tank, and I even fought him once. I think. I lost track of the people I'd punched. "Or...maybe not. Might just be my imagination."

"Too bad, bro," Lee told me. "There's a reward."

A reward?

My evening just got interesting.

Stay alive.

Prevent Tank from hurting Katie.

Stay alive.

Prevent Tank from hurting Katie.

Those were my goals and capturing Guns to claim a reward didn't help accomplish either one. So maybe this was a bad idea. I paced the bedroom for over an hour, talking with myself. I'd completed my homework at the kitchen table while Dad flipped channels in his chair. Now he was asleep, and here I was pacing. It was the disease talking. I recognized the familiar euphoria, the distant siren call of the night beckoning. I should just go to sleep, give my brain plenty of downtime. But I could hear the illness whispering, leaking epinephrin and energy into my body, transmuting my bed into a completely unacceptable option, an utter waste of time.

Earlier in the day I'd visited a motorcycle shop near Memorial Park. I found red peel-off decals for my bike and helmet. With them I could transform the motorcycle's color scheme from black and orange to black and red. And when the Outlaw finished rampaging around the city, I'd simply peel the red decals off and save them for future use. Camouflage! I also cut out some white decals so I could alter the license plate.

Screw it. I was going. This would be fun! The illness and the night and the rush were irresistible. Wooooooooo!!

I looped around Natalie's and Tank's building twice and then expanded my search to include other city blocks, hunting for trouble makers that might lead to Tank or Guns. But the city is vast and my chances were small. After the fruitless search I decided to investigate one more spot. The house. *The House.*

I'd been in The House three times; once when I was searching for Katie's phone, once when I was reclaiming a stolen locket, and once when Tank had kidnapped Katie. Tank owned the house, probably through one of his holding companies. He was rich and invested in property and often visited this one in particular. He used it as a base for illegal operations. It was a two-story mess, situated on a run-down street not far from downtown.

My bike moved in silence behind the row of dilapidated houses, twisting between trashcans in the alley. It was midnight and nothing moved except the breeze. And the Outlaw. I climbed off (but left the battery engaged, ready to jet) and snuck up to the rear porch of the hated house.

Bingo. Activity. Men were lounging on the chairs and a couch, watching boxing. A couple occupants were asleep. The air was hazy.

No sign of Tank.

In the past I might have been afraid to enter such a room. Too many guys, too much muscle, too many possible weapons, too much could go wrong. But that was when Chase was in control of his body. That was when Chase's fears and rationalities ruled the day. Now? Now the Outlaw was in full possession. The Outlaw did not fear a den of lazy, clumsy crooks.

I walked brazenly into the room, picked up an unopened bottle of liquor and threw it through the television. The bottle and television both disintegrated, shattered glass flying, and the room reacted like a bomb had gone off. I picked up the first man to reach his feet and I hurled him into the other room. *Hurled* him. He traveled over fifteen feet in the air, crunched the far plaster wall, and landed like a sack of dirty laundry.

After that, nobody moved.

"Evening, gentlemen," I said to my captive audience. I recognized a couple of them from previous interactions.

"The Outlaw."

"El Diablo."

"That's me," I confirmed. "You boys enjoy the big fight last night?"

"Not us, man," a little due spoke up. "No way, Outlaw. Didn't go near it."

"That's not what I heard. And how are you, Beans?" I asked. "Remember when I carried you to the hospital?" I'd had multiple run-ins with this particular character. He was all mouth, no heart. He nodded. "Good times, Beans!"

"Why don't you go away," he said with every scrap of nerve he possessed. "We ain't bothering nobody."

"Ah, poor grammar and a double negative. How I love the ruffians."

"We didn't start nothing, man," he said. "We don't go south anymore. Getting loco down there, Mr. Outlaw."

"What do you mean?" I asked.

"There's a crazy man, yo. You heard of him? He controls everything with his new drugs," Beans said and he tried to marshall support from his silent, sullen companions. "Nobody don't mess with him."

"What's his name?"

"Don't nobody don't know, man. Rumors about rumors, right? But people talk. He's crazy."

"Speaking of crazy," I said. "Where my old pal Tank?"

Stoney silence. No response.

"You know," I encouraged them. "Big guy? Ugly? Wears gloves all the time? You call him T."

Nothing. Angry stares.

"Oh well. Tell him I said hello. I'll just take Guns and be on my way," I said, and I pointed at the man in the green hoodie near the television. I'd spotted him immediately.

"The hell you want with me?" Guns asked. He gave the impression of being high. Or drunk. Or aggressively stupid.

"I'll tell you when we get there," I said as cheerfully as I could in my deep snarl.

Just then, the house shook, as if from a small earthquake. Dust drifted from the ceiling. Wooden boards everywhere groaned, and a tyrannosaurus rex came down the stairs. Or at least that's how it sounded, based on the deep booming footsteps.

"Who is making the noise?" asked a voice so low it could have been vibrating out of a subwoofer.

Someone whimpered. Actual whimpering.

Tank, if possible, had gotten bigger, but he looked terrible. In the past he'd dressed immaculately and taken great care of his appearance. Now his hair was a mess, he had bags under his eyes, and his clothes were rags. He squinted against the light. Sometimes I forgot that he wasn't a super villain; he was a teenager with homework and football practice and parents.

"Beans made the noise," I answered, rolling my eyes. "You know him. He's a chatterbox."

"You," he said, his baleful eyes alighting on me.

"Not me," I said, hauling Guns to his feet. "Beans. Now go back to sleep."

"New outfit," he said, and he shook his head like an invisible fly was bothering him. "Looks stupid."

"You don't like the vest? I like it. Makes my arms look great. By the way Tank, have you been having headaches? Stomach aches? Trouble with stress? Things like that?" I asked on a whim. "Feel like you could die any minute?"

He didn't answer. He came after me in a rush, like a furious freight train. I jumped away, hauling Guns after me, but I couldn't move him fast enough. Tank plowed into us, his gloved hands going for my throat. We crashed *through* the rear wall, sprawling and rolling out into the backyard. Tank and I were both temporarily disoriented by the sudden darkness. Guns was knocked out cold. My head was killing me.

"Tank, you big dummy," I shouted. "How will you explain that to your mortgage insurance?"

He tried to stand but stumbled on the rubble. I grabbed a long section of a broken 2x4 and hit him in the head, using the busted wood like a baseball bat. The board shattered and Tank fell over again, but he appeared to barely feel it. Oh well.

I hefted Guns up on my shoulder like a big sack of potatoes and ran for the bike. Getting on wasn't easy. I held his inert body between my arms and knees like I would a child, and I opened the throttle. Gravel flew and we leapt out of the alley.

"Man, I hate that house!" I shouted, steering onto the adjacent street.

Tank materialized out of nowhere like a nightmare, landing heavily on the sidewalk. He roared unintelligibly and sprinted after us. I should have been able to speed away from him, but I couldn't. He was miraculously keeping abreast of my bike, his thick legs pumping steadily, his mouth pulled into a vicious grimace. My speedometer read **35 mph**. Isn't that faster than humans can run?? I tried increasing our speed but Guns slipped out of my grip, forcing me to decelerate and readjust my cargo. Tank veered off the sidewalk and swung an olympic-sized fist at me. I jerked the handles, barely evading him, and we lost even more speed. His next swing would destroy us.

I glanced up, just in time to see the Los Angeles Sniper rise up like a ghost on the house ahead of us. The Sniper! The Shooter! It had to be. He stood tall, poised, slender, rock solid, feet planted on either side of the roof's incline, death incarnate silhouetted by the moon. The figure raised a rifle to his shoulder in slow motion.

Time   slowed   down   to   heartbeats.   I'm   dead...the Shooter...Infected...Maybe he'll hit the vest...Lee's kevlar plates better work...Katie...Katie...

The Shooter fired, an angry flare bursting from the weapon's maw. I flinched instinctively. No noise. Silencer! Did he miss??

Tank's head snapped back! One second he was towering over us, the next he was on the ground, holding his face. He groaned and roared and shook his skull from side to side. He was alive?? A wax bullet!

This is madness! I gunned the engine, popped a wheelie that almost tossed

Guns, and streaked away from Tank and the Shooter.

"That was a bad idea….and kind of awesome!"

"…hello?" Lee's slurred voice came over the headset in my helmet.

"Wake up, Lee," I barked into the receiver.

"Outlaw?" he asked.

"I just deposited a fugitive into the back of your car. He's on the police's wanted list," I shouted. I was close to fainting. The pain! "He's tied up. Take him to the police station immediately. Collect the reward. Don't mention me. It's a Thank You for the vest."

I clicked off and almost crashed. The pain was blinding. I could barely see, barely process, barely move. Tonight had been too much. Too much excitement, too much stress, danger, exertion. Every joint ached. Skull about to crack.

I braked to a clumsy halt. Where am I? Lots of lights. I know this place. Safety. Through a fog of delirium I tore off the helmet and pulled on my long-sleeved shirt. I left my bike illegally parked in a handicap spot and staggered up the steps to the Holy Angels Church. I remember this. I remember my mother's funeral here. I remember spending the night here once. The soft music was playing over the speakers instead of the organ pipes. The smell of incense permeated everything and wafted up from the pew cushion when I collapsed in the back. There were no other midnight pilgrims, just me, no more sounds. Most of the light came from candles burning near the alter. Quiet. Peace. Safe. Heaven.

Sleep.

I didn't hear Carter enter the church.

Chapter Ten
Wednesday, January 18. 2018

My phone was beeping. Unread text messages from Puckdaddy.

>>**Shooter requested permission 2 waste u last night**
>>**Carter said No**
>>**u 1 lucky dude**
>>**u dead?**
>>**hey dummy. u there?**
>>**u have a few more hours to respond b4 i erase all data on your phone**

I stared bleary-eyed until the words made sense. I'd just woken up at five in the morning on a pew in a church under a blanket most likely provided by our football team's offensive coordinator, Todd Keith. He worked as a Deacon at this church.

I'm not dead, I typed. **Why would you erase all the data on my phone?**

>>**good morning stoopid. thought the virus got u**

Not yet, I typed, and I sat up. Mercifully my headache was gone but my neck was intensely sore. I rubbed it and groaned.

"Your neck is sore because you had an aneurism."

I almost jumped out of my skin. Carter was sitting on the other side of the pew, legs stretched and ankles crossed. He still wore tactical gear, and he was still smoking cigarettes.

"And you had an aneurism because you didn't take my advice," he said a little hotly.

"Missed you too," I croaked.

"Not a joke, hero. You almost died last night. Should have," he shouted and it echoed throughout the towering sanctuary. "Perhaps I failed to express myself previously. Drop the machismo act. It'll kill you."

"How do you know I had an aneurism?"

"You have blood in your cerebrospinal fluid," he said and he flicked his ash on the floor.

"You shouldn't smoke in church. And I have blood where?"

"Smoke wherever I want, boy. I checked your subarachnoid. I've done it a lot over the years. You didn't even wake up. Found traces of blood. You had an aneurism. I'm shocked you're alive."

"An aneurism? That sounds awful. Shouldn't I be in worse shape than I am?"

"Your body is trying to both kill you and heal you at an enormously fast rate," he explained. "After the aneurysm failed to kill you, your brain began repairing itself."

"How'd you find me?" I asked, gingerly massaging the muscles around my spine.

"One of the Infected. He thought you were dead. Triangulated the wifi signal off your motorcycle. Or so he tells me." Carter waved his hand in the air to indicate he didn't understand the technology involved.

"Puckdaddy?"

"Call him what you like. He's the best alive. And he's hoping you'll stay that way. For some reason, he's rooting for you. I brought you breakfast."

I located a McDonalds bag under my seat. Five breakfast sandwiches. I could cry.

"How'd you know I'd be hungry?" I asked after finishing the first. "Like, really hungry. I'm starving."

"I'm Infected too, just like you," he said simply. "We get hungry, that's how it works." After I finished the third, he leaned forward and said, "Listen, hero. You're right in the middle of this thing. All the symptoms are here. I want you to make it. We need you to pull through. Gotta get yourself under control."

"You were right," I said, my mouth full of food. "My body is addicted to excitement. It's like the Outlaw is in control of my decisions half the time."

"Not the Outlaw. The virus," he barked at me. "You get no more chances. Not from me, and probably not from the virus."

"Got it."

"You must learn self-control. You *must*. The virus can kill you several ways."

"What do you mean?" I asked.

"Many Infected die even though they survived the virus. They live through post-adolescence but die in their twenties. That's one of the reasons why there are only nine of us."

"What happens to them?"

"Those of us that survive through the end of adolescence face two common pitfalls. The first is if an Infected decides he's Superman. Most of us do. We get drunk on power. And then we do something stupid. Like you did last night. For example, an Infected died last year. Let's call him Ten. Ten believed himself indestructible and so he jumped out of an airplane at fifteen thousand feet with no chute. There wasn't much left of him after the mountain got through," he said and he shook his head in disgust.

"Okay. Makes sense. Drunk on power, do something stupid. What's the other way the Infected die?"

"The second way. Like I said, we're a private group. We do not tolerate publicity. When one of the Infected threatens our anonymity..."

"You put a bullet in their temple?" I guessed, remembering his prior words.

"Exactly. We stay secret. And we enforce the secrecy. Remember that, mate." He stood up, took a final drag from his cigarette, and flicked the butt onto the ground at my feet.

"Wait," I said around a bite of eggs.

"What?" he demanded. He looked obscene and sacrilegious standing in the multi-hued stained glass light of the church, smoke still leaking from his nostrils. His gloved hands were clenched into fists.

"Tell me more about the Infected."

"There's nothing else," he snapped.

"Do you guys hang out? Like on a heli-carrier or something?"

"What is a heli-carrier?" he asked.

"The big flying ship the Avengers have."

"Get it through your head," he growled. "There are no such things as heroes."

"So you don't have a secret headquarters at the top of a tower? The Infected don't all live together? Christmas parties? That kind of thing?"

He glared at me a long time and then strode out without another word. I finished breakfast and texted Puckdaddy.

Thanks for the help. Again.

>>yeah yeah sure whatev

Why will you wipe all the data off my phone when I die?

>>ill erase the data so no1 asks questions about the virus. All virus evidence will vanish from phone after u die.

Can you really do that?

>>childs play

Where are you? Are you in the Infected's secret headquarters?

>>hah. i wish only infected Ive ever met is carter

Why don't you hang out with the others?

>>carter

What about him?

>>he doesn't let us

>> and that's all ill say if ur smart u wont piss him off

I thought Carter said he wasn't the boss

>>suuuuuuure lol

I'll try to be more careful. But if I survive the disease, I'm taking you out for a pizza. My treat.

>>hah sounds good

Hey. Do you ever talk with the Shooter?

>>duh. texting with Shooter right now

Good. Tell him thanks for helping me last night

>>tell him thanks???

>>hahahahaha lol

What's so funny?

>>u stupid but i like u

But tell him to quit shooting innocent people. It's freaking everyone out.

>>hah. u so stupid. u don't know the Shooter. Would never listen 2 me. Shooter's crazy.

Your grammar is terrible. Shouldn't the world's foremost computer hacker use better syntax?

>>u make fun of puckdaddy's texting and puckdaddy will empty ur bank account

>>anyway i need 2 use my wpm on other programs

>>right now im texting u, texting Shooter, counter attacking some cracker in moscow, helping an infected in austrailia, and writing code 4 new software. and watching sportscenter. go yankees. busy day, dummy. i rock. don't mess with puckdaddy!

I smiled and put the phone away. I liked that guy.

Good thing I woke up early. The world hadn't risen yet to see my Outlaw bike. I peeled the red decals off the motorcycle and then drove it home. Or at least I tried. The machine ran out of battery power two blocks away, so I pushed it the remainder. I bet Batman never has to do this.

My girlfriend Hannah Walker was complicated. Her GPA was currently a sparkling 4.2. She's captain of the Varsity cheerleaders. She'd never done drugs and refused to drink; she seldom attended parties at all. Despite her popularity, she was kind to everyone and never used her influence to rampage over any other girl's life. She took excellent care of me when I'd been hospitalized in November.

Despite all that, she had serious quirks. Our relationship was primarily a logical and convenient arrangement based on mutual respect. In other words, we used each other; I got to date a pretty cheerleader and she benefited by being attached to the Varsity quarterback. Unfortunately there were very few other benefits, especially now that football season was over and I reverted to social unimportance. She was mildly affectionate but usually distant, because affection wasn't really necessary in her life. Her parents never showed her any and she didn't see the need to express it herself. But, on the occasion when she decided to turn it on, it was an invigorating romp of the senses.

Today was one of those days. She informed me before classes that we needed to make a splash on social media. This was a periodic task on her agenda. These days were the closest we came to being a normal couple. She took selfies of us kissing for Instagram. She greeted me with hugs in the halls after each class. We sat at a table alone during lunch and Snapchatted pics to everyone. She racked up the Likes and Favorites and declared the day a success.

But it wasn't a success to me. The romance was clinical, not organic. Forced, not genuine. After school I sat on our school bleachers, watching Cory and Samantha practice football, and I took my 'relational temperature,' as my therapist once told me to do. Introspection. Self-evaluation. If I spent any time at all being real with myself, the truth was obvious: our arrangement was no longer meeting my emotional needs, even though I had very few. In fact, I was really only a prop to my girlfriend. To be fair, she generously offered to be my prop, and she was a shockingly attractive prop. However, I no longer cared about possessing a prop.

I just wanted Katie Lopez, but I couldn't have her. She had never returned my affection and she was dating someone else. But even so, my relationship with Hannah wasn't working and it was because I wanted Katie to such a degree that I'd rather be with her or else be with nobody.

I drove to her apartment but didn't go in. I sat astride my bike outside, wanting her, aching to be with her. Correction: I sat astride Hannah Walker's father's bike. Ugh. So confusing.

Katie's mom, a pretty middle school teacher, opened the front door and waved me in. She kissed my cheek and hugged me a long time. Her hair smelled like delicious, like seasoned peppers and chicken.

"Buenas noches, guapísimo," she smiled. "Thank you for visiting. We do not see you much."

"I know," I nodded, feigning shame. "I apologize. I've missed being here."

"Katie, she still talks about you. Always she talks about you. She still loves you," she poked me in the chest. "But..."

"But it's complicated now."

"But it's complicated," she agreed. "You want dinner?"

"Yes!"

Katie came in and we all ate. I had four helpings of fajitas because I was still hungry from last night's Outlaw episode. For thirty minutes the world was simple and happy and we were kids again. I kept hoping Katie would eventually break her promise to the Outlaw and tell me about his visit, but she hadn't yet. I was both pleased and disappointed.

We went back to her bedroom and I asked, "What do you think of Samantha Gear?"

"I like her. She's good for Lee and Cory. Keeps them on their toes."

"She's pretty intense. Coach Garrett could tell immediately that she'd be trouble."

"Will she make the team?" Katie asked, sitting down on the bed in the midst of her homework. I assumed my usual position in her desk chair. My neck ached. In the past, Katie would have massaged it. But no longer.

"Of course. She has a bionic leg, basically. What's all this? Are you preparing for your model U.N. event?"

"Yes," she sighed, surveying the extensive pile of papers. "I had to miss Young Life tonight. Too much to do."

"Good. That leaves no time for Tank," I grinned.

"Chase," she warned. "There will be no Tank bashing tonight."

"Do you have another date scheduled?"

"No," she admitted. "He's not the best communicator. We just live in totally different worlds, you know? That's what makes it exciting, but that's also what makes it frustrating."

"Frustrating," I said. "That's exactly it."

"What do you mean?"

"My love life," I said, tossing her stuffed bear into the air. "Frustrating. Complicated."

"Oh? Things not going well with Hannah?"

"You don't have to look so smug about it," I smiled.

"Smug? This is not my smug face," she smiled back. "This is my 'I told you so' face."

"When did things get so…weird? Remember when we spent every night in here, just being friends? Talking and laughing and being normal."

"We're getting older," she agreed.

"Let's make a deal."

"I'm listening," she said.

"I'll break up with Hannah. You call it off with Tank," I said with a sudden surge of courage. Let's live dangerously.

"Why would we?" she smiled, leaning forward towards me. Her sudden sensual interest in my deal seemed to actually draw the light towards her, like she had a gravitational pull.

"Because," I said, my brief burst of courage faltering as she grew more beautiful. I didn't deserve her. I never have. She deserved…everything.

"Tell me why," she repeated.

"Things could go back to the way they were."

"The way they were?" she asked. Neither of us could look directly at the other very long. The eye contact was brilliant and unbearable. This was scary uncharted territory. "Exactly the way they were?"

There was a loud, rapid knock at her back door. We both jumped as the room's enchantment shattered.

"Who is that?" I asked.

"Yo no sé," she said in Spanish. "Answer it."

"It better not be Tank," I said. "I'm going to knock his teeth out, if it is."

"What??" Katie cried, scrambling to her feet and cascading papers to the floor. "You can't just punch him! He's twice your size!"

I yanked open the back door, almost hoping the visitor was Tank. Empty. Nothing. Nobody in sight. Katie peered around my shoulder.

"This happen often?" I asked, scanning the lawn.

"Never. Oh, look! A note! I hope it's from him," she said and retrieved an envelope from the welcome mat. "That would be so romantic."

"I'm going to vomit," I said under my breath as she read it. "Well? Is it from Tank? I bet he wrote it in crayon."

"It's not from him. It's…I don't understand. This makes no sense," she said, puzzled. She held the note out to me.

Dear hot latina girl. sorry to bother u. no trouble. U know the

Outlaw right? tell him to call me. I gotta talk to him bout T. T gone crazy. this is important. beans.

"Oh man," I sighed, reading it again. This wasn't good. Tank had gone crazy enough for Beans to be worried? That's a new level of insanity. At the bottom was a telephone number.

"Does it make sense to you, Chase? What could 'beans' mean?"

"That's his name," I told her. "I mean, I guess it is. Right? That's how he closes the letter."

"What kind of a stupid name is Beans?"

"Stupid name for a stupid guy," I shrugged. "His handwriting is awful."

"And who is T? That sounds familiar," Katie said, looking off into the distance while she searched her memory. When she wasn't looked I saved the number into my phone.

"It should sound familiar to you. Unfortunately."

"Why? Why should…oh," she gasped. "Oh no. I remember now."

"Yeah," I sighed. "This is trouble."

"Oh no. T? The guy harassing me last year kept signing his name T."

"Right," I nodded. "And T is probably the guy that kidnapped you and escaped."

"T is back? Who's Beans? And why would he think I knew the Outlaw?" Katie asked, hugging a teddy bear to her chest. I won her that teddy bear at a fair. "This makes no sense."

"I have a theory," I said carefully. I had to reveal enough of the truth for her to be careful, but I had to postulate the facts like guesses. I could tell her the whole truth but she wouldn't believe me.

"Tell me."

"You and Beans are the middle-men between T and the Outlaw. Last year the Outlaw reclaimed your stolen phone from T. We already know that. It infuriated T so he kidnapped you in order to get the Outlaw. My theory is that this guy Beans knows T. They're buddies or business associates or something. Right? And Beans is worried about T going crazy so he wants to…tattle on T to the Outlaw, and he thinks that you could deliver the message."

"Oh," she said, processing. "That's complicated."

"Yes. Welcome to my life. Or I could be wrong and it's a trap."

"I don't know what to think," she cried. "Last time the police were absolutely helpless with this."

"And it's not like you *actually* know the Outlaw," I said, scrutinizing her carefully for a reaction. "Right?"

No response. She kept staring at the back door.

"Maybe I should just call this number now and tell Beans he should rat T out to the police," I suggested. Not a bad idea, actually. "Or give this telephone number to the police."

"Lee knows how to contact the Outlaw," Katie said.

"Maybe. Lee claims he made the Outlaw a vest or something, right? But, does that matter? I mean what can the Outlaw really do? Go beat him up?"

"I don't know," she said in a big breath of air as she laid down on the bed. "I thought this was all behind me. There's no way I can tell Mami. She'd freak out. But Chase, how does Beans know where I live?"

"Because of T. Because of the Outlaw. The stupid stupid Outlaw," I said, rubbing my temples with both hands. "He should never have returned your phone. He's caused nothing but problems."

She disagreed with me, strongly. But I didn't hear it. Natalie North had just texted me.

>>The FBI wants to help with your disease.

Chapter Eleven
Monday, January 23. 2018

I went to bed early four nights in a row. Two of the nights I didn't sleep a wink, tossing and fighting the covers until daybreak. But for those ninety-six hours I had no significant headaches or stomach cramps. The word 'aneurism' sent shockwaves through me and I swore to do anything to stay alive, to see my grandkids grow old. The grandkids I'd share with Katie, my wife. That was a fun thought until I remembered my girlfriend. I really gotta figure all this out.

Thoughts of Katie and Hannah and the aneurism forced me to a mall kiosk on Monday night, where I purchased a disposable cellphone with a temporary number. I thumbed off the new phone's location services, synced it with my bike helmet, drove to Beverly Hills and called Beans.

"What," Beans answered.

"Tank's gone crazy," I rumbled inside my helmet. "Explain."

"The hell is this?" he yelped.

"You wrote that Tank's going insane," I snarled. "Talk fast."

"Oh!" he cried. "Oh. Waitwaitwaitwaitwait a second," he panted, and I could hear him running. "Hang on

hangonhangon…gotta get somewhere I can talk." I rolled my eyes and kept motoring up and down extravagant streets teeming with extravagant shoppers and extravagant cars. Anyone trying to track this phone would have a hard time pinpointing me because I was in perpetual motion. "Okay," he gasped, sucking in air. "This the Outlaw?"

"The Easter Bunny," I corrected him. "Tell me about Tank."

"He gone loco, yo," Beans said. "He started using drugs, mano, and that ain't Tank. He's clean. Never touched the junk before, yo. Now he's snorting up blow by the shovel."

"Tank on coke," I sighed. "Just great. Because the world isn't broken enough."

"What?"

"He's trying to manage his pain," I reasoned, partly to myself. "I think he's sick. And in a lot of discomfort."

"Yeah, mano, always talking about a headache," Beans agreed.

"Has he ever passed out?"

"Hell yeah he has. Anytime he starts talking about you. Just falls on his ass, yo."

Aaaaaaaah crap. That confirmed it. Tank was Infected. I didn't know whether to offer him help or pray the virus killed him. I need to tell Carter.

"And, yo, he's straight obsessed with you, pana, you know? His parents gonna cut off his cash if he goes out anymore, you know, at night."

"You know about his parents?" I asked, shocked. "I thought you guys didn't know who he was."

"Nah. Told you. Gone crazy. Talking in his sleep, homie. Stumbling around like a zombie, saying weird crap."

"You need to turn him in," I said. "Let the police handle it."

"Not a snitch, yo. Be trippin."

"Honor among thieves?" I asked, taking another lap down Rodeo Drive.

"What?"

"Nothing. Anything else?"

"Yeah," Beans said. "The Chemist's been after him."

"The Chemist? What's that?"

"Yo. You don't know about the Chemist?" Beans asked. I grew weary of people pointing out how little I know. "The homie in south LA? Started the rumble, yo."

"Tell me about him."

"Don't nobody know," he said. "Just this guy south. Chemist. Controls all the drugs, got some kinda new recipe. He sent us a batch, but T threw it out."

"Smart move," I observed.

"But he's after T, mano. Wants to be allies or some crap."

"So there's a guy living in South LA that has a new type of drug, and he starts big city-wide fights, and he wants to be allies with Tank. That right?"

"Yeah man."

"Okay. Thanks for the info. Now do me a favor. Forget where the Latina girl lives," I said, and I parked my bike in an open spot in front of a designer boutique. It must have been a famous shop because girls were taking selfies in front of it.

"Yeah, Outlaw. Yeah mang. You got it."

"I'm serious."

"Alright alright," he shouted. "A la gran!"

"You need to stay away from T. It's going to get worse. If you need to talk to me, don't drop notes off at her door. Post a note on Craigslist. Use codeword Beans. I'll scan it every few days."

"Aight."

I hung up, searched through my contacts, located Isaac Anderson's number, called him on the new phone, and continued my itinerant motorcycle trek through downtown Beverly Hills. Just me and the luxury cars.

"Isaac Anderson," a brisk voice said on the other end.

"Captain FBI," I grinned, picturing the handsome agent's surprise. "This your cell phone?"

"It is," he said. "Who is this?"

"Don't try to track me," I said. "I'm mobile and I'm using a disposable phone. It'd be a waste of your time. So let's just talk."

"Outlaw," he identified me. "I can't track you from my cell anyway. You have my word. I'm in my kitchen chopping vegetables, that's all."

"Are you keeping tabs on the Chemist?"

"You know about him, huh," he chuckled.

"Of course," I lied. I didn't know anything. Ever.

"That was a pretty slick stunt you pulled," he said. "We still can't determine how you did all that magic."

"You are referring to your pathetic attempt at arresting me? And my easy escape?"

"I wouldn't call it pathetic," he said. I could hear him frown. "We weren't prepared for…all the tricks you have up your sleeve. I got chewed out by both the Deputy Director and his Assistant."

"That's a shame. Now tell me about the Chemist."

"Yeah, he's a problem. Fortunately for you he's turned into priority number one."

"What are you doing about him?" I asked, remembering to mask my voice just in case he was recording our conversation.

"Our section, and the U.S. Marshals, and the Sherrif's office, and LAPD have formed a temporary joint task force. It's been a real picnic, all us buttheads in one boat. But the Chemist is bad news and we want to grab him before it gets worse. To be honest I was hoping you might have some intel."

"What's in this new drug of his?"

"I wish I knew," he sighed, sounding exasperated. "Neither our forensics team nor Los Angeles Vice can figure it out. First of all we can't get our hands on much of the stuff, and secondly it's a designer cocktail we don't have experience with. Probably originating out of Europe. Seems to be effective. His thugs are unbelievably loyal to him."

"He's sending the drug to different gang leaders around the city as a present," I told him. "At least that's the way it appears."

"We suspected as much," he confirmed. "The Chemist is particularly effective because he's a good marketer. His gang is spreading fast and absorbing other groups."

"Ever seen a picture of him?"

"We think we have a few grainy photos. But what we have doesn't fit the profile. He's making inroads with gangs like Bloods, Crips, and MS13. Black and latino gangs. But our photographs are of a caucasian. A big white male, identity unknown. A handful of guys in lockup confirmed he's the mastermind. We thought for a while the Chemist might be the LA Sniper too."

"No. Different guys," I said.

"Yeah?" he asked. He sounded like he was drinking something. "You know the Sniper?"

"The Sniper is not the Chemist," I said. "Trust me. From what I know, the Sniper arrived recently to Los Angeles."

"A portion of our team believes *you're* the Sniper."

"Hah," I cracked. "The Sniper about took my head off the other night."

"He shot at you? The Sniper *missed?*"

"Not exactly."

"What were you up to?" he asked, and I heard a smile in his voice.

"Saving the world. The usual."

"You told Natalie North that you're sick," he changed the subject.

"Yep. How do you propose helping me?"

"Come to my office."

"No chance," I said.

"I played the recording for a physician in our Laboratory. He said it sounds like you have an unknown form of progeria."

"Progeria. The aging disease?"

"Right. Patients with progeria age rapidly. Simplistically, they have the body of a thirty year old when they're eight. You spoke as though your body is doing similar things. Am I right?"

"Not...really," I considered it. "Not aging. More like improving at a fatal rate. But I don't know much about it."

"How do you know you have this disease?"

"You saw me jump off the roof," I reminded him. "Right?"

"Oh, I'm aware you're a weirdo," he said, and to my shame I laughed. Dang it. The Outlaw doesn't laugh. "Thankfully Natalie and I are the only two who saw the full extent of that jump. But how do you know your diagnosis?"

"That's not your concern."

"It'd be easier to help if I knew."

"Sorry."

"I have an idea, then," he sighed.

"I'm listening."

"Leave a blood sample with Ms. North. Let my guys examine it," he said.

I didn't respond for several blocks. I wove in and out of traffic, examining his offer from all angles, until I finally came to rest at a red light. His idea had merit. Carter certainly wasn't much help with my disease. Carter was basically a vulture, waiting around until I finally kicked the bucket. Could the FBI actually help me survive? I'd have to do it in secret, because the Shooter would waste me the instant my betrayal was discovered.

"I'll think about it."

Chapter Twelve
Wednesday, January 25. 2018

Back in October I agreed to participate in a televised high school quarterback competition. I'd been having a good season and I didn't realize all the changes that were happening to my body then, otherwise I'd never have agreed to it. But at least I got out of school. Now the day of the competition had arrived, and Mr. Desper, our school's director of public relations, personally drove Andy Babington and me to a football stadium in Santa Monica. Andy sat in the front. Fox Sports had set up cameras and tents and interview stations around the field, and it was a typical gorgeous clear California afternoon.

Babington had several buddies in attendance but I didn't. While he talked and joked with the other alpha males, I sat by myself and stewed.

What was I going to do? I hadn't really thrown a football in two months, but I could now probably chuck it across town. Thanks to the bizarre disease I could win this competition easily and break all the records and get myself on every television set in America. But I wouldn't be playing on level footing. I had an unfair advantage. All the quarterbacks began throwing to loosen up so I played catch with Mr. Desper. I spun the ball in my hands and smiled grimly. This ball and I could do anything. It would go anywhere for me. In my mind's eye, visions of passes appeared, paths I could use to deliver the football anywhere, including through car windows a mile away.

"Hey, Chase," Mr. Desper called. "Take it easy. Save it for the cameras. You're stripping the skin off my hands."

This competition was only open to Californians and the surrounding states. Fifty guys had been invited. A pretty reporter introduced us one by one to the camera and rattled off our statistics from last season. I politely answered a few questions and then returned to my seat.

There were three challenges. An obstacle course. An accuracy contest. And a long distance throw. The contestants began cycling through them. Each of us had a name and number pinned to our shirt so our progress could be tracked. Two former professional QBs I didn't recognize sat in the stands, commentating into microphones for the camera.

My turn. How fast should I go through the obstacle course? Several cameras were recording me; I didn't want to embarrass myself but I also didn't need to draw extra attention.

The buzzer sounded and the Outlaw violently seized control of my body. I hadn't realized how fast my heart was beating, how much adrenaline I had pumping. I practically flew through the obstacle course, far too fast! My legs refused to listen. Chase Jackson was merely a passenger trying to wrench command away from the virus. I was moving like the fate of the world depended on it. Near the end, after scorching through a shuttle run, I made a desperate attempt to sabotage the virus and throw my body at the ground. It partially worked; I stumbled. I gasped and panted, pretending I was out of breath, telling myself, "Slow down, slow down, slow down." Despite the costly stumble I finished the course in second place, behind a state finalist sprinter.

I stalked to the coolers, gulped down some Gatorade, and returned to my seat. "Stupid, stupid, stupid, stupid, stupid," I scolded myself. "What is wrong with me?"

"What the hell *is* wrong with you, son?" Mr. Desper asked, sitting down in the adjacent seat. He appeared upset. "You just got second place. Which is good. But you walked right past the girl trying to interview you. You're talking under your breath, like you're crazier than a jack-in-the-box. You keep shaking your head at nothing. Your eyes are twitching!"

"Ugh," I groaned. "Sorry. I'm not myself today."

"You should go act chummy with the other contestants," he said, pointing at the crowd. A handful of the guys were watching me. "For appearances' sake. Everyone thinks you're insane. Which means they think I'm a jackass. And our school is a bunch of jackasses."

"I'm not talking to anyone," I said and pressed my face into a towel. "I already know too many people. I just need some peace."

"You've no time for peace, Mr. Jackson. You have two more events."

The accuracy event was easier to fake. I just simply missed on purpose. I wanted a respectable score, so my misfires weren't far off target. Instead of dropping the ball into the trash bin, I knocked it over. Instead of throwing the ball through the hoop, I threw it straight over it. Andy got a better score than me and he snickered with his friends when the scores were posted. I finished middle of the pack, and Mr. Desper was obviously disappointed.

Last, the event I'd been dreading, was the long distance toss. How do I *look* like I'm throwing as hard as I can while actually only throwing *a fraction* of that? Most of the other athletes had completed all three events and were milling around, killing time until the winners were announced. The ball spun in my hand as I stared down the field, stalling. Markers had been pinned into the turf, designating the current farthest tosses. They appeared ludicrously short.

"Let's go, Chase," Mr. Desper clapped behind me.

Okay. I'm just going to land the ball on the marker of the current leader. One of the flags was a lot farther away than the rest, so someone here had a cannon for an arm. I'd tie him. Brilliant. This way, I wouldn't be much of an anomaly. I took a three step drop, gathered and threw a long tight spiral.

While the ball was in flight, the marker moved. It wasn't a flag at all! I had aimed at a piece of trash scuttling across the field. I held my breath. This could be a disaster. The ball thumped down and all the guys started cheering. The announcer called out, "76 yards!" I let my air out in relief. Okay, that wasn't too bad. I beat the other throws by seven yards, which was within reason. I waved to the audience and the cameras, and I declined to throw again.

My combined score earned fourth place. Perfect. No interviews. But probably good enough to keep college scouts interested in me. I grabbed my gear and went to wait in the car. Like all superheroes do.

"Did you see the riots?" my father asked when I arrived home. He was watching television, drinking a soda. I dumped all my bags on the stairs.

"No. There's another one?"

"Yeah, closer this time," he said. "I thought you might have seen it, driving home from Santa Monica."

"Wow, it's that close?"

"Yep."

I dropped onto the couch beside him. I'd been spending as much time as possible with Dad ever since I found out about the disease. If I died, I didn't want him to have any regrets. "How was work?"

He shrugged and said, "Boring. I miss my old job. Look. The Governor called in the National Guard, but that'll take hours, if not the rest of the day. There," he pointed at the screen. "A mob ten thousand strong is heading north from Huntington Park."

"That's south of downtown," I said, scrolling through Twitter on my phone. "So like...fifteen miles from us?"

"About. Ten thousand people," he whistled. "Glad I'm not a cop today."

"People are going to get hurt. A lot of them are probably hopped up on drugs, too. I'm glad you worked the morning shift."

My phone chimed.

I had THREE phones now. My personal line, which I paid for. The Outlaw's phone, which Natalie paid for. Very few people knew that number. And the disposable phone that I used just once to call Beans and the FBI. I left that one upstairs under my mattress.

This was a new text message from Natalie North.

>>The Outlawyers have offered me $5,000 to come speak at their next meeting. LOL! Think I should go?

"The Outlawyers?" I said to myself. "What are the Outlawyers?"

"Outlawyers are fans of the Outlaw," Dad answered, looking at his phone. His buddies from the police force always kept him updated. "S'what they call themselves."

"How do you know?"

He shrugged and said, "Everyone knows."

"I cannot believe Outlaw fan clubs actually exist. Outlawyers. That's a stupid name."

"Why do you hate the guy so much?"

"I don't *hate* him," I protested and stood up to get a better view of the screen. "I just have a more realistic impression of him than most people do, that's all. Is that...? Are those protestors *burning* an Outlaw doll??"

"Yep. Burning him in effigy."

"What? Why?! What'd he do? The world's gone mad."

All evening I monitored the television in my room with mounting trepidation. The mob had crossed the Santa Monica Freeway and was flooding into the Fashion District. The task force was slowing fragments of the tide but the full might of the National Guard hadn't arrived yet. The ocean of angry humanity kept surging north. There appeared to be no rhyme or reason to the crowd; the police were hauling Blacks, Whites, Hispanics and Asians away in droves, young and old. Reports claimed drug use was obvious and rampant. None of the channels mentioned the Chemist, but that might be because he wasn't public knowledge yet.

On a whim I texted Puckdaddy, **You heard of the Chemist?**

>>of course dummy, came the instant reply on the Outlaw's phone.

Know anything about him?

>>nope. hes completely off the grid. well hidden.

Can't the Shooter do anything about him? Shoot out his tires? Blow up his house?

>>cant find him, stoopid. just told u that. thats not really how the Shooter operates n e way not exactly a public defender

>>also carter wants u 2 stay out of the city 2nite

No problem. I was going to bed early. Nothing on earth could get me into the city.

But then Natalie North texted me an hour later.

>>Hey... I'm reluctant to bother you. But...could you come help? The mob has surrounded my building. They're breaking in. Yelling something about the Outlaw. I'm really terrified...

Chapter Thirteen
Thursday, January 26. 2018

"Thank you for tuning into Channel Four News, and our on-going coverage of tonight's dramatic events. The mob's retreat south continues, as you can see here live, but many of our callers are asking for an Outlaw update. There's a lot we don't know yet, but here's what we do know. Police report last night that a man on a motorcycle broke through their barricade around 9:30pm, driving into the downtown area. The description of the rider fits that of the Outlaw. The cameras on our Channel 4 helicopter caught this fleeting glimpse of a figure leaping from the top of the a parking garage and landing on a hotel roof across Broadway. That bears repeating: this figure, which we presume is the infamous Outlaw, jumped _across_ Broadway, a span of perhaps fifty feet, from several stories up. As you can see here, several minutes later our cameras spotted the same figure on top of the condominium building that should now be familiar to Outlaw enthusiasts. This is Natalie North's building, the same roof on which the Outlaw fought for Katie Lopez's safety. It's also the location of the FBI's famously unsuccessful attempt to arrest him.

What's on your screen now is a collage of all the pictures and video footage we have. All the residents of this building, including Natalie North herself, had taken shelter on the roof and were waving their arms for help. We can clearly see the throngs of angry protestors below, breaking the windows and the doors of this building and surging inside.

From the information we've gathered, it appears this building was the ultimate target of the entire riot. Channel 4 news has no other reports of similar, concentrated attacks on any other building downtown. This apartment complex was the focal point, and hundreds of rioters swarmed it.

Regina Woods, an apartment owner in the building, offered us this insight. "I don't know why they attacked us. None of us do, do we? It has something to do with the Outlaw, we know that. They started knocking down our doors, like they were looking for him. It was scary...all the screaming. My husband and I live on the second floor so we ran up here to the roof as quickly as we could. It's like the world was ending. The people...they were acting...inhuman, I guess is the right word."

Our cameras had also been tracking the arrival of the National Guard. The combined might of local law enforcement was not enough to repel the riot. This panoramic shot from our helicopter illustrates how close the National Guard's forces were. Those are the headlights of the incoming military jeeps you can see driving into the city off of Highway 10.

"We thought we could survive until help arrived. We saw their caravan lights a few blocks away. My husband thought so, anyway. I was having trouble thinking anything. But...oh yes, that was when the Outlaw jumped off the roof. He was talking with Ms. Natalie, and then he was gone. I still don't know why he did that. I feel sure he's dead, the poor man. I hope not, but...that's a long fall."

Those two figures centered on your screen are Natalie North and the Outlaw. Natalie hasn't yet commented on what exactly happened, but we can see they are talking and pointing downwards. And then...well, just watch. We lose sight of the Outlaw because he simply jumps off the building into the street below. If there was any doubt before that this person, the Outlaw, is either a world-class athlete or using some form of unknown technology or....or something exceptional that we can't explain yet...well, that doubt has been removed, at least in this reporter's mind. These are not camera tricks.

Captain Luke Boas describes what he saw.

"Our company entered the city at approximately twenty-one hundred hours. We were boots on ground at the scene of the incident five minutes after that. We engaged the civilian protestors using non-lethal crowd dispersal techniques, and they proceeded south without offering resistance. No casualties. Few injuries. And no, we did not encounter any vigilantes."

In other words, we don't know why the Outlaw jumped into the streets and we don't know where he went. There's a lot we don't know, to be frank. We don't know why the rioters were attacking this building. Or perhaps I should rephrase. We can make an educated guess that the rioters were looking for the Outlaw in that apartment building, but we don't know why they thought he would be there. Does he live there? Does he...

...wait. I'm just receiving an update. We're about to put a graphic onto your screen. Apparently Natalie North has taken to twitter. There it is now. She tweets, 'I'm fine. Scared, but fine. The Outlaw was rescuing people being dragged out of our building. I don't know what happened to him.'

Okay, so there's another piece to this puzzle. According to Natalie North, the protestors were dragging residents out into the streets and the Outlaw intervened. If anyone has pictures of this, Channel 4 news would like to see them. This story..."

Natalie North turned the screen off. We had been watching the news report on her iPad. Now everything was dark and silent. I could have been at the bottom of a well.

"Where am I?" I asked. I could see nothing but the vague outline of her face. I didn't even remember waking up. Maybe I was dreaming.

"We're alone. In my storage unit, under the apartment building," she answered, stroking my hair. "I knew that if I took you to my apartment you'd be discovered. So we came down here to protect your anonymity."

"Thank you," I said. My voice came out in a croak. "What time is it?"

"Seven in the morning."

"Do you have any water?"

"I do," she responded hesitatingly. "But you'll have to remove your mask."

"You haven't taken my mask off? Not even once? While I was asleep?"

"Well, the doctor did. He had to give you mouth to mouth," she said, and she unscrewed the top of a water bottle.

"Mouth to..." I repeated, confused.

"But I never saw your face. It was too dark."

"Why was a doctor giving me mouth to mouth?" I asked, feebly ripping off the loosely attached mask. My anonymity felt completely unimportant in this moment. Besides, it was suddenly stifling. If I could barely see her then should barely see me. She poured several gulps of succulent cold water into my mouth.

"I knew it," she smiled in the dark.

"You knew what?"

"I knew you'd be gorgeous."

"Hah. You'd say that even if I was an ogre," I chuckled.

"Probably."

"Why was a doctor giving me CPR?"

"What do you remember?" she asked.

"Nothing. I remember...I couldn't reach you...I remember parking...a few blocks from here. And then...nothing."

"You jumped off the roof, Outlaw," she grinned and poked me gently in the ribs.

"I did? Why?"

"You and I were watching the mob below us. They captured a kid who lives in my building. The Wares' son."

"The Wares' son," I frowned. "Do you mean Tank? Why'd they capture him?"

"How do you know Tank?" she asked, clearly surprised.

"Oh. Well. Because. He's a pretty well-known football player. Still in high school, right? I've heard of him."

"Yeah, that's him. There was a rumor going around that Tank was the Outlaw. I even wondered that myself once," Natalie said. She was pressing a wet washcloth onto my face. I actually didn't feel that bad, now that I was waking up. But having someone care about me was pleasant.

"So the mob grabbed Tank because...they thought he was the Outlaw?" I puzzled. "Is that right?"

"I believe so. That's what it sounded like. Imagine their surprise," she snickered, "when the real Outlaw landed in their midst. I hope someone got video of that."

"What happened?"

"You freed Tank. I don't know how you survived that fall. It's five stories."

"Nothing feels broken," I commented, wiggling my feet.

"Tank was unconscious. You drove all the rioters back. You fought like a hundred guys. And that's when the jeeps started rolling in."

"Then what?" I asked. This was a fascinating story, especially because I participated in it.

"You found me in the lobby and then..." she paused.

"Then what?"

"Well, not to sound dramatic but then you died."

"Then I died?!" I cried.

"You just fell over," she nodded. "You grabbed your head and collapsed. You had no pulse. One of my friends, the chief of medicine at General Hospital, helped me pull you down here, and he revived you. CPR."

"Whoa," I breathed.

"He did *not* want to leave you here. He's checked on you three times, and I'm under strict orders to call him immediately if you act funny."

"He should have let you die," Carter said, his voice ringing out like a hammer, shattering our private conversation. Both Natalie and I jumped.

Where'd *he* come from?? "Woulda saved me the trouble." Carter stepped into our dim circle of light that came from an emergency bulb in the corner. Natalie started to scream but he calmly drew his pistol, thumbed the hammer back, and placed the muzzle against her jaw. "Not sure if you have to die yet, Ms. North," he said gruffly. "So try not to give me ideas. Don't get ambitious, kid," he barked at me when I started to rise. "I'll kill you both before you get halfway."

"What are you doing here?" I demanded.

"Told you," he snarled. "Told you to keep your head down. Go to bed early. No extra attention. Now you're on every TV on the planet."

"Let her go, Carter," I warned.

"Maybe. Maybe not," he said. He shoved Natalie and she fell onto the blanket beside me. And then to my surprise he sat down on a box, like weariness overtook him. He sighed and rubbed his face. Nobody spoke for over sixty seconds. Finally, "This whole thing is getting out of hand."

"What whole thing?"

"There's much you do not know, kid. So much. Shoulda trusted me. Now…now it's gone to hell. The entire…all ruined." He was talking into space, his eyes far off, thinking about things unseen. Natalie and I glanced at each other but kept quiet. I wanted him to keep talking. "What you don't realize is that I'm protecting you. From yourself. From everyone."

"I can take care of myself."

"You're a mess, hero. You've basically died twice. Realize that? I'm not mean. I'm realistic. I don't *pre*scribe, I *de*scribe. I'm pragmatic. I wanted you to make it. Really wanted it. A grand experiment of enormous magnitude. Thought I could control it," he kept droning to himself. "Thought I could manage. Still might. Maybe… Variables…too many variables… But it's falling apart."

"Nothing's falling apart," Natalie said. "He's one of the most beloved people on the planet. My publicist takes calls daily from reporters wanting to interview him."

"Really?" I asked.

"Of course. They all want me to introduce you. I keep telling her No.

She's even hired a ghostwriter to compose our story into a novel that will be released the day after you sign off on it," she rolled her eyes.

"You see, kid? This is a disaster," Carter said.

"Just relax, Carter. Everything's okay."

He laughed bitterly and said, "You're losing parts of your memory. You can't handle your emotions. Or your body. Soon you'll be out of control. Everything is not okay."

"I'm not insane."

"You're wearing a clown costume, jumping off buildings, and you have no memory of it. Exactly what further evidence do we need? Soon you'll start hurting people."

"I'm helping people," I reasoned. I was vulnerable, on my back. He had all the power. Keep him talking. "What do you do with your ability? Nothing that I can see."

"Tried helping you," he said tiredly. "But you didn't listen. Really wanted you to make it. Wanted it to work. Exhausted with failure. But it's a no go. You're just grist for the virus. All the time…all the years…and the planning. It gets all of us, eventually."

"The virus? Not the surviving Infected," I said.

"Especially the survivors," he grunted. This was Carter's weary soul. He was spilling out his thoughts, and for the first time I fully understood he wasn't 100% sane. He hadn't escaped the virus unscathed. "Gets us too. Us most of all. We're not really alive."

"The Infected?" Natalie asked. "What's that?"

"The Infected is a group that needs to be protected," he said and jabbed a finger at me. "From him."

"You're protecting the Infected? I thought that was the Shooter's job," I pointed out.

"Yeah," he chuckled darkly. "Supposed to be. Shooter shoulda dispatched you. Days ago. I have scheduled a long talk with the Shooter."

"The Shooter knows I'm a good person," I told him. "Just like PuckDaddy. They like me. Ask them. I'm not insane. I'm not crazy."

"You're halfway there. And just because you earned some pity from two of the Infected…doesn't mean you get to live," he waved his pistol at us.

"Not pity. Approval. Acceptance."

"I decide who gets accepted, hero!" he yelled suddenly, and the thin metal walls of Natalie's storage unit rattled. My whole body clenched, expecting a gun shot. Was I still wearing a vest? "Not them. They do as they're told."

"Apparently not."

"I don't understand," Natalie breathed.

"Let Natalie go," I repeated. "You and I can figure this out."

"No go, mate," he said. He shook his head. "She's heard too much."

"No she hasn't. She'll be quiet."

"What are you two talking about?" she asked, and I could feel her trembling.

"Sorry, kid," he said with no smile. The gun leveled. At me. "I liked you. You had potential."

"Wait…" I said, with mounting desperation.

Then he cocked his head, listening. I heard it too. A sound. A door shut. Footsteps. Two sets of feet. Coming closer. Carter stood up and put his gun behind his back.

Our door opened, spilling in light, and a man entered, smiling. He looked fifty, tall, slender, well dressed. His smile faltered briefly when he saw Carter. Carter's face hardened. He looked ready to bring his gun back up but in walked a little girl. She had to be six years old or less, wearing cute red pajamas. She had just woken up. Oh no. Run! Go! Carter was frozen, his eyes flicking between all of us.

"I wanted to bring my niece," the man said, glancing at Natalie. "To check on the patient. Is now a good time?"

No one moved. No one spoke. Natalie was holding her breath. The man, the doctor I assumed, started looking more and more concerned during the long pause. The granite in Carter's face slowly softened.

"Now is a great time," Carter finally spoke. Everyone let out a big breath. "I'll make you a deal," he said, addressing Natalie and I. "I'll leave you now. I'll leave you and the little girl in peace. But please remember what I've said," he said and he patted the little girl on the head. "So that there will be no more accidents. Innocent people could get hurt if you don't take my advice. Am I being explicit enough?"

"Yes. Now go."

"That sounds great," Natalie nodded, her voice strong and friendly. She was an actress, after all. "We'll see you soon."

He left.

The doctor promised complete confidentiality. In his professional opinion I had a major cardiac event and I needed immediate medical attention. He wasn't wrong, I knew, but my body had probably already healed itself. Soon afterwards he and the awestruck little girl left.

It took me ten minutes to convince Natalie not to call the police on Carter. There was absolutely nothing that could be done about him.

I was starving so Natalie fetched some food. She was thrilled to know what I looked like, even though my appearance didn't help her discover my identity. She rejoiced that we were approximately the same age, and she demanded payment for my rescue. We stayed on that blanket for another thirty minutes while we talked and she covered my face with kisses. I resisted her but she was persistent and my arms weren't moving very well. Besides, my girlfriend didn't care about me and the girl I really loved was dating another man.

That was too many girls.

That night I worried over the Shooter, the riots, football practice, Samantha Gear, Katie, Hannah Walker, Natalie North, my grades, Andy Babington, my fatal disease, my secret identity, my father, my new physical condition, my lack of money…everything. There really was only one solution.

I needed to simplify. And I knew just where to start.

Chapter Fourteen
Friday, January 27. 2018

Katie

I'm alone.

Well. Not really. I'm not alone. That's too dramatic. But I *feel* alone.

I know that's silly. Mami loves me. I have a great mami. My brother Anthony loves me, even if I never see him.

Chase loves me. Sometimes I think he even loves me romantically. He's changed recently. He's taller, broader, muscular, dark, and...beautiful. My heart flip flops just thinking about him! He used to be so scrawny, so timid. Now I can scarcely focus in Spanish!

I have friends like Lee and Cory, too.

And I'm dating a handsome guy! He's really really hot, actually. I really shouldn't be into Tank, but I am. There's something magnetic about him that I cannot escape. He's funny when we're together. He has a very impressive GPA. He's extremely busy, so he only contacts me once or twice a week. He's crazy rich, which isn't important...but it helps!

But I still feel so alone. No one really *knows* me. My Model UN friends are more like business associates. I love Young Life but rarely get to attend. Everyone is so busy. Like we're in a competition.

On the bright side, apparently the world's only true superhero has a crush on me! I have to fan myself when I remember that magical night.

Someone knocked on my door. What time was it? Eight o'clock? Could only be Chase! Chase was here! I glanced at myself in the mirror, rearranged, rubbed some lotion onto my arms and hands, and answered the door for my favorite guy.

…it wasn't Chase.

It was Chase's girlfriend, Hannah Walker. Surprise! Augh!

"Hannah? Uh, hi!" I said.

"Hi Katie," she said. Gosh she's pretty. I loved her and hated her for her beauty. She stood there, wearing more money than my whole closet cost, effortlessly looking like everything beautiful. "I'm sorry. It's late."

"No! That's okay. Come in. How do you know where I live?"

She came in, and I felt very conspicuous about my room. It was too girlie. Like a little girl lived here. Hannah Walker was not a little girl and my room looked shabby in comparison. Must fix! Immediately! No more kitten posters! I wonder what posters Hannah had in her room? Maybe I should get my hair colored like hers.

"Chase pointed out your apartment once," Hannah answered, playing with her rings. "I'm sorry for coming so late."

"It's fine. Are you okay?"

"No," she answered simply, and then I realized she was bursting with emotion, barely holding it in. Her eyes were pooling, her lips pouting.

"Hannah! Ohmygosh, what's wrong?"

"Chase," she squeaked.

"Chase? Is he okay?"

Then she fell apart. She stood like a beautiful statuesque carving, crying into her hands until I hugged her. She pushed her face into my shoulder, getting my new sweater all wet. She's tall, almost as tall as Chase, and clearly not good at hugs. Most white people are bad at it, actually. "We broke up. Chase did…Chase broke up with me."

Whoa!! Huge news!

Broke up? Why??

Chase doesn't have a girlfriend! The whole school would be after him now.

"Oh Hannah," I said, walking a tight-rope with my emotions. "I'm so sorry. I thought you two were happy."

"Me too! Please don't tell anyone?" Hannah asked.

"Oh. Sure. Of course. It's a secret?"

"Mmhm. At least, you know, until I figure out how to get dumped gracefully. Right?" Hannah said, backing up and wiping tears away with her fingers.

"When did this happen?"

"Just now. I went over to surprise him. I bought him some designer supplements, to help him put on muscle. And...he just told me," she sighed and sat down on the edge of my bed. Perched, more like it.

"Guys are such jerks," I commiserated. But I was lying. Not Chase. Chase was one of the nicest guys I knew.

"Yeah. But really? Chase isn't," replied Hannah, snatching several handfuls of tissues out of my unicorn tissue box. Embarrassing. "I'm sure you know. You two are best friends. He is so good for me. *Was*. *Was* so good for me. I never had to worry about him, even when I knew he was coming over here to see you. You're like...the prettiest girl on earth, but I never worried. Not with Chase."

"Yeah," I said. I sat beside her and rubbed her back. I didn't know what else to say. She was right. She didn't have to worry about him. Chase was an open book. Almost...boring.

"Do you ever worry? About the guy you're dating? Tank?" she asked.

"Well..." I stammered.

"I feel so stupid. About getting him the present, the muscle supplements. Sometimes he looks huge. Don't you think? When he's working out or playing football or something? Like, so big! And sometimes...he looks like he did a year ago, normal-sized Chase. Your boyfriend is going to kill normal-sized Chase on the football field next year. I thought the supplements...might help? I don't know. I'm pathetic. So lame."

"No no," I said. "I get that. But Tank is not my bo-"

"I don't blame him. Chase, I mean, for breaking up with me, you know?" sniffed Hannah. "I'm *not* a good girlfriend. I have too much baggage. Too many issues. It's my fault. I know it is. But do you know what?" she said with sudden energy. "He's changed, too. He's different recently. Have you noticed?"

"I have! Like he's distracted, or thinking-"

"Exactly!" she interrupted me. "He's always somewhere else, do you know what I mean?"

"Complaining about a headache?" I *had* noticed. Chase's whole disposition had changed in the past month or two. It was like he'd become constantly feverish. Tired. Stressed. Always wanted to hold hands. Which I didn't exactly mind.

"Yeah. Maybe. I don't know. A good girlfriend would have noticed."

"I'm glad you came over. You can even spend the night, if you want. No one should be alone on days like this. Mami won't mind."

"Wow," she laughed through her tears. "You really are very nice. And your house smells delicious."

"Why'd you come here? And not go see Erica or some of your other friends?" I asked.

"Oh. You know. I'm not sure I have any real friends. I have…allies, is perhaps the right word." She dabbed her eyes and looked ashamed at having to admit that.

"I was just thinking the same thing!" I cried. "Right when you knocked! Being friends with girls is hard."

"Ugh. I know. We're the worst," she agreed.

"So catty."

"And do you know who I really hate? That new girl. The kicker. God, I hate her. I know she's after Chase. Speaking of being catty. I want to run her over."

"Oh," I managed to say. "Samantha. I-I don't think she's after Chase."

"I do." She laid down, head on my pillow, and was asleep almost instantaneously. I watched her for a while, feeling uncomfortable and awkward in my own room. Now what?

My phone was on my desk, next to the laptop, beckoning. Chase, it whispered. Chase is single. Call him. Call Chase.

Chapter Fifteen
Tuesday, January 31. 2018

Katie

I did not call Chase. I fought with my phone for five days. But I never gave in. Two of the nights I told Mami to hide my phone, so I could avoid temptation. She seemed to understand.

He didn't call *me* either. Which crushed me. Why wouldn't he want to talk about it? I'm right here. Aren't we best friends? Don't we talk about everything?

Sigh.

Tank hasn't contacted me either. Also distressing.

Boys are so so so so stupid. Blah. Can't stand them. Can't focus. I've been working on the same easy math problem for twenty minutes. Stupid stupid stupid boys.

Chase looked terrible today at school. And yesterday. He hardly talks anymore. Looks like he hasn't slept in days. Could he be doing drugs? He only perks up when I hold his hand. I'm not complaining. He says that it makes him feel better. But it's strange. Very unlike him.

Hannah has been asking to sit alone with me at lunch. Everyone stares at us. It's nice having a girl friend, even if she does most of the talking. But I miss my guys, even Lee. Even Samantha Gear. Kinda. No one knows about the big breakup. Hannah is determined to keep it quiet. She's even trying to win Chase back.

I have no idea what to think about that. I'm so torn. So conflicted about everything. She's really not good enough for him. No one is. Chase is perfect. Even when he's acting like a drug addict. He's been changing in other ways, too. Chase is no longer the little boy I grew up with. He's become…harder. Like the same guy but made out of steel. Sexy. I *have* to stop thinking about this every day.

"Ugh!" I threw my pencil across the room. Dumb math problem. Dumb boys.

Knock knock. At my door.

Chase! Has to be him. It's late. Or…actually, it could be Chase's ex-girlfriend. That happened too.

I went to the door and pushed aside the curtains. It was dark out, and I still hadn't put the lightbulb back in. Nothing out there. I hoped I wouldn't find another note…wait. Oh my gosh. I tore open the door and jumped out, into the waiting arms of my very own superhero. The Outlaw is here!

"Hello!" I chirped into his chest. He's SO big! "I've missed you."

"Let's go," he said in that massive, impossibly deep voice of his. Before I could respond a blindfold was wrapped around my eyes and tied in the back.

"What?" I giggled, but he shushed me. He took my hand and placed it against his neck and we just stood like that for a moment. I know I was trembling and I think I could feel him tremble too. He was like Aslan, from Narnia; he didn't feel safe, but he was *good*. I hoped. "Where are we going?"

"Flying."

He plunked a motorcycle helmet down around my head and before I knew it I was holding on for dear life as we drove…somewhere. The news stations had reported the Outlaw was using a motorcycle as his mode of transportation; it hadn't occurred to me I'd get to ride on it! I've never been on one before. Even if I wasn't blindfolded, I'd still have my eyes squeezed shut. Hannah Walker bought Chase a motorcycle but I hadn't even seen it yet, much less ridden it. We've both been too busy.

Suddenly his voice erupted inside my helmet, like a radio. "Can you hear me?"

"Yes!" I said.

"You okay back there?"

"This is so cool! Our helmets can talk!"

"Do me a favor," he said. "Put your hand under my vest. Onto my stomach."

"Why?"

"It helps me concentrate."

"No it doesn't!"

"Please?"

"I can't! I'm trying. It's too tight."

"Then unzip my vest at the neck. I just like our skin to touch," he said and his voice sounded entirely sincere. So I fumbled with his vest until I found the zipper and carefully pulled it down. It might have been the hottest moment of my life. I slid my hand in until I felt his body and I almost melted. I kept reaching and then my palm was flat on his chest. "Thank you," he said.

No no no. Thank *you*.

We parked. No idea where. But judging by the sounds, we were downtown. He took my helmet off, positioned my arms around his neck and then picked me up on his back, like a piggy-back ride.

"Hold on. Really tight. Okay?"

"Okay," I answered. This was a little scary. Or a lot. I still couldn't see. And then we were moving. His shoulders and arms were working. I clung on tighter because I was swaying and bouncing and then…then…then I realized my grip on his neck was the only thing keeping me from falling! He was climbing something, and I was dangling off his back! Where *are* we?

As if he could read my mind, he chuckled and said, "Don't worry. I won't let you fall."

"Are we climbing?? What are we doing?" I gasped, and I managed to get my ankles crossed around his waist. If I adjusted my eyes just right I could peek under the blindfold and see his neck. He has neck tattoos. Never noticed before.

"It's a secret. Almost there." He didn't sound like he was exerting much effort.

And then he was lowering my quaking feet to the ground. He untied the blindfold. I blinked against the city lights and got my bearings.

"We're on a roof," I said, turning in a circle.

"Yes."

"This is so exciting! Which roof? It's not a very tall building. Wait! Is it Natalie North's building?" I asked, and I walked to the edge and peered down at the face of the structure and at the street below. We weren't on a skyscraper, just a normal sized building, maybe five or six stories. It was dark up here but well lit below.

"No. But her apartment isn't far."

"I know those windows," I said, examining the tall, pyramid shaped skylight in the middle of the roof. "We're on top of the Bradbury Building!"

"Yes. Very good," he said. His voice came soft and deep.

"Did you just…did you just climb the side of the wall?" I asked.

"I did. I tried it yesterday to make sure I could."

I wanted to wave to the people below. Call to them. Yell, hey I'm up here with the Outlaw! A steady stream of people below were walking into the Subway restaurant but no one noticed me.

"No one ever looks up," he said, joining me at the edge. "Not unless you do something ridiculous."

"Too full of their own comings and goings." He frowned at me. I smiled and said, "It's from a book. But it applies."

"Oh."

"Is that why you brought me? You get lonely up here?" I asked.

"I brought you so we could fly."

"What does that mean?"

"See that building over there?" he said, indicating a structure on the other side of a tuxedo shop. "Let's jump to it."

"Absolutely not!" I cried.

"We can do it. I tried it last night. It's easy."

"This building is, what? Five stories tall? That one is only three. And it's forty feet away," I explained, my voice cracking with incredulity.

"Do you trust me?"

"Implicitly so, Outlaw. But I also trust gravity."

"Watch." With no further warning, he ran to the edge and jumped. My breath caught in my throat. He *soared* into the air! He leapt so high and so far that I had to track him across the sky by watching the stars wink in and out. Gracefully he landed on a taller apartment building across Broadway. Our eyes met and held and he shrugged.

"Absurd," I whispered to myself. "Ridiculous. This is crazy." I blinked and he was gone. What? Where'd he go? Then a rush of air and he landed beside me, his knees and ankles absorbing the fall like it was nothing. "I can't believe you can do that," I said lamely. I couldn't even think.

"Me either."

"How? How can you?"

"That's complicated," the Outlaw said. "But it's not magic. The simple answer is, I was born weird. My body is many many times stronger and faster than average."

"Why?"

"That's a great question," he chuckled. "I wish I knew."

"Does it hurt?"

"No. When I exert myself I get both queasy and hungry, though. I'll eat several pounds of food later. Ready?"

"Ready for-ahh!!" I screamed as he pulled me onto his back. I didn't have time to fight him. He got a running start and jumped.

We flew! The initial surge of takeoff nearly jarred me loose, bruising my arms, but the otherworldly sensation took my breath away. The city dropped from our feet and swung crazily, like a piñata below us. The air was an ocean in my ears as we crested, and then the ground came rushing back. My stomach jumped into my throat! He was laughing, I was screaming! We didn't crash, but rather touched down effortlessly in a run that absorbed all our momentum.

"You don't have to hold on quite so tight," he said, stretching his neck.

"I can't stop," I said through chattering teeth.

"Hitch yourself a little higher on my back."

"Why?" I asked.

"Let's do it again."

We jumped forever, plunging upwards into the stars and diving back, successively higher with each leap. The earth danced under our shoes, the city lights twirling magically. I was weightless for hours, flying closer and closer to the clouds. On the last leap I let go at the zenith, briefly, and held my arms out wide, like an angel, before snatching him back again.

"Why are we doing this?" I asked when I could breathe again. We sat on the edge of the Bradbury roof. The world was warm and aglow, and I was in ecstasy. His vest was still partially unzipped. His eyes were afire and the black ink on his neck looked silver. "I love it. But why?"

"I wanted to show you. To share this."

"Why me?"

He took his time responding. His voice was cavernous and choked with emotion. "Katie. There are big chunks of my life I can't share with anyone. This is as close as it gets. I wish I could be with you. In your real life. Without my mask."

"Why can't you?" I said. I picked up his gloved hand and put my other hand on his arm. His shoulders sagged and his neck relaxed.

"Because of...a lot of things. But I wish you knew. If only you knew," he said, and I think he was crying! "How much I think about you. How much I adore you."

"Take off your mask, then," I pleaded. I reached up and touched his jaw, covered in the stretched black fabric.

"I can't. It's a curse. But it also protects you. Protects me, too."

I nodded. I hated it, but it was true. People raged against him, despised him. For no reason. People might come after me, like T.

"Plus. We shouldn't get too attached," he said as an afterthought, shaking his head. "I don't think I'll be around much longer."

"What?" I cried. "Why not?"

"Many reasons," he said in a grunt. "One reason is, I've already tried to quit the Outlaw gig several times. And if I stay alive, I still plan to."

"Of course you'll stay alive," I pointed out. "You're the Outlaw. You can do anything. Even jump buildings!"

"I wish it was that easy," he said, and through the disguise I could see his smile. I touched his masked lips. "I'm going to blindfold you again."

"Oh. Is it time to go?" I asked, crestfallen.

"No. I'm going to take off my mask."

I sucked in air. My heart stopped. "Why?"

"I want to kiss you. Just once. None of this is real. It's not real life. The Outlaw is imaginary. But you're real. And I want to kiss you, at least one time, before it's over," he said, watching me the whole time.

"Hurry," I breathed. "Blindfold me."

He did. We were so close his face touched mine when he reached his hands behind my head. I pressed my fingers against his chest. He finished tying the blindfold on...but he made a mistake. I could see through one of the thin folds over my eyes. Not well, but if I closed my other eye then I could clearly discern his features. I could see him!

I reached up with both hands and felt his mask. It was soft and cool. I curled my fingertips over the edge and began to tug downwards...

He stiffened. I panicked and let go. Too fast? His head cocked to the side. I could make him out well enough to see his eyes widen and eyebrows skyrocket. He wasn't looking at me. He was staring at something behind me. What was...

"Watch out!" he shouted and he shoved me sideways!

I heard a soft crack as I was falling to the roof. A noise like an angry bee snapped at my ear. Through my mask I could see him twist and rock backwards, like a huge invisible hammer had crushed him. I screamed.

The Outlaw had been shot! He rolled on the ground, groaning.

"Are you okay?" I cried.

"Yeah," he coughed and then he staggered to his feet, hauling me after him. His breath was coming in ragged gulps. "I'm going to kill that guy."

"Is that the LA Sniper?" I asked as he pulled me onto his back. "What are we doing?"

"Getting out of here. Yes, that's the Sniper."

"Now? Like this? Augh!" I closed my eyes. Everything was happening too fast!

He took two steps and jumped into the atmosphere.

Chapter Sixteen
Friday, February 3. 2018

Katie

"Katie? Are you even listening, bro?"

"What?" I asked, reality coming back into focus. Lee was frowning at me. My lunch sat unopened. Chase's head was on the table and his hand was clamped firmly around mine. Cory was eating and watching television. Samantha Gear was smirking at me. "What'd you say?"

"I said…" Lee huffed. "What is that you're playing with? You've had it three days in a row."

"Oh," I said. I'd been daydreaming about that magical night on the rooftop. Well, it was magical until the gunfire. "It's…it's…"

Samantha answered, "It's a wax bullet." Chase's head came up and he blearily examined the pink bullet in my hand. "I recognize it, even though it's obviously been fired."

"Yes," I admitted. "It's a wax bullet."

No one spoke. I could feel my face redden. I brainstormed a reason for me to have a wax bullet but nothing surfaced. I certainly couldn't tell them it was a memento from my night with the Outlaw. I'd pulled the bullet out of his vest before he'd abruptly left, and I hadn't heard from him since.

"Dude," Lee finally said. "Are you the LA Sniper?"

"Yes, Lee," I laughed, relieved. "That's me."

Samantha Gear asked me, "What were you day-dreaming about?"

Lee said, "I bet it was the Outlaw."

"Hey, that reminds me," Chase said, looking up. "Lee, have you heard of Outlawyers? The Outlaw fan club?"

"Course, bro."

"Are *you* an Outlawyer?"

"Heck yes I am."

"Of course you are," Chase groaned and put his head back down.

"But I'm not an Outlawgiver," he clarified.

"An Oulaw *giver?*"

"Outlawgiver," he repeated. "One of those stupid Outlaw imitators."

Samantha observed, "That's a ridiculous name."

"They call themselves Law Givers, for short. True amateur vigilantes. They mostly cause trouble and get hurt falling off roofs," Lee said.

"Soooooooooooo dumb," Chase said, his voice muffled by his arm.

"Anyway, Katie," Samantha rolled her eyes. "Were you daydreaming about your big beautiful Latino boyfriend?"

"No," I sighed. "He's not my boyfriend. I haven't even talked to him in a few days. I miss him."

"Ugh," Chase said.

"S'wrong, Chase?" Cory asked around some meatloaf. "Another headache?"

"Nah," Chase said, rubbing his eyes. "Best I've felt in three days, actually. Just tired."

Lee asked, "Dude, why are you holding Katie's hand?"

"Because shut up," Chase said and put his head back down.

"Taking notes in Spanish class has gotten crazy challenging," I said, playfully trying to shake him off.

Samantha Gear said, "Thanks for sitting with us today, Katie." Her lunch today was a carrot and a chocolate bar. No wonder she looked like pure muscle. "Instead of sitting with the Queen."

"She really doesn't think of herself as a Queen," I said in defense of Hannah Walker. Today was the first day she'd gone back to sit at her old table. Truthfully, I kind of missed her.

"How's she doing?" Chase asked from his position, face down on the table.

"Hey, sit up," Samantha Gear said and she whacked him solidly in the side. "You look ridiculous. Quit slouching."

"Um, kicker? Hush your mouth. Katie, how is Hannah?"

"Ask her yourself," I said.

"Noooooo," he said, sitting up and looking pained at the idea. "It would be so weird. Just tell me."

"She misses you."

"No she doesn't," he scoffed.

"Yes. She really does," I shot back.

"Do *you* think Hannah and I should get back together?" he asked me, and he gave my hand a squeeze. My Chase. My sweet wonderful Chase.

"That's...up to you," I said carefully, even though I wanted to shout 'No!'

"Yo, Katie, how's she feel about you always holding his hand?" Lee teased.

"She knows he's initiating it," I said. "And she's kind of pissed at him."

Chase yawned, "It's no big deal. Sometimes friends hold hands."

"Dude. No we don't."

―――――――――――――――――――――――――――――――――――――

Chase texted me that night, after supper as I was doing homework.

>>Katie. I've decided I need to tell you something. Something big. Something important. Can I come over in about ten minutes?

Sure! I replied. I FLEW into my room and changed out of my old t-shirt. Hair looks great. Make-up, done. Room, messy, but that's okay. I popped a breath mint and was rubbing lotion onto my arms when he knocked.

That was fast! I opened the door for him.

But, once again, I was fooled. It wasn't Chase.

Chapter Seventeen
Friday, February 3. 2018

I texted Katie that I was coming over and then I looked in the mirror. Oooof. Wow, that's bad. I hadn't been sleeping recently and it showed. I looked like the After Photo in an anti-drug campaign.

I had to tell Katie. She must know. She must know she's everything. I don't have much longer, I can feel it. The virus was everywhere and I was constantly fighting a war between headaches and bouts of insane energy. The pain and the irrational unstoppable urges to go flying off buildings were closing in each day, both threatening to kill me. The nights I managed to stay in bed were spent tossing and turning.

I'd already written Dad a letter, for him to find in case I lost the fight. A letter explaining how much he meant to me, my hopes for his future, etc. I kept the details vague on why I wrote the letter, on how I knew I was dying.

Now, Katie. I practically floated to her house. I'd wanted to tell her for months. I love you. I think I always have. I want you. I want to be with you. There's only you.

I knocked on her back door.

No answer.

I knocked again.

And then Tank opened the door.

Tank!

Tank ducked his head and emerged out of the sliding doors, one arm draped around Katie's shoulder. They were both pink and had flushed lips.

They'd been kissing.

Katie looked affectionately at Tank, then at me, and then back at him. Tank smiled victoriously. No one spoke for a long moment. Time slowed. I could hear every animal within a mile. I could see both their pulses palpitating faintly in their neck. I could smell her lotion, his deodorant, and supper from both tonight and last night. In that instant, in that blast of startling clarity and acuity, I was confident I could count the blades of grass in her backyard with a single glance. I almost tore her whole building down.

"Hi Chase!" Katie giggled. Since when did she laugh like that? "I forgot you were coming over."

"Yeah, I was going for some ice cream," I lied smoothly, somehow. "Didn't realize you had company. Some other time."

Tank sneered at me.

I made a quick list of all the secrets. I knew Tank was Katie's abductor. He knew I was the Outlaw. We knew each other knew. Tank was probably Infected, but might not be aware. Katie had been with the Outlaw, but wasn't telling anyone. But Chase Jackson knew. And I knew they'd just been kissing.

"Tank, good to see you," I said.

"Yeah," he chuckled maliciously. "I bet."

"I'll go make some popcorn," Katie said and she vanished into her bedroom.

"Popcorn?" I asked. "You eat popcorn? I figured you just ate little kids."

"I like popcorn," he grinned. "And Latinas."

"How's your forehead?" I asked, peering at an imaginary spot on his face. He'd apparently healed from the gunshot. "Looks pretty ugly. But it matches the rest of you."

His face clouded and he said, "The Sniper saved your miserable life, pajamas."

"Miserable? Seems a little harsh. How about a 'Thank You' for saving your life the other day? You know, when the Chemist's goons were about to rip you apart?"

"The Chemist," he thundered. "You know him?"

"Nope. Not a clue."

"I'm looking for him. Won't be long," he said, and he started rubbing his temple. His skin tone was fading to white and then flushing. "I'm going to burn both him and the Shooter alive in the middle of the Dodger's Stadium. Done it before. Might bring you along to watch. Or use you as kindling."

"What's the Chemist want with the Outlaw?" I asked.

"Don't know. Don't care. He's dead."

"Fine by me," I shrugged. "I'm not a big fan of his, either. You have a headache, by the way? Trouble sleeping recently?"

He didn't answer. He pinched the bridge of his nose and started taking deep breaths. I commiserated with his pain. Watching him was fascinating. I could hit him. He wasn't ready. I could break his nose. I could drive his nose back into his brain, and then dump his body somewhere. Maybe I could find a rock and crush his skull. But. I wasn't going to.

"I heard you started using cocaine," I said. "Coke help with the pain? Maybe you should go home and sleep it off. Far…far away from Katie."

"Nah," he smiled even though his eyes were watering. "Got a date. Watching a movie. On her bed. How's that for pain?"

He went back inside and slid the door closed.

I bounced on my toes outside her door, grinding my teeth. My imagination tortured me as I pictured them on her bed. Nothing would happen. Probably. Katie wouldn't let it. Maybe. Tank wouldn't try anything with her mom home. Hopefully. But what could I do? I couldn't manipulate Katie's will or emotions.

So I drove to a downtown pharmacy and bought two needles and a pack of glass vials. Then I climbed to the rooftop next to Natalie North's building, staying in the shadows and out of sight.

Nine at night on a Friday, and I was hiding on a rooftop, learning how to draw blood. My life sucks. But maybe I could find a way to stay alive.

The phone rang inside my helmet.

"What?" I answered it.

"Yo, dummy. How come you keep wearing the motorcycle helmet?" the voice sparked in my ear.

"What?"

"I think the black and red mask looks better. Pretty badass."

"PuckDaddy," I said.

"That's me, baby."

"Are you always watching me?"

"As often as I can," he answered. "You're priority number one. For Carter. And, well, your life is pretty fascinating. Even though you're stupid."

"Can you see me now?" I asked, scooting closer to the brick wall. "I thought all those stupid cameras wouldn't be able to find me here."

"Yeah, dummy, I can see you through about a dozen cameras. I see everything. But I'm erasing the data."

"Great," I said, examining the needle and vial in my hand.

"What are you doing? The picture is too fuzzy."

"It's a secret," I said.

He sighed and said, "I could pull up your bank account, or I could scan the pharmacy security tape to see what you bought. Or you could not be a total newb and you could just tell me."

"Secret," I repeated and I jabbed the needle into my finger. The needle...bent. I jabbed again. Nothing. I tried scraping the point across my skin. No luck. Again. Jab. Again. Jab. Katie. Jab. Tank. Again. No blood.

"Oh crap," PuckDaddy groaned into my ear.

"What?" I said, blinking away tears of frustration.

"I see what you bought. You idiot. Why are you collecting blood?"

"Shut up," I said.

"Oh boy. You're not smart."

"You know what else isn't smart?" I asked through a tight throat. "Waiting around to die."

"The FBI guy, Anderson. I heard his plan. You're giving him a blood sample."

"Come on!" I shouted and I hurled away the destroyed needle. "Do you listen to *all* my phone calls??"

"Not that night. You used a disposable phone, remember? Pissed me off. But I listened to Anderson talking to his superiors about it. He said you were considering providing a blood sample. Which is totally stupid."

"It's not stupid," I said. "I'm trying to survive."

"It won't work, dummy."

"It might," I said, losing the battle to keep desperation out of my voice. "Might find a cure."

"No, not that. You won't be able to draw blood right now. You're upset. Your skin is probably hard as a rock. That's how the virus works. When you're mad or under duress or excited or upset or something, the virus kicks in, begins manufacturing adrenaline. That epinephrine makes your muscles tense, skin turn hard, blood start pumping, you can see better, you know. All that stuff. No way can you pierce your skin right now."

"Ugh," I groaned and laid flat on my back. Tears leaked and spilled in hot rivulets down the creases around my ears. "This sucks. This sucks so much."

"Sorry, man. The virus is cold. Merciless, like a machine."

"Yeah," I sniffed. "I've learned. I can't sleep. Can't think. Can't function."

"You're doing better than most," he said and I could hear him drink something. "I monitor a couple kids like you every year. They all die. You've lasted the longest in five years."

"How old are you?"

"Thirty-three."

"How'd you get through the virus?" I asked. I wanted to talk, to distract myself, calm down.

"Cause I'm awesome," he replied.

"Oh. Wow. Thanks."

"It's true. But your situation is weird. Our whole world is on hold, waiting to see what happens to you. Lots of manpower, lots of money, lots of precious hours spent deleting data, accessing phone calls, moding fan websites, really deep magic stuff on my end. It's like nothing we've ever done. Most guys like you drop dead pretty quickly, or commit suicide, or do something stupid, like a girl last year thought she could swim across the Pacific. You're still here and still pushing through with your daily life, even with this bizarre hero gig. Crazy legit. Mad respect."

"Yeah," I sighed, fogging the visor of the helmet. "Crazy legit. How many sick kids has the Shooter put out of their misery?"

"None last year. Pretty rare. The virus is effective. You were *supposed* to get shot. Twice, actually. Because you were being a dumb ass."

"He got me once," I said. "Right before I could kiss this girl. *The* girl."

"He got you once," PuckDaddy mocked me. He did that a lot. "Yeah, I was watching from a security camera. Carter ordered a real bullet. Shooter decided to just warn you, though. Used wax. I thought Carter's head was going to explode."

"Shooter and Carter don't get along?"

"It's...complicated, man," he laughed again. "I stay out of it."

"Is Carter the boss? He gave me the impression he wasn't."

"Oh he's the boss."

"What, did you guys elect him or something?"

"No." A chuckle. "It's a monarchy. He's the king, not the president. Something like that. Crazy control freak. But he's aight. Usually. PuckDaddy too busy to complain."

"What are you doing right now?"

"Monitoring the escalating war between North Korean hackers and NSA's cyber ops team, and toying with ways to requisition NOAA's satellite cameras without them knowing. Harder than it sounds, amigo, but nothing's impossible for PuckDaddy. By the way..."

"Yeah?" I prompted.

"Don't know why I'm telling you this. Really don't care. I guess I do, but whatever. I think you should tell Katie who you really are."

"Hah!" I laughed. "Oh man. You are all up in my personal life."

"Yeah, kind of pathetic. Don't know why I'm so hooked. It drives me crazy when you two talk in real life and I can't hack in."

"If I survive this thing," I said, "I might tell her. It'll be a lot to explain."

"Yeah, definitely. Trust PuckDaddy. I read your text to her tonight. How'd that go?"

How'd that go? It went awful. Really awful. Tank was there.

I sat up straight, grabbed another needle, and tore open my finger. The wound turned white and puckered when I pressed it open, but then it began spilling thick red drops into the waiting vial. My skin had softened during our conversation. Because of the lack of adrenaline? Who knows. My body is so freaking weird.

"What are you doing, noob?" he asked.

"How'd it go tonight?? It went *so* bad. I'm dying and Katie is dating a monster," I said, fresh emotion welling up. "And I don't know what to do about it, so I'm doing this. I'm trying to live. Looking for hope. It's all I've got." I pressed the green stopper into the opening and examined the full vial. "Maybe the FBI can help me. Because you and Carter sure can't."

"Okay. Well. Close your eyes, stupid," he warned.

"What? Why?"

The vial in my hand exploded. Snap, *crash*! Glass and blood all over the bricks beside me. A gun shot! Someone shot the vial out of my fingers!

"NOOOOO!" I screamed.

"Sorry man," he said, and he sounded sincere.

"No no no no!!" I screamed again and put my fist straight into the outer layer of bricks, splintering them in all directions.

"Carter would kill you if he knew, Chase. And he'd find out. Shooter's doing you a favor."

"I'm just trying to survive!" I bellowed, my voice almost cracking the helmet. "I just want some help!"

"Chase, Outlaw, chill out-"

"No!" I cried. "I can't chill. I'm losing everything! I'm so tired, my head hurts so bad, Katie is in bed with a monster, I'll be dead soon, and my family, and everything..."

I curled up next to the wall and cried openly and fiercely. Deep sobs, building for weeks, forced their way out. I ripped off the helmet and buried trembling fists into my eyes and wailed in anger and despair and loss. Visions of my future kept slipping away. I couldn't hold on to them, to hope. Everything slipping away, slipping...

I must have cried myself to sleep because when I woke up my head was in Natalie North's lap. My motorcycle helmet was off and she was stroking my hair. My mind was foggy and it took me a second to remember where I was.

"Hello, sleeping beauty," she smiled at me, upside down.

"This is a little embarrassing," I sniffed. I had a moment of panic when I realized my mask was off, but she'd already seen me without the mask. She still didn't know my identity.

"Are you hurt? I don't see any wounds. Against my better judgement I decided not to give your body a thorough examination."

"No," I smiled. "I'm not hurt."

"Then why, superhero of mine, are you up here crying in your sleep?"

"Oh, you know," I sighed. "I thought I'd give it a try. Sounded like fun."

"Are you upset because of your malady?"

"If malady means disease, then yes."

"Have your symptoms gotten worse?" she asked.

"Not much. Not since I saw you last."

"Since that day you died?"

"Right," I chuckled. "Things have not gotten worse since I died."

"Did you come up here to see me?" She lowered her face until her lips were touching my nose and she quietly said, "I hope so."

I was about to push her away. But then again, I didn't have a girlfriend. And Katie was with someone else. So I let her kiss me.

"I'm very glad to see you. Honestly," I said. "But I came up here to provide a blood sample for the FBI."

"Oh! A fantastic idea!"

"I think so too. But I can't."

"Why not?"

"Several reasons," I sighed. "Some of which I can't explain. But, part of the problem is my skin. It's become very difficult to get a needle through it."

"That's part of the disease?" she asked, picking up my hand and examining it.

"Apparently."

"What a fascinating illness you have. I bet scientists all over the world would love to examine you," she said. "Maybe you should let them?"

"I can't. Hopefully one day I'll be able to explain why not."

"There's other stuff going on," she said, watching my face. "Other stuff than just the virus, right? Conspiracies and secret clandestine groups and things like that?"

"Natalie North," I smiled. "You are one of the most perceptive people I know."

"No," she said, lowering in for another kiss. "I just obsess over you."

Chapter Eighteen
Monday, February 6. 2018

I spent Saturday with Cory. We played video games and ate dinner and did things that teenagers do when they're not wearing a mask. On Sunday Dad surprised me taking us to church. I love that place! It's quiet, it's peaceful, it smells good, it's beautiful, the people are polite, and the Bible really makes God sound like He knows what He's talking about. Love each other. Live peacefully. Take care of the poor. I dig it.

On Monday my peace ended.

Hannah Walker met me as I walked into the school. There is NO way her outfit met the dress code. We hadn't spoken since the breakup. I'd texted her about returning the motorcycle, but she hadn't replied.

"Hi handsome!" she chirped. Before I knew it she was in my arms, hugging me.

"Hi…Hannah," I said. I was confused. "You look nice."

"I haven't told anyone yet," she whispered in my ear. "About the break-up."

"Oh."

"Besides." Her lips were brushing my earlobe. "I miss you. And I'm going to get you back."

Uh oh.

My head pounded with this new bit of stress, until Katie held my hand in Spanish. Her hand is so great. It's small and smooth and fits easily into mine and she rubs my thumb with hers. I would rather hold hands with Katie than make-out with Natalie North. And just like that, my headache was gone.

"Are you okay?" she asked me.

"Getting better." I squeezed her hand. The teacher, Señora Richardson, always shot me dirty looks when we held hands. "How was your date with Tank? Did you have a nice time in bed?"

"We weren't in a bed, stinker," she snickered. "Why would you think that?"

"He told me you were."

"You two," she shook her head. "Silly boys. And he didn't stay long. He got a migraine and had to leave. I almost called an ambulance. And you don't have to look so happy about it!"

Lee appeared exhausted. At lunch he could barely keep his head up.

"What's wrong, good-looking?" Samantha Gear asked him.

"I'm tired, dude."

"Lee," Samantha growled softly, "You better find something else to call me. Soon."

"Samantha, I mean. Sorry. I'm tired, Samantha," Lee yawned.

"Me too," she said. "Cory kept me up too late."

"What??" Lee, Katie and I all blurted in unison.

Cory, the humble giant, looked mortified. He put his container of pot roast down, wiped his hands, picked his food up again, set it down again, and took a long drink of water. Then he cleared his throat and said, "I just cooked her dinner."

"And...?" Samantha prodded wickedly. Katie was beaming.

"And we watched some basketball," Cory said.

"And...?" Samantha prodded again.

"And I rubbed her feet." He shrugged and went back to eating.

"He's got strong hands too," Samantha shivered.

Katie and I didn't know what to say.

Lee said, "This sucks so bad. I'm a great foot massager."

"Why were *you* up so late?" Katie asked Lee.

"Working on a project," he answered. "Top secret. And watching the Compton lockdown."

"The what?" I asked.

"I swear!" he shouted. "You people! Watch the news! Or check your twitter feed!"

"Okay okay," Katie shushed him. "What happened in Compton?"

"Total lockdown, bro. Martial Law declared."

"Why?"

"Civil unrest. Fighting. That kind of stuff. Plus," he yawned again, "the FBI is trying to track down some kind of criminal mastermind."

"They think he's in Compton?" I asked. The FBI was looking for the Chemist!

"Dunno. Maybe."

Cory, Samantha and I walked onto our practice field, along with half the varsity team, to find Coach Garrett with his hands on hips.

"Well, team," he grinned behind his glasses, chomping on his gum. "Today we're going to practice in our stadium, instead of the practice field."

Great! We all loved the stadium and it's FieldTurf. Someone asked him, "Why?"

"Because," he said, his grin growing wider. "I invited the Patrick Henry Dragons to use our practice field."

Silence. Disbelief. Someone snorted in the back.

"For real?" Jesse Salt asked. He was our running back, and he was heading to San Diego on a scholarship to play football.

"Yes, Mr. Salt, for real."

"Why?"

"The Dragon's field was recently commandeered by a government task force for a weekend exercise and subsequently ruined. It won't be ready for several weeks, despite Uncle Sam footing the repair bill. The Dragons have nowhere to practice. So they'll be circulating between a few fields, including ours. I extended the invitation myself."

"Coach, for real, though. For real, I hate you," Jesse said.

"Come on, Salt," Samantha Gear said and smacked Jesse on the butt so hard his eyes teared up. "Not scared, are you? I say we scrimmage them."

We didn't scrimmage them, but we did stare at them a lot through one of the stadium's entrances. About twenty Dragons, including Tank, came on a school bus to work on football drills. Tank was going to be ranked as the best high school football player in the nation next year, and our guys kept sneaking peaks at him. He was a man among boys and we all knew it. The Dragon's coach brought in former college players to help him practice and he was already better than them. After twenty minutes of practice he laid down, put a towel over his head, and started massaging his temples.

I knew *that* feeling.

Samantha walked up and said, "I could punt a ball over the bleachers and land it right on his face." She indicated Tank with her chin. I was spinning a football in my hands and didn't realize I'd been staring at him through a gap in the seats.

"Probably not a great idea," I said.

"Plus she couldn't get close, anyway," Andy Babington said. He was nearby, working on timing routes with senior receivers. "No way."

"I can kick farther than you can throw, second-string," she said casually.

He shot at her, "No. You can't."

"Jon!" Samantha Geared called. One of the receivers looked over at her. "Jon, Andy and I just made a bet. Help us out, handsome. Run up to the top of the bleachers and tell us who gets the ball closer to the the big ugly guy laying down over there."

"Maybe you should just try hitting the far goal post," I suggested. "Instead of the angry freak of nature?"

"Too late. This is happening," Samantha said.

Andy looked like he'd been caught in a bluff. He couldn't throw the ball all the way to Tank, and he knew it. Unfortunately for him, the challenge attracted interest and a small crowd gathered to watch.

Samantha went first. She lined up and glared at her target for a few heartbeats, running calculations in her mind. She took a step, dropped the ball and punted with that beautiful strong motion of hers. It was a powerful blast and the ball sailed smoothly up and over the high stadium wall into the blue sky.

The football thumped down on the practice field behind the stadium, about ten harmless yards from Tank's prone body. We couldn't see it land, but Jon delivered the news. Her kick probably traveled fifty-five yards, an absurd length for that height.

Andy's turn. He shook his arm loose, took two steps and threw the ball on a line to the top of the seats where it bounced against the back retaining wall. He didn't even clear the stadium. Jon threw it back while everyone chuckled uncomfortably. Andy fumed.

"Nice try, kiddo," Samantha laughed. "You lose. Thanks for playing. Okay Chase. Your turn."

Andy said, "Hah. Yeah right. My little buddy has a good arm, but he can't throw farther than me."

I hated when he called me that. Plus, secretly I was itching to try the throw. I could clear the stadium easily, but I wasn't sure how close I could land it. This wasn't a good idea. But...

"Toss me the ball," I said. Samantha grinned.

Like always, I spun the football in my hand, and I rolled my shoulder twice while everyone watched. I stared down my target, gathered, and shot a high tight spiral up and over the wall. I watched it disappeared beyond the seats and then I dropped my eyes to Tank. This was going to be close. The trajectory looked perfect... I was going to hit him!

Through the stadium seating, we could all clearly see Tank's hand punch up and snatch the football out of the air before it connected with his face. His fingers pierced the football's hide, deflating it within his fist.

He crushed it like a grape and we all scrambled back to our drills before he could look up and identify the culprit.

After practice Lee and I studied math at his house. I finally drove home at 9:30pm, exhausted, head pounding. I kept thinking about that throw, the one that almost hit Tank. Just how far *can* I throw it? And how hard? Carter had thrown quarters straight into the cement.

Just outside my neighborhood, I braked next to a new home construction site. I'd wanted to try something for weeks, and tonight would finally be the night.

I stepped over the orange tape and approached the house. The night was quiet and still and my footsteps sounded alien. I rooted in the dirt until I uncovered a handful of heavy nuts and bolts. About ten total. I juggled them in my hand, intentionally dropping a couple, until they felt comfortable. Three sheets of plywood were leaning against a tree near the back of the site. The plywood sheets had been spray-painted and cut up and were clearly waiting to be tossed into the trash dumpster.

I set my feet ten paces from the upright sheets of plywood and shifted the metal in my hand. The evening was silent and the house loomed over me. Taking a deep breath, I went into a pitcher's throwing motion and hurled the scrap metal into the wood.

CRASH!

All three sheets of wood splintered, buckled, and collapsed as the metal ripped holes through them. The sound of destruction was preposterously loud. The echoes bounced around the stark walls of the vacant house. The plywood had disintegrated.

"Wow," I breathed. That would've killed a person. My arm was lethal. If Carter tried to kill me again, I would have a weapon of my own.

I scanned Craigslist that night, looking for any posts from Beans. The Outlaw had received a lot of messages but none that interested me. None from Beans.

Before going to sleep I powered on the disposable phone. Two voice mails from Isaac Anderson, the FBI guy. No way. I turned it off. Then I checked the Outlaw's phone. I had a text message. From Lee.

>> Outlaw!! I made you something! TWO things!!! Come try them out! -Lee

Chapter Nineteen
Thursday, February 9. 2018

The Dragons returned on Thursday. The previous three days had been pleasant and stress free, other than Hannah Walker's advances, and now the Dragons were back to ruin everything.

Tank and I stood on opposite sides of the field, glaring at each other while our coaches arranged a scrimmage. He and I were living in such a strange existence. We knew each other's secrets. We hated each other. We were fighting over the same girl, both in the news for various reasons, and both very sick. And yet we were both just teenagers living at home with our families. He had the world fooled and he would kill me if he could do it cleanly. But I didn't know what to do about him, and he knew it. Our cold war continued.

We forewent pads and helmets during our 'friendly' scrimmage because there would be no hard hitting. Yeah, right. During the second play a Dragon creamed Josh Magee, almost knocked his head off. Josh limped off and the Dragon received a scolding from his coach. The rest of his team congratulated him.

Cory was the only Eagle capable of even partially blocking Tank, and so Tank never lined up near him. Tank chased me on every passing play, knocking blockers aside. I ran for my life and threw the ball early every play before he could maim me. One of the Dragons knocked me down and stomped on my hand while the coaches were distracted. He walked off laughing, and I sat there steaming, thankful I didn't have access to any nuts and bolts.

Our punting unit came on the field. Samantha Gear was trying out to be the punter too, and as she trotted past she said, "I see why you hate these guys."

"Real classy, aren't they?" I asked wryly.

"Watch this," she said and winked.

Uh oh. Samantha was trouble. This was going to be…inflammatory.

The ball was hiked to her. The play should have been a routine punt. The Dragons didn't attempt blocking the kick because she was a girl and they were astonished by this. She took a step and punted the ball straight into the face of the nearest Dragon defender. Boom! She crushed him! Her kick rebounded twenty yards off his face. He snapped backwards, his feet flying over his head before he landed on his neck.

The Eagles laughed until tears streamed down our faces. We could barely stand. The Dragons appeared to be suffering from a mixture of outrage and mirth. Did the new girl do that on purpose?? The injured Dragon's nose was busted and his coach helped him stagger off the field. He might have a concussion.

"Kick it again," Coach Garrett ordered. "Everyone else, put on helmets."

"You got it, Coach!" Samantha Gear chirped.

Oh no. She was going to do it again.

Another kick. Even though they were wary of her now she still managed to knock one down with a solid blow to the helmet. He stumbled backwards and fell over.

A fight erupted instantly, like a starter's pistol had been fired. The indignant Dragons were furious and the proud Eagles were defensive and all forty guys jumped on each other. Immediate mayhem! Punches and kicks and face mask grabbing and dog piles as the coaches blew their whistles and tried to drag us apart. Cory stood in the middle, a boulder in the storm, tossing Eagles and Dragons apart.

Tank came snarling, his dark face a mask of malice. I could outrun him but I couldn't outfight him, not without drawing unnecessary attention. He closed the distance and I dove, putting my shoulders into his shins. He somersaulted over and landed in a howling heap.

Wump! Wump! Samantha Gear found a hopper of footballs and she was blasting rockets one by one into the Dragons. Wump! Solid punt, Dragon destroyed. Wump! Another Dragon sprawling. Wump! She wasn't missing!

I admired her too long. Mistake. Tank gained his feet and smashed my skull with an enormous fist. Pow! The lights dimmed and I hit the turf hard. I should've worn a helmet! My head swam. Tank towered over me and raised a foot. He was about to crush my sternum when his face slackened. He had enough time to grab his temples before he collapsed. He just fell over, like his power had been cut. I yanked my foot out from under his dead weight. He didn't respond.

"Hey. The hell happened to Tank?" someone shouted.

"Tank! Is he okay? Yo Tank!"

The fight ended as quickly as it began. Tank wasn't moving and I was on the ground, holding my head, which felt like it was about to split open. A crowd gathered.

"Is Tank breathing?"

"What happened? What's wrong with Chase?"

"I think they killed each other, yo."

"I'm okay," I said through clenched teeth. "I think. Tank might need an ambulance."

"What'd you do to him?"

"Nothing," I barked. "I think he had an aneurysm."

Cory helped me up and guided me towards the locker room. I kept my eyes closed against the awful light. My lip was split and my cheek was swelling. As we walked indoors an ambulance began wailing nearby. Wow, that was fast! Maybe Tank had a chance.

Somehow, someway, the fight made the six o'clock local news. I didn't see it, but Lee texted me afterwards. The anchor announced two local football stars got into a fight during a scrimmage and both suffered injuries. No word on their condition. Pictures and videos had been taken with phone cameras, Lee said.

Great. I'm sure the Patrick Henry Dragons all blamed me. There'd be an outrage if Tank died. Nooooo, I'll tell them. It wasn't me. He was suffering from a Super Hero Virus that gave him all those muscles and then killed him. I'm sure they'll understand.

My headache was NOT going away. I felt as bad and as ragged as I had in weeks, a miserable shell of my former self. None of my painkillers were effective.

I watched the news at eleven to distract myself. The anchor began by warning us the lead story contained a graphic video and viewer discretion was advised. She was right. It was the worst thing I'd ever seen.

Multiple people had used their phones to film a man going insane. He was running around Gardena (about ten miles from here) without a shirt on. He was screaming. Two police officers attempted subduing him but their mace had no effect, and he tossed them aside like they were children. A minute into the video, the poor dude actually flipped over a Nissan! He was a short, skinny white guy with no business over-turning a car. He was about my age. Finally he ran into the street, grabbed his eyes, and fell down.

The news anchor said that he was taken to a hospital and pronounced dead. Police suspected his erratic behavior was due to an over-dose of illegal bath salts.

Bath salts. Maybe, but I doubted it. The strength, the insanity, the aneurysm…I bet he was Infected.

I got up and started pacing the room. My own head was throbbing. Oh crap oh crap oh crap oh crap. I really don't want to lose my sanity. How long do I have?

I grabbed the Outlaw's phone and texted PuckDaddy, **Did you see the video of crazy man in Gardena today?**
>>affirmative
Think he was Infected?
>>probably got no intel on him tho
What are the odds of three guys being Infected in Los Angeles at

the same time?

>>ZERO who is the 3rd guy?

You don't know?

>>i know about the third guy. PuckDaddy knows all. Im just surprised u know about him

So...what's going on? Why are there three of us?

>>no idea my man u stay chill stay calm stay alive

I wanted to keep texting but I could no longer concentrate. My stomach was churning. Stars were flashing in my vision. This was bad. This was scary.

What I needed was a way to relax. So I grabbed my helmet with shaking fingers and navigated to my motorcycle through squinting eyes.

Somehow I safely and slowly wobbled all the way to Holy Angels Catholic Church. I love this place. I started to unclench immediately as I shouldered through the heavy wooden doors. I dropped to my knees on the rear pew's kneeling bench and tried to pray the virus out of my pores. This church was the best. Were all churches this great? I especially loved the candles and the smell. However, the aroma was faint. I need more than intermittent wafts.

I moved deeper into the mostly vacant sanctuary. A handful of other pilgrims sat alone in their own pews. Soft recorded worship music drifted down from above. The closer I approached the alter the closer I came to the candles and to the incense and to peace, so I didn't stop until I reached the front row.

This is what heaven must be like. Peace. No pain. No worries. No stress. I was about to drift off when someone sat down beside me.

"Nice to see you again, Mr. Jackson." It was one of my football coaches, Todd Keith. He worked at this church, and he helped break up the fight today. "You're here late."

"So are you. But I don't blame you. This place is the best."

"Oh yeah?" he chuckled quietly. "I've found you sleeping here twice, you know. Everything okay at home?"

"Yes sir. No problems at home. My life has been wild, and this church...I don't know, Coach. It's keeping me sane. Keeping me alive. God's the best."

His eyes widened and he laughed. Everyone frowned at him. I frowned too and said, "What's so funny?"

"Nothing, Chase. Kids your age don't usually think God is the best because of a church." He wiped tears out of his eyes. "You caught me off guard."

"Other kids don't value peace as much as I do. They don't realize how precious it is, you know?" I said, staring at the flickering candle flames. "You know how teenagers have all these hormones that make us feel and act weird? I have that too. More than most guys, and it sucks, and this place calms me down. Isn't that what church is for? That's why God invented them?"

"Sure, partly," he nodded.

"I should probably come more often."

"Your face doesn't look so bad," he noticed, indicating my bruises. "I thought you'd be black and blue for a week."

"I heal quickly. How's Tank, do you know?"

He shook his head and said, "No. You two sure seem to hate each other."

"It's so bad, Coach," I sighed. "It's so much worse than people know. I wish I knew how to make it stop. He despises me. He would truly kill me if he could."

"Wow. That part of the reason your life has been so wild?"

"Yeah."

"The last time we talked here," he said and he screwed up his eyes trying to remember our conversation last fall. "You were struggling with dual identities. You are the real Chase Jackson but also someone else. You still feel that way?"

"Absolutely."

"You feel pressure to live up to people's standards? To be the star quarterback and the perfect student and everything else?"

"Yes. Definitely everything else," I said.

"I know the feeling," he said. He was sitting sideways on the pew with his hand resting on the seat back near my shoulder. "That's a good way to be lonely."

"You get lonely?" I asked.

"Sure. It's part of the human condition."

"Explain."

"All the things we humans have in common," he waved his hand to indicate the people in the big sanctuary. "We all love. We all get lonely. We make mistakes. We sin. We all will die."

"What's going to happen to me when I die?"

"Well," he took a deep breath and thought about his answer. "No one knows for sure. But the New Testament tells us that God's children will go be with Him. And the rest...won't."

"I like the New Testament. It seems to be right about everything. And here in this church? I don't hurt at all right now," I realized.

"Are you often in some kind of pain?"

"A lot of the time. There's just so much stuff going on. And things like today's fight don't help."

"I bet."

"And the secrets," I groaned. "So many secrets."

"Is there a chance that keeping your secrets bottled up is contributing to your pain?"

"Maybe? I don't know. We probably all need an outlet, right? I used to be able to tell things to my friend, Katie. But...you know, things change."

"Would you like to try Confession?" he smiled.

"Maybe sometime. I'm not really Catholic, and I think that'd be a very bad idea right now. The confessional might catch fire if I really unloaded."

"Perhaps not," he smiled. "I've heard some doozies."

"Coach. Trust me. You've never heard anything like this."

Chapter Twenty
Saturday, February 18. 2018

Los Angeles was becoming nightly global news. Even though there'd been no Outlaw sightings recently, except for a few grainy photos of Katie and me jumping between buildings, the city was ripping apart at the seams.

A law enforcement task force was quarantining sections of south LA, trying to contain the spread of a new strain of highly addictive bath salt designer drugs, while also searching for a criminal mastermind they believed was behind both the new drugs and the recent civil unrest. Riots were spontaneously breaking out all over the sprawling city and the government could neither stop them nor determine if they were caused by the communities' revolt against new immigration legislation or the drugs.

To top it off, the LA Sniper was on a roll. He shot an average of three people a night for a week and the police were stumped. The Sniper was still using non-lethal wax bullets, but the public was petrified. Anytime I texted PuckDaddy and demanded he tell the Sniper to stop, he just laughed at me.

I didn't know how to help with the drugs or the riots or the criminal mastermind. But I had an idea how to make the Sniper stop. I was going to meet him.

I knew Sniper attributes that the police didn't. The police believed the Sniper was constantly roving, due to the wide dispersal of his targets. But I knew the Sniper was really Infected and could hit targets at an unheard of distance; he didn't have to move as much as the police assumed in order to make those long range shots. I also knew the Sniper had shot Tank, shot me, and shot the vial of blood all within the northern limits of downtown. The Sniper had reached those venues extremely quickly, so I deduced he had a favorite perch with an excellent view and easy access to Natalie's building. After all, he was in LA because of me so he wouldn't stray far from my favorite haunts.

I purchased a map of downtown and marked the locations of all known attacks, including mine and Tank's. After glaring at the markings for three nights I decided he was setting up shop on the roof of either the Plaza skyscrapers or Los Angeles City Hall. An even better guess was that he rotated between them. Tonight I would investigate City Hall, for several reasons. First, the City Hall tower was much older than the Plaza towers so there was less chance of roof-top security cameras, which the Sniper would want to avoid. Second, it was closer geographically to two of the locations where I'd been shot. Third, the Plaza towers were nothing but floor-to-ceiling windows, like big single-sided mile high mirrors, so I didn't know how I'd scale the side without being seen. City Hall looked much easier to climb. And fourth, the 450 foot City Hall tower was several hundred feet shorter than the Plaza towers. Much less scary. Hopefully.

Last night I visited Lee as the Outlaw. He breathlessly showed me his two newest creations. The first item was a new black mask. This design had no velcro. It pulled down over my head like a sleeve, and still covered my nose and mouth. He said it was made from thin breathable lycra and I wouldn't have to worry about it coming loose. He'd also made me a new vest with some of the remaining bounty he received in exchange for Guns. The vest was the same black North Face design but with dramatic red stitching that gave it a "more dramatic flair, to match the red bandana." He'd also designed it with a built-in shoulder harness attached to a small parachute stuffed into an unused compartment located in the back.

"I got the idea after watching you jump off Natalie North's building, you know, dude?" he said. "After the chute's been deployed, you can pull it back in with these two strings feeding through to the front chest pockets. The chute is small and if you were normal it wouldn't decelerate you enough to prevent broken bones. Keep a sharp knife on your belt in case you need to slice the ropes. It's smaller than a normal chute with fewer strings to get tangled, so it'll be easier to stuff back. But next time you need to jump off a building it might come in handy, bro. Uh, Outlaw."

And that's just where I was going. To the top of a building. I thanked Lee and told him I'd use his inventions when I ambushed the Sniper. He nearly passed out. On the way home that night I scampered up the side of my school, tossed the parachute in the air and jumped. The chute snapped open, almost ripping the vest off, right before I hit the ground. I pulled on the strings to retrieve the chute, which slowly gathered in a bunch at the back of my neck, and I stuffed it home. The contraption worked…kind of.

Three o'clock Saturday afternoon, I texted PuckDaddy from the Outlaw's phone.

I'm going to visit Natalie North tonight. See if you can delete the evidence from…you know…everyone's computers and stuff.

>>not a good idea

Tough. I'm going. Nine pm. Might get steamy. Don't watch.

>> dont go stoopid but if u do then im watching

Hah. I grinned and stuffed both phones under my pillow. The trap was set.

I walked out of my house at 3:30 wearing the Outlaw gear under my jogging suit.

"Hi handsome!" Hannah Walker greeted me.

"Whoa!" I shouted in alarm and almost fell off my front porch.

"That's just the type of greeting a girl wants," she smiled wryly. She was learning against her convertible Audi, looking like a million dollars. People shouldn't be allowed to look that good; it puts the rest of us at an awful disadvantage.

"Hi Hannah," I stammered, recovering from the shock as rapidly as I could manage. "This is a nice surprise."

"I thought it would be," she smiled and hugged me. Her hands began curiously probing the strange lumps in my vest so I backed away quickly. "Going somewhere?"

"No! Well, yeah, I guess. Over to see…Cory."

"You're not off to meet Samantha?" she asked and gave me a piercing, searching glare that I didn't understand.

"Samantha? Samantha who?"

"The kicker." She said the word 'kicker' with severe distaste.

"Samantha Gear? No. Why would I? I don't even know where she lives."

"Good. Can we talk?"

"Ah, yeah, sure. I mean, for a little while?"

"I miss you," she said simply with the force of slap.

"You *do*?" I asked incredulously. "But...but we never...we never did anything. We never went on dates or...hung out or anything."

"We went from making-out to broken-up like that," she said and snapped her fingers. "Of course I miss you."

"But we never really made-out either."

"Well," she said and she stepped into me. "Let's do that. Right now." Her lips hovered inches from mine and her blue eyes were everywhere.

"You want to?"

"Very much," she whispered.

"I don't know, Katie," I said, trying to think clearly. "This is all..." I stopped when I heard her breath catch. She stepped away from me and expelled a short, chopped laugh. Disbelief, hurt, and anger all clouded her face. "What's wrong?"

"You just called me Katie."

"Oh. Sorry. Force of habit. She's my best friend."

"That's *all* she is?" she asked. She hugged herself and shivered, despite the relatively warm afternoon.

"Yes. I promise. She's dating someone else," I said.

"But. Do you love her?" she asked, again searching my face.

I took a deep breath and said, "Yes. I do, very much. I'm sorry. But please don't tell her." Hannah would have known the truth if I tried to lie. My face would have revealed it.

"Did you two ever...?"

"No. Never."

Actually. That wasn't exactly true. Just remembered. Katie and the Outlaw *almost* kissed, after I'd broken up with Hannah. Buuuuut that'd probably remain a secret.

"Ugh. This sucks," Hannah said. "You're in love with Katie but I'm in love with you."

"You're...you love me?"

"I guess," she rolled her eyes. "I could have any boy at our school, Chase. Any. Boy. But I only want you. I suppose that's love."

"That's what I feel for Katie."

"I think I also hate you, too. Does Katie know?"

"She does not. Please don't tell her?"

"That's a pretty juicy tidbit, Chase Jackson," she said slyly. *Uh oh.* "I'll cut you a deal, quarterback. Your secret is safe with me, until you tell her. Up until then, you are my boyfriend."

"I can do that. No problem."

"With benefits," she clarified.

"What does that mean?"

"My god, Chase," she cackled, her hand over her mouth. "You are so adorable. I mean, I want you to kiss me."

"Hannah, you can't be serious."

"Dead serious, handsome. Otherwise I'm off to see Katie." This was messed up and we both knew it. I just stared at her. She glared back. "Obviously this isn't ideal. I concede that. But I've invested a lot of time into this and it still might work and I want your mouth on mine this instant."

So I did. I grabbed her face and mashed it into mine. It was false and uncomfortable but it was a kiss.

"Whatever," she sighed, wiping her mouth with her hand. "Just make it look good at school until I replace you. Got it?" I didn't say anything. "And if you ever want more? My door is always open."

PuckDaddy could track my phones so I left them both at home. He could also follow my bike because the dash was a tablet with wifi. So I *ran* to the bus stop, over two miles away, and caught a ride downtown. If my plan worked, he'd assume I was in my bedroom for the next several hours.

I sat on a bench looking up at City Hall until after dusk. The tower is flanked by two shorter wings, each about ten stories tall, and the whole campus is stylish and well manicured, like most of Los Angeles. I grew dizzy staring up at the peak. Nothing moved up there except an American flag flapping in the breeze.

At six thirty, I jumped over the campus hedges and hid in a corner of the lawn. Everything was dark. Everything was still. I took off my track suit, stuffed it into the bushes, and pulled out my mask.

The new mask Lee made was a dream. It slid perfectly into place over my mouth and nose. It was tight but very light, almost like air. I tied on my trusty red bandana, Rambo style.

I became the Outlaw.

This was truly living. I filled the Outlaw's lungs with air and had to smother a triumphant roar. Being the Outlaw was intoxicating and addictive. He was determined, quick, strong, furious, and unafraid. The Outlaw can do anything! This is life!

I needed to gain the roof before the Sniper arrived. With a quick jump I reached the second story egressed windows and began leap-frogging the protruding sills. I zigzagged up the building, gloves and feet finding solid purchases, glancing into windows I passed. I saw a dark office with an empty desk. Jump. Dark hallway. Jump. Lighted empty office with full bookshelves and an open Diet Pepsi. Jump. Dark hallway. Jump. Bathroom, maybe? Jump. Dark hallway. Office. Office. Bathroom. Conference room. Vacant observation deck. I wasn't even breaking a sweat.

An outdoor service walkway, cluttered with big circular antennas, surrounds the tip of the tower. To be safe, I circumnavigated the breezy pinnacle twice. Empty. Perfect. Even though I discovered no evidence of recent occupancy, I had a sixth-sense inclination that the Sniper frequented this aerie.

Wow, what a view! No wonder the Sniper liked coming up here. I'm not afraid of heights, but this was a heady outlook. Far below, Natalie's building looked like a miniature model dominated by tall skyscrapers. I also located the street where Tank's house was.

I found a suitable hiding spot behind a big antenna disk and settled in to wait for the Sniper's arrival. If this didn't work then I'd try again soon, and if that failed then I'd switch towers.

Very quickly I made a discovery; man, I was addicted to my phone! I missed it so much! Ugh. I felt like I was going through detox. I tried sorting out my train wreck of a love life. Simplifying obviously hadn't worked.

Twenty minutes later, in the midst of my self-pity, I heard a noise.

I'd been unlucky for months. Contracting the disease was unlucky, so was meeting Tank, and falling in love with my best friend, and dating Hannah, and my Dad's injuries, and a thousand other things. Well, unlucky or stupid. But tonight, finally, I hit the jackpot.

The Shooter climbed over the parapet. The Shooter! My pulse quickened. He was wearing night-vision goggles, a black knitted cap, and a leather shooting jacket. A powerful rifle was slung over his back. He moved effortlessly, efficiently, and the long climb had clearly not taxed him. It was impossible to judge in the dark from my angle but he looked shorter than me. He was trim and wiry.

I pressed further into my cleft, anxious about those night-vision goggles exposing my hideout. So far, however, the Sniper was oblivious to me, secure in his solitude. He rested the rifle against the outer rail and he stretched while looking over the city. I waited and tried not to breathe. His hearing was probably heightened, like Carter had once explained. After a few minutes he pulled out a small telescope and began scanning.

Well, I was here. I had him. Now what? ...no idea. So I did nothing. And then I continued to do nothing. Forever. And ever. I didn't dare look at my watch.

After a million hours of cowardice, the Sniper answered a phone call by pressing a button on the headset in his ear.

"Yes?.........okay. Is he still at home? Both phones? Good.........I don't understand. Explain.............got it. Understood, probably just asleep..............Maybe? I need more intel...........well, Carter will have to come up here and tell me that, then. If the old man can make the climb then I'll listen............that's his fault........."

Fascinating! I'd bet anything the Sniper was talking to PuckDaddy. Another Infected, right in front of me! His voice was serious and stern, but not deep like mine. The breeze was snatching most of the sounds away but I heard enough.

So this was a terrible plan, it turns out. Now that I was up here it was obvious too much could go wrong. He could fall. I could fall. We could be seen. One of us could get hurt. This might finally be my last straw with Carter. But it was too late and my best chance at getting the rifle away from the Sniper was now while he was distracted on the phone.

Utilizing every bit of care and caution I possessed, I crept forward. Small steps. Shallow breaths. No big movements. Seven feet away.

"I don't care," the Sniper said, voice pitched high in frustration.

Five feet away. Sweaty hands inside my gloves. Stepping on the outside of my soles to avoid scrapes.

"I won't clean up his messes forever. Tell him that. Or I can."

Two feet. Reaching out for the weapon.

He saw me. He hissed in surprise and anger, my fingertips frozen on the stock of the gun. Like lightening he kicked away my empty fist, spun, and struck out with the heel of his hand. I smacked the blow aside using reflexes I didn't know I had. Another kick, another parry.

"Stop!" I shouted, backpedaling desperately.

Kick, kick, kick. Block, block, boom! Too fast! A boot connected solidly with my chest, propelling me up and over the security parapet and out into the endless night.

My ambush had gone downhill fast.

Free falling!

I somersaulted backwards through the void. On instinct I reached over my shoulder, released the parachute clasp and hurled the fabric into the air. A rush of wind and then the material filled with a Pop! The chute caught the air and jerked me upwards. I hauled furiously on the right hand cords, changing the angle of my dangerous descent. The parachute tilted and swung me around underneath, like a ball on the end of a string, and I slammed into the tower wall.

"Big mistake," I growled, using one hand to hastily stuff the small chute back as best I could. "Now I'm mad."

Thirty seconds after I'd been kicked off the roof, I leapt back over the security rail, ready to break something. I approached from a different direction. The Sniper was silhouetted against the city lights, head in his hands.

"No! That's what I'm telling you! I think that was Chase! His texts were a trick...oh god..." the Sniper was saying into the ear piece as I ran up, left my feet and drove them through his body. I caught him by complete surprise. His thin frame collapsed like paper machete. That kick would have killed a normal man. I landed, pinning his arms down with my knees.

"Now," I snarled, "we talk."

The Sniper was sucking air, dazed and trying to form words. I tore off the night vision goggles and balled up his knitted cap in my fist. But in that instant I couldn't speak either. I was staring down into the wide eyes of Samantha Gear.

Chapter Twenty-One
Saturday, February 18. 2018

Later that night

"How could you not figure it out?" she asked again. We were perched side by side on the rim of the sky, the upper-most part of the tower, staring down on normal humanity. To my surprise, Samantha had risen and hugged me in a fierce embrace during those first few moments of deep shock. Then she punched me *really* hard and now we were trying to talk things through.

"I realized the LA Sniper was also the Infected Shooter," I said. "But I never dreamt he was a girl that went to my school."

"Hah," she smiled victoriously. "I told them I could pass for a high school junior."

"How old are you?"

"I'm twenty-nine. So you really shouldn't be checking me out so often. How'd you survive that fall, anyway? Thought I'd killed you."

"Parachute. In the back of the vest." I indicated the compartment with my thumb.

"You're full of surprises."

"If you're twenty-nine, you really shouldn't be hitting on high school kids like Cory and Lee," I pointed out.

"Touché. But nothing happened between Cory and I," she laughed mischievously. "I was just having fun, trying to fit in."

ALAN JANNEY

"Why were you at our high school in the first place?"

"Lots of reasons." She took a deep breath and blew it at the sky. "I murder teenagers as a profession, Chase. Sometimes older adults, but most of them are your age. It's hard, grinds me down. You know? It has to be done. The kids are sick and dying and sometimes they're hurting people around them. I don't know them, I just...alleviate their pain. Right? But you. I felt like I knew you because of the Outlaw gig. I couldn't just kill the Outlaw. He's the *Outlaw*! I was as intrigued by him as everyone else. So Carter calls me in and spills the beans about my next target, but I told him I'd only do it after I verified for myself that you'd gone insane. So I had Puck enroll me," she shrugged.

"PuckDaddy's pretty good, huh. I imagine he fabricated a full official academic history and fake kicking statistics."

"Puck is the best," she nodded. "I don't know what we'd do without him."

"It's like he never sleeps."

"He doesn't, hardly. One of his Infected traits is that his brain never turns off. I think he just...goes comatose for a few hours a day." She pulled out her telescope again and glared at something in the distance with one eye screwed shut.

"Where does he live?"

"Got no idea. Never asked. Carter wouldn't want me to know."

"Jeez, freaking Carter," I scoffed. "Why do the Infected jump whenever he says to? He seems so unreasonable."

She closed the telescope between her palms with a soft smack and said, "He is demanding."

"So...why? Why is he the boss? Does he pay you?"

"Actually, he does pay us," she grinned wryly. "He's Michael Jordan rich. We get monthly 'allowances' to support ourselves without getting into a real line of work. That way we can assist him full-time or be on constant stand-by. But that's not the real reason why he's the boss."

"So? Then why?"

"He's old, Chase. Our Infected *symptoms* grow stronger the longer the we live. Carter is ancient. I'd wager over a hundred years old. Maybe a hundred

162

fifty. He's extremely powerful. Much more so than the rest of us. And he's temperamental, so we've learned to tread carefully."

"So it *is* a monarchy," I mused. I was dropping small pebbles between my feet and watching them twist and whirl out of sight.

"He likes to pretend it isn't," she nodded. "But he's in total control."

"I overheard your phone conversation. Sounded like you were breaking ranks."

"Kind of," she said. "He trusts my judgement. Or he used to. Recently he's been less than pleased. After tonight I might go into hiding. There's a rumor of an Infected living on a yacht in the middle of the Pacific Ocean for the past ten years, where Carter can't find him. I don't know what he did. Or if it's true. Maybe I can go live with that guy."

I frowned and said, "That doesn't sound like the arrogant Samantha Gear I know."

"Arrogance is worthless against an avalanche. And that's what Carter is."

"Is he the oldest living Infected?"

"Seven years ago PuckDaddy let it slip that Carter's mentor was still alive, but that he was a hermit. Permanently hidden. He'd have to be old beyond belief, so he might have died recently. Who knows. Natural causes, like heart disease or renal failure, will eventually claim all of us who live long enough. Skin cancer? Something like that."

"Maybe that's why Carter never lets all the Infected gather together," I said. "Because then you'd have enough strength to defy him."

"Perhaps, champ, but you're getting it wrong. He's not a villain. Carter is not an evil dictator that we must over-throw to preserve ourselves. He's a man that takes this disease more seriously than anyone else and he makes the hard choices to keep us all safe. And besides, there's nothing we could do about him anyway. Not only is Carter much stronger than us, he's never alone."

"What do you mean?"

"He has a Shadow. Wherever Carter goes, someone else goes too. Like a body guard. I've seen the guy just once. Puck and I don't know what to call him so we call him Shadow. Puck knows about Shadow because he's had to erase pictures of him at Carter's insistence. He's Infected and his sole purpose is keeping Carter safe. If Carter meets with you inside a church, you can bet the Shadow is outside. Shadow was probably on the roof with you that first night, but you never saw him."

"That's the creepiest thing I've ever heard," I said and I actually shivered. "But also kind of cool."

"Wait till you meet Carter again," she scoffed. "You'll be looking everywhere for the guy."

"Has it occurred to you that Carter could be the Chemist?" I asked.

She took a long time answering. She stared into the stars, as if she hadn't heard me, and then she scanned the city again with her scope. Finally she replied, "Yes. It's occurred to me."

"And?"

"And…I doubt it."

"Me too," I said. "But maybe? Right?"

"Carter is a mystery. He's doing things I can't guess at, and he'd kill PuckDaddy if he tried spying on him. But I don't think he's a drug lord. Or a gang leader."

"I talked with the FBI about the Chemist. He said the profile they have of the Chemist isn't what we'd expect of an urban general. The witnesses describe an older white guy."

Her face cracked into a grin and she shook her head. "You're so stupid."

"What?"

"Amazing you're still alive. You talked with the FBI??" she howled in laughter. "What is *wrong* with you?"

"Shut up."

"Really," she wiped her eyes. "So dumb. You never stop doing the absurd. You're threatening our very existence. I should probably kill you now. Carter definitely would." She made a gun with her finger and thumb and pointed it at my skull. "Bang, quarterback. You're dead."

"Hah. What makes you think I'd let you kill me?"

Her face grew serious and she leaned in. "Has Puck told you that you're advanced?"

"Uh…no? I don't get it."

"Any Infected that survives is like a newborn Bambi. All elbows and bravado. Too much ability, too few brains. Stumbling around, falling down, doing stupid stuff. They don't have the capacity to control their enhanced bodies yet. Follow? But not you. You have a very advanced harness on your body, for lack of a better analogy."

"Yeah, I'm the best."

"No really, Chase," she glared. "It's wild. You're stronger and faster and in much greater control than you should be."

"Why?"

"Why? How the hell should I know? Carter doesn't know either."

My stomach growled. I realized I was famished. "Do you ever get crazy hungry? Like after climbing a building?"

"Of course, Chase. You're human and you are burning through a truck load of calories." She pulled out a handful of granola bars from her pocket. She handed me two. I could have eaten a thousand. "You'll learn to keep food handy. Otherwise you'll go into shock, almost like a diabetic."

"Thanks," I said, chewing gratefully. "Oh good. They're chocolate."

"I bet you love chocolate. We all do. All Infected crave it. I dunno why."

"I *do* crave it. Change of subject. Does Carter know why all these Infected are popping up in Los Angeles? LA is turning into a zoo."

"We don't know why. It shouldn't be happening. Another one died last night, went crazy, but thankfully I got there quickly," she said and she indicated southeast LA with her telescope. "The odds of this many Infected in a localized area are astronomical."

"Carter doesn't know why?"

"If he does he hasn't shared it with me or Puck."

"You know, you're not helping things, Sniper," I said. "Why are you terrorizing the public with your wax bullets?"

"Because it's awesome," she grinned. "And I'm bored."

"You cannot be serious. You're shooting people because you're bored?"

"Oh come on, Outlaw!" she laughed. "Surely you've been in bed at night, practically on fire, just itching to do something dangerous! That's the disease, and those urges don't do away. Being Infected is the BEST!" Without warning she leapt to her feet, balancing on the rail. She screamed at the top of her lungs with such physical force it hurt my ears. "Sometimes! Sometimes I want to jump off this tower and FLY! Spin off into the stars and NEVER come back!" She'd undergone an instant transformation. The quiet girl beside me had been replaced by a wild eyed maniac. Power pulsed inside her, physically radiating off her body. She closed her eyes, arms wide. "God, Chase! How I envy you your jumping ability. I can't do that. I can climb, but not jump like you," she said between deep breaths. "You see this, Outlaw? This is the disease. The insatiable desire to fly, to risk, to die. I have so much adrenaline pumping in my ears and in my limbs that I can't even think straight. This is why we die. This feeling I have right now. It's intoxicating. It's everything."

"Maybe you should step down."

"This is why you wear the mask. This is why you venture out at night, why you keep risking your life. The Outlaw, the disease, forces you to. This is why the Infected perish after surviving adolescence. We want to. Because the chance to cheat death is euphoric," she said. The slipstream around the tower was tossing her hair. She quit talking, eyes still closed, and began leaning forward. Then back. Then farther forward, like a diver, but before she slipped past the edge of balance she came back again. "Worried, Outlaw?"

"Very! Please sit down."

"This is why I shoot people," she said and she squatted down beside me. Her eyes were feverish and her breath was sweet and hot on my face. "It's why I'm still alive. It gives me something to do while I'm sitting on a tower, fighting the disease, trying to keep from leaping. Make sense?"

"It does. Why is your face so close to mine?" I asked.

"Because you're a boy and I'm a girl and I've never found that bandana so sexy before," she said huskily.

"I'm in high school," I chuckled uneasily. Her passion was contagious and I'd always found her pretty. We needed to change the subject. "And you're old."

"You're eighteen," she said. "It's legal. And also," she said and she hit me so hard I nearly slipped off the ledge. "Don't call me old. I've barely aged since I was nineteen."

"Ouch," I growled.

She sighed, returning to rest on her perch. "But you're right. Shouldn't mix business with pleasure. It's hard to think straight if you give the disease an inch. But maybe you should find an ugly mask. The one you have gets a girl's blood hot. Also, the new red accents on the vest? It should look stupid but somehow it works. I like it."

"Thanks."

"You're special, Chase. And not just because of the mask. PuckDaddy agrees, and we both think Carter realizes it. You're different. The virus makes us all mean. We grow selfish and secretive. We're arrogant and too serious. But you seem able to resist that. You're generous and you care about others. You're the *only* one of us that genuinely tries to protect the civilians, the people without the disease. One of the reasons we're not unified is that we naturally don't trust each other. There's no camaraderie, only suspicion. You're the first Infected that's actively sought out the company of others."

"You have no desire to meet PuckDaddy in real life?"

"No. Well, not until recently. Maybe now I do, I'm not sure. All the Infected are interested in you. Carter, me, PuckDaddy, and Puck said a couple of the others asked about you too. The Outlaw is something we all have in common. We trust you, for whatever reason. We're fascinated that you're so public and...heroic. I've been ordered to kill you and...and I just can't. And when I don't? Carter seems relieved! Like he was hoping I wouldn't! This is the longest conversation I've had in ten years, Chase. By a mile. And I hope it never ends, you know? It's hard to explain. Puck concurs. He digitally spies on you as often as possible, because you're such an anomaly. You're special, Chase." She finished in a reverential whisper, as if fully processing the implications of such a change in her world.

"Maybe you're all just jerks?" I suggested. She glanced sharply at me but I was smiling. She rolled her eyes. "So now that I know who you are, will you quit attending our school?"

"No way, quarterback. It's getting too good. I've got a front row seat to the drama. Katie is one in a million, and I adore her. But I bet Puck a thousand dollars you'll die before working up the courage to tell her how you really feel."

Chapter Twenty-Two
Wednesday, February 22. 2018

"Dude, you see the magazine article about you?" Lee asked me at lunch.

I groaned. "Oh no. What now?"

As if on cue, Hannah Walker strutted by and smacked a high school football magazine down on the table, already open to the correct page. "I couldn't have said it better myself," she purred, close enough that her lips brushed my ear, and walked off.

Samantha Gear slid over and said, "Let me see that." We read it together.

Hidden Spring's Hidden Gem

Hidden Spring's junior quarterback Chase Jackson is a bad man.

I heard the rumors so I went to see him play against the Burbank Bears last September, only his third game as starter. Words do not do him justice, but I will give it a shot. The kid *swells* as the game goes on. After a forgettable first quarter, the seventeen-year old appeared to grow taller, straighter, broader. He started the brutal mid-season clash as a boy and ended it as a demigod.

I presumed my enthusiasm was simply playing tricks on me until I witnessed the phenomenon again in the divisional championship against the Patrick Henry Dragons, and then again recently at a quarterback competition. It was not my eyes. It was Chase Jackson. Guy just seems to get bigger in big moments.

Obviously his actual physical dimensions do not increase, so what is the deal? Why does he *appear* to increase in size? Because he is other-worldly good at football, that is why.

Let me describe what I saw.

He makes professional throws. I saw him almost out-throw senior burner Adam Moseley. He chucks fifty yards on a line. He *snapped* a receiver's fingers, and I would bet the deed to my house the ball was screaming at over fifty miles per hour. He won the long-distance toss without trying. I was there. I saw it, his effortless pitch that sailed nearly seventy yards.

I saw him outrun every player on the field against the Bears. He runs at minimum a 4.5 forty-yard dash. At minimum. He *jogged* the quarterback obstacle course and finished third, and I know that I know that I know he wasn't trying to win. He was coasting, and his coach knows why.

"Yeah, kid's a humble guy. Doesn't like the spotlight. Watch him long enough and you'll realize he doesn't want you to know how good he is, like he's embarrassed." Coach Garrett smacks his legendary gum even harder when discussing Jackson. "He won't have that luxury for long. The word is getting out. He's special."

His teammates know. I attended several recent practices. They know. They would face a firing squad for him. The team loves its reluctant superstar-in-the-making. On the field, his word is law, even if he does not realize it.

I saw him change directions so fast it *broke* the ankle of all-planet linebacker Tank Ware. I saw him cross the goal line with most of Burbank's population hanging on his back.

His school knows. The Hidden Spring public relations director has stopped fielding requests from college coaches, due to sheer volume.

His father knows. He declined to comment, but he did mention that he preemptively trashes all the football mail Jackson receives, so the junior will have less to stress about.

His girlfriend knows. The sparkling bombshell of a cheerleader gushes, "He doesn't even know how many followers he has on Twitter. It doesn't matter to him. To us."

So why did Chase Jackson's team lose the divisional championship game? According to the medical records, he suffered injuries similar to those of a bad car wreck. The notorious Dragons took so many cheap shots that the refs had to eject one of their players in the first quarter. Jackson *still* almost won the game on a last-second heroic drive, despite being rushed to the hospital afterwards for treatment to *life threatening* injuries.

Go see this kid play next year. If you can wrestle a seat away from the college scouts, that is. He will be the guy throwing lasers and lapping the field. He will be the player you can not take your eyes off, the one you subconsciously recognize as different. He stands differently, runs differently, almost dangerously. His bark is louder, his bite is unbearable, a preternatural predator. You will know it is him. Just like I did. He will be the guy that is growing bigger than the game itself.

"Way to go, dummy," Samantha growled.

"What?" I snapped at her, balling up the article in my fist. "It's not my fault. I didn't know. And I can't believe dad is throwing my mail away."

"Walker never gonna let you go now," Cory noted sagely.

Samantha scoffed and said, "Speaking of the sparkling bombshell that obviously paid to get in the article, why is she eating with our Katie again?"

Lee, Cory, Samantha and I stared glumly across the cafeteria at Katie, wondering what we'd done to drive her back to Hannah Walker. They were deep into an animated discussion, leaning towards each other, food forgotten.

"I don't know," I sighed. "But it can't be good for me."

"Why not?" Cory mumbled around a chicken sandwich.

"So so many reasons."

"Like what?"

"Like he loooooooves Katie," Samantha said. This was astonishing news to Cory and Lee, both of whom choked on their food. And I should have been furious with Samantha for voicing my secret. But I had too many secrets and I no longer cared if the world knew. I loved Katie. Loved her fiercely and jealously.

"Dude! Is that true?" Lee said. "Because I saw you making out with Hannah Walker this morning."

"It's true," I said. Hannah had greeted me in the hallway that morning, wrapped me up and kissed me passionately. I didn't participate, just tolerated. I'd play along until I could tell Katie how I felt. Sooooo I'd probably end up marrying Hannah. "Please don't tell her, okay? I haven't figured out how to completely screw this up, yet."

"Okay," Cory said sacredly.

"This will change everything, bro."

"Yes," I said. "Yes I know."

"Why are you rubbing your head?" Lee asked.

"He has a headache," Samantha replied.

"A bad one," I said. And then…nothing.

Dreams. I remember Katie. My parents and I used to rent a house across from her building. When we were little we'd leave notes on her older brother's car and run behind the pine trees when he came out of the apartment. We rolled tennis balls back and forth across the street until one day a car stopped. It was a police car. He told us to stop. Katie cried. She kissed me on the cheek once when I wasn't ready. I think we were seven. She told me she just wanted to kiss a boy.

Now she was dating a ticking time bomb. And I was…asleep?

Waking up took forever. I clawed to the brink of consciousness several times and even when surfaced I was swimming through strange memories of voices, confusing images, colors, tastes, and smells. A lifetime's worth of dreams were forcing themselves on me, pretending to be reality, posing as remembrances. The whole universe was inside my eyelids.

"You awake this time, kid?"

That voice was real. I think. Blindly I tried brushing away the false emotions but all I found were sheets. I was thrashing around in a bed.

"Wake up, Chase."

"Okay," I groaned. "Where am...?"

"See for yourself."

I was in my bed, my bedroom, my home. I squinted at the person talking to me.

"Carter," I said.

"You realize that me being in your bedroom is a bad thing," he said simply.

"Did you hurt my dad?"

"No. He believes I'm your physician."

I took a closer look. Carter was dressed like a doctor, complete with a bag of medical instruments. He was leaning against my dresser. He held a revolver.

"Doctors use six-shooters?" I started to laugh. Or at least wheeze. It shouldn't be funny but it was. I felt drunk or high, even though I'd never been either. "You a doc from the Old West?"

"Chase, you're on the verge of insanity," he said quietly. My blood ran cold and I quit laughing.

"Oh."

"What do you remember about today?"

"...nothing?"

"The Shooter found you right before you picked up a drink machine. You also threw a knife that pinned Babington's shirt to a wall and heaved another football player halfway across the cafeteria. Fortunately there's no known video. Yet."

That wasn't good. I didn't remember any of that. On the bright side, it sounded like he didn't realize I knew the Shooter's identity.

"The Shooter gave you a shot of tranquilizer and got you out before you hurt someone," he continued. He appeared grim. As he talked he kept spinning the revolver's chamber, click click click click. "Only because killing you in a public school is against our rules."

"Very kind of you."

"PuckDaddy sent forged medical records to the school, indicating you suffered a stress-induced episode of temporary psychosis, from all the football and school work. Your school believes this is a treatable and preventable malady, and that it won't happen again. The principal called your father earlier and you are suspended tomorrow."

"Good. I need a day off."

He squinted at me, jaw locked, for a long moment. I fidgeted. He said, "She *told* you."

"Who told me what?" I asked. Oh shoot, he knows! Run!

"Don't lie to me. I can tell."

"Okay fine," I admitted. "Samantha didn't *tell* me. I caught her."

"How?"

"I figured out where her nest was, tricked PuckDaddy into believing I was still at home, and then surprised her in the tower."

He didn't say anything.

"Don't be mad at her," I said. "She *tried* to kill me. Kicked me off the roof and everything. But eventually I won the fight."

"Why were you looking for her?"

"I was looking for the Shooter. I didn't know it was Samantha."

"Why?" he asked again.

"To make her stop shooting people."

"Why?"

"Because it's messed up! She was scaring people."

"It's so strange," he sighed, scratching an itch on his forehead with the barrel of his gun, "that you care about others. None of the rest do."

"Yeah, well, you should."

"What did she tell you?"

"She says you're not *that* big of a jerk. She says you're just doing what you have to."

"Which is why I'm here, mate," he said. Click click click click. Each click sent a shiver down my spine.

"She also said that if you murder me she will kill you in retaliation," I said in a rush. My brain was scrambled, and all my thoughts were loud and incoherent.

"Liar," he sniffed.

"Yeah, that was a lie."

"Here's why I haven't killed you yet..."

"Because I'm so likable."

"Because you are quite advanced in your physical abilities, and I may need to use them," he said and then he clarified, "If you still have a grasp on your sanity."

"How can you use me?" I asked. I wished I could get up out of bed. Laying there while he lectured me was really emasculating. I could tell I was being too flippant, but I couldn't stop. My mouth wasn't obeying orders.

"To begin with, you could assist me with Tank."

"You know about him?"

"Of course. Like you, he's an overly developed young Infected. And he's a problem."

"I think so too!" I cried. "Let's ship him to Antartica."

"I've already tried to kill him, kid. The night he almost disemboweled you on the motorcycle?"

"Right," I remembered. "Samantha shot him. It was so great."

"Yes she did. And with a real bullet."

"Not wax?"

"Not wax."

"But..." I said. "But...that makes no sense."

"Exactly. He's a problem."

"Wait. No. No way. How could he survive?" I said, staring at him in horror.

"He shouldn't have. He's impossibly strong. His bones must be as hard as steal when his adrenaline is going. I'm sure the bullet fractured his skull, but he survived."

"Wow we *are* in trouble."

"It gets worse," he said. "We tried to kill him again and failed."

"When? How?"

"The Shooter...er, Samantha purposefully started that fight on the football field. I was lurking nearby. We were hoping you two would injure each other, so I had an ambulance ready to finish you off quietly."

"Okay. You're an awful person, but keep going," I said stonily. I wondered where his Shadow was. On the roof? In the spare bedroom? Under my bed?

"Don't take it personally. Just business, kid. So you stumble away and we load Tank into the ambulance, and I drive off. I find a quiet street and go into the back to inject pure oxygen into Tank's veins, to make sure he's truly dead. But Tank wakes up, even though he should be toast, surprises me, rips a hole in the ambulance, and escapes."

"Holy moly. Destroyed an ambulance?"

"Yeah. Very impressive. If he wasn't such a nightmarish loose end I'd leave him alive. He'd be a powerful ally," he said.

"He sounds indestructible."

"Remember, we don't have super powers. We're sick. His sickness is messing with his body and will probably kill him. I hope. But he's still human. We could drown him, or poison him, or burn him alive, or shoot him in the temple. You get the idea. But no way could he be beaten to death when he's angry."

"You're morbid," I said, feeling a little queasy.

"You asked. And he hates you."

"You want to use me as bait, don't you?"

"Maybe," he nodded. "We know where he lives but we Infected like to keep a low profile. Storming into a condo to murder a kid isn't exactly our modus operandi."

"I won't help you kill someone. Not even Tank."

"There's another problem too. This one might stir your deep well of foolish nobel intentions, hero."

"Okay," I said.

"You heard of the Chemist?"

"I have," I said slowly and carefully. I had suspicions Carter WAS the Chemist. Time to keep my mouth clamped shut. If I could.

"He's building an empire in southern Los Angeles, and he's largely doing it through a new drug he's created," Carter said, oblivious to my deeply dubious expression.

"I heard."

"But here's what you don't know, kid. The Chemist is Infected. And he has some Infected soldiers with him."

"Whoa," I said, sitting up in bed. My heard swam. The FBI didn't know *that*.

"That got your attention?"

"How do you know?"

"I have many avenues of information. I traffic in information."

"So the Chemist," I said, "is Infected, and he has an army of drug addicts waiting in the rougher neighborhoods, and he also has some Infected. How many Infected?"

"I'm not positive. There's been an unexpected explosion of them in this city. Depends on how many he's collected. But my earlier estimate of ten Infected *total* is way off."

"Why does he want an army in the first place?"

"Because he's power hungry. And, just a guess, he's bored," he shrugged. "Boredom is the primary scourge of the Infected. We grow restless and anxious, like a kid with a new bike he hasn't ridden yet. My intelligence suggests he'll strike soon against the rest of Los Angeles."

"Like start a war?"

He nodded and said, "I think so."

"He can't win a war against the United States government with a bunch of drug addicts," I couldn't help but laugh.

"He doesn't care about winning." His face darkened. "He cares about causing mayhem. And don't forget his Infected. They change everything."

"That's why you want my help," I realized.

"Correct."

"To help you fight his Infected."

"Correct again."

"That sounds…really…really…really awesome," I said. Wow! A chance to actually DO something. I knew it was the disease talking, but finally being able to test my body, take it to the limit and see how far I could go, would be exhilarating. I was sick of hiding and pretending. I thought it over. He remained quiet, probably debating my lucidity. "You think if I help you that I'll get killed, either by the Chemist or by an aneurysm, and that I'll be one less loose end for you to worry about, but maybe I'll be of some assistance before I die."

"Once again, you are correct."

I crawled out of bed, which suddenly felt too small, and started pacing. "I have a contact with the FBI. I can alert them about the Chemist and his upcoming war."

"No," he said abruptly. "No outside help. We handle our own business. Privately."

"Carter, no way. This sounds huge," I reasoned. My body had swelled with adrenaline. I was clearly closer to the ceiling and my clothes were all much tighter, despite the fact that I'd started wearing baggier stuff. "You can't fight an army with just a handful of Infected."

"I don't need to fight an army," he said and his voice was edgy. "I just need to go in, remove the Chemist, and get out. Everything else will fall apart in his absence."

"He's going to start a war. You said so yourself. That means a lot of people will get hurt."

"Yes. Thousands," he nodded.

"You look like that idea is appealing," I commented.

"Like I said, mate. Boredom."

"Well I'm not okay with it. We could warn the people. We *should* warn the people," I pleaded.

"If we did then the Chemist would know we're coming."

"Do you know the Chemist?"

"I've run into him before," he replied, looking out the window and scratching that invisible itch on his forehead with the gun again. "Not for many years, though. I think he's bored and perhaps now fully insane. A megalomaniac. He's not being careful and he's going to expose us. He's become a loose end."

"What do you propose we do?"

"I'm searching for him. Every day. But he's very careful and very well hidden. As soon as I find him, we'll move. If he starts a war, we sit tight unless there are Infected that need to be eliminated. We wait until he reveals himself and then we take him out."

"Me, you, and Shooter? Samantha?"

"Right," he confirmed.

"Anyone else?"

"We won't need anyone else. Assuming you're still alive and sane."

"I don't see why your plan precludes warning the police? Or the FBI?" I said.

"Because," he snapped. "We don't need to. It would warrant additional attention from agencies that we avoid."

"It could save lives."

"We're not in the business of saving lives," he said with an air of finality. "And neither is the Outlaw, if you want to live."

Let's do it, the disease whispered. Let's warn the people. We can't let thousands of innocent people die. Besides, it would anger Carter and that's always fun!

That DOES sound like fun.

Chapter Twenty-Three
Tuesday, February 28. 2018

The Outlaw *should* warn Los Angeles. Right? I wrestled with the decision for five days. Was this actually a good idea? Who should I tell about the impending war? Would Carter really kill me?

Samantha Gear was plainly on edge. She kept checking her phone and watching the news. PuckDaddy was only answering my texts with one word responses. Two different Outlaw impersonators (called Law Givers) tried to sneak into Natalie North's building, and the Outlawyers (Outlaw fan club) were raising money for her to come speak at their meetings. Katie reported Tank was acting even crazier than usual, and she was considering calling things off with him. Woohoo! She and Hannah Walker continued lunching together, which made it hard to hold her hand. We were all sitting on a bomb, with the fuse slowly burning away.

My headaches had largely abated but I could feel insanity creeping in. I'd hear voices or see visions or wake up and realize I'd been unconscious for a few minutes. Mundane happenings seemed hilarious or completely confusing. I assumed the disease was applying more and more pressure on my brain, causing these problems. Cory and Lee kept looking at me askance, like I was a stranger.

No Carter. No Chemist. Nothing happened. I slept as often as I could.

At the end of five days I was ready to explode. This was why Samantha took shots at innocent targets; she was insanely bored, almost literally. I was raging, jumping around my room, breaking rocks in my fist, anything to keep from erupting. I needed to do SOMETHING.

You could warn Los Angeles, came the gentle tug in my mind.

Or I could tell Katie how I truly feel about her.

Which one, which one, which one, eeny meeny miny moe, catch an Infected by the toe.

I was going to warn Los Angeles. Katie was MUCH scarier.

I pulled on the Outlaw outfit. The Outlawfit. Hah! I'm so funny. I zipped up a jacket over the vest to avoid being recognized, because I'm sooooooo famous and awesome. I stuffed the mask and bandana into my pocket. I grabbed my helmet. I got on the bike. And then I rode off to save the day.

First! I needed to get control of my emotions and thought processes. Done! Maybe! After I'd driven several miles from my house I turned on the disposable phone and called Isaac Anderson, Captain of the Universe, Mr. FBI himself.

Straight to voicemail. *This is Special Agent Isaac Anderson, please leave me a detailed message. Beeeeep.*

Noooo! I called again. *This is Special Agent Isaac Anderson, please leave me a detailed message. Beeeeep.*

"What kind of FBI agent are you?" I shouted through the phone. "You'll have to read about this on the front page like everyone else, because you wouldn't answer your phone. This is the Outlaw, by the way." I hung up.

Well, now what? I didn't want to do an interview on television. So that left the radio, or the newspaper, or the internet. Newspaper sounded good, but I didn't know any writers. In fact I only knew the name of one reporter, and she worked on television. Oh well, she could write, couldn't she?

I dialed the news station.

"Channel Four News. How can I help you?"

I said, "Put me through to Teresa Triplett, please."

"I'm sorry sir, but she's gone for the day. Would you like her voicemail? Or can someone else assist you?"

"This is urgent and I need to speak with her," I growled as I drove past an ice cream shop teeming with parents and their children.

"May I ask who is calling and what this is in reference to?"

"I'm the Outlaw and I need to warn Los Angeles," I said. As soon as the words spilled out, I realized it was the lamest thing I would ever say even if I lived to be a million.

"Sir," the lady sniffed. "You're the third Outlaw that's called in today."

"What?? Ugh! What is *wrong* with people? Hang on. I'll call you back." I hung up, switched phones, and rang Natalie North. This was so dumb. Spider-Man never has this problem.

"Well hello there stranger!" Natalie North bubbled into the phone.

"I need a favor."

"Anything," she said. "Come over."

"I need you to call the Channel Four news station and tell them I'm about to contact them. They don't believe it's me."

"How do I know it *really is* you unless you come over?" she teased.

"Natalie!" I yelled at her.

"Okay okay!" she squeaked. "I'll call them. If they don't believe me then I'll have my agent yell at them. Give me three minutes."

"Thank you."

"Come over when you're done?" she asked.

"No. Maybe. Isn't it a school night for you? Nevermind. I can't. Well, maybe. Just call."

I drove around a ritzy shopping mall for five minutes, which should give Natalie plenty of time, and then called Channel Four again.

"Channel Four News," said a shaky voice.

"Believe me now?" I asked, perhaps a little too hotly.

"Yes sir, and I'm sorry about that, sir."

"No problem," I grinned inside my helmet.

"I have Teresa Triplett waiting for you."

"Great! Put me through."

"One more thing, sir. Miss Natalie North asked me to give you a message. She wants you to come visit later."

I sighed and said, "Please don't repeat that to anyone. And put me through to Teresa."

I told Teresa Triplett to keep this a secret but she didn't. I was hiding on one of the L.A. Times' lower roofs, well before our rendezvous, and I spied three cameramen sneaking around. They remained far enough away from our meeting location (the very top of the building, under the flag pole) that I didn't worry about them.

Now I had to figure out what I wanted to say...

...and then I woke up. I yawned, shook my head and looked around. I hate it when that happened. Without warning, boom! Knocked out.

I glanced at my watch. Whoops! I'm late. I yanked the mask up from around my neck, tied on the bandana and JUMPED! I sailed into the black sky and over the uppermost roof of the many tiered building. I didn't blame Samantha Gear for being jealous; this was awesome. I plummeted down and landed beside the dark, still form of Teresa Triplett. She jumped and gasped, which was wonderfully gratifying.

While I stifled another yawn, she looked around wild-eyed, searching for something to say. She had interviewed Chase Jackson once, before the previous football season, so I kind of knew her. She was pretty and seemed much more confident when I used to be a normal seventeen year old.

"Hello," she said finally. I nodded in reply because I didn't know how to start and also because I'd discovered people *expected* me to be quiet. "So why'd you choose me?"

"What do you mean?" I growled at her.

"Why do you want to talk to *me*?" she asked and her voice was shaky. I suppose this *was* an intense experience for her, meeting on the roof of a tall building in the middle of the night with guy in a mask. "Instead of other more famous reporters?"

"Oh," I shrugged. "I don't know that many reporters. And you seem nice."

"How'd you get up here? Do you have abilities that I don't have? That question sounds absurd, even to my ears," she said. I frowned, wondering how I could phrase this, debating how much I could reveal to her. She continued, "Did you fly up here? Like a superhero?"

"No," I chuckled. "That's hilarious. No. There's no such thing as super heroes. In fact, I'm sick."

"What do you mean?"

"I mean I'm very sick, and it's possibly fatal," I said and I decided not to elaborate. Carter was going to be pissed enough already.

"Fatal?" she asked, writing things down on her notepad. I'm sure she was recording the conversation too. "With what illness?"

"Nevermind," I said, dropping my voice to a deep growl again. "Shouldn't have said anything. That's not why I'm here."

"Then why are you here?"

"I want you to pass along a message."

"To who?" she asked, looking mystified.

"To everyone."

"What message?"

At that instant the bluetooth headset in my ear blared to life. I didn't even answer it; the device just turned on somehow. The very distinguishable voice of PuckDaddy yelled, "You fool! You idiot! What are you doing?"

I didn't say anything to either of them. I stared into space. This was it. I was crossing some sort of threshold from which there could be no return. I was making powerful enemies.

"Chase. Outlaw. Just stop. Abort. Don't do this. You're dead if you do. Seriously, stupid. Carter will waste you for sure," PuckDaddy said.

"Are you okay?" she asked. "Is something wrong? What message?"

"Outlaw. No way. Don't. Cancel, cancel," in my ear.

I took a deep breath and told Teresa, "I'm not the only one."

"Oh no," PuckDaddy groaned. "You're toast. Damn it. So dumb. You're dead."

"You're what?" Teresa Triplett asked, leaning towards me.

"There are others," I said, stronger. This felt...correct. This was good. I was doing the right thing. "There are others like me. And they are already here. Lots of them. In Los Angeles. And we're all in danger."

PuckDaddy sighed loudly.

"Wow, okay," Teresa babbled. "You mean, they can jump like you? We have video of you flying or jumping or...something."

"Yes. And other things."

"Like what kind of other things?" she asked. She was no longer taking notes, simply staring intently, urgently.

"Anything a human can do, they can do much much better. And some of them are not nice."

"Who are they?"

"They are hidden, living in the shadows. I don't know their real names, but I can tell you that one of them is called the Chemist," I said, emboldened by the truth.

"The Chemist? The gang leader in south Los Angeles?"

"Right. I'm still learning too. But I believe the Chemist and his army will revolt soon, and our law enforcement agencies need to be ready."

"Ready for what?" she asked.

"War. In our streets."

"Wait!" she cried as I turned to go. "This...this is a lot to absorb. Do you have to leave?"

"Yes."

"What you just said is insane. You want to warn the city but all this is...impossible. How can this be true?"

"You'll have to trust me," I said simply.

"Will you help us? If there's a war in our city?"

"Of course."

I jumped into the clouds.

"You should have consulted with me first," PuckDaddy scolded as I walked south on Alameda. My mask was stowed in my pocket.

"You'd have just warned me not to."

"Affirmative. Now listen close. This is the last time we're ever going to communicate. Otherwise I'm dead too. You can't return home."

"I bet Carter bugged my room," I said.

"Your room's been bugged for two months, dummy. He'll kill you tonight in your sleep. Go somewhere else. Off grid. Forever. Don't go back to school. Move far away and burn your phones. Both phones. Turn off the wifi on your bike. I can't track you if you disappear. Live in a desert. Okay?"

"This isn't goodbye, Puck," I laughed. "Once the war starts, Carter will realize that I'm on his side."

"You'll be dead by then, Outlaw. I'm sorry."

"Talk to you soon, buddy."

"No. You won't. PuckDaddy out." Click. The line went dead.

I smiled, shook my head, and called Natalie North.

"Yeeeees?" she said.

"Hey. I'm downstairs in your lobby and I need to hide for a while. And it can't be in your building. Help me find a place?"

"Funny you should mention that. I have just the spot," she said. "But it's not ready yet. I need a few more days."

"Meet me down here in five minutes. And bring some food, I'm starving."

Then I turned off the Outlaw's phone, perhaps for the last time.

Chapter Twenty-Four
Friday, March 3. 2018

Katie

"Has Tank texted you yet?" Hannah Walker asked. We were sitting together at our usual table, heads together conspiratorially. It was great! I think authentic friendship with another girl was so novel to both of us that we might be over-indulging in it. I missed sitting with my guys, but Chase wasn't here today anyway. Neither was Samantha Gear. Chase had been absent yesterday too and he wasn't answering my texts. School was no fun without him.

"No," I admitted.

"Katie! Do you see? That's so messed up of him!" Hannah said with surprising vigor. "Boys are the worst."

"They ARE the worst! Ugh. Besides-"

"He can't just show up, make out, and then not call you. You're Katie Lopez, gorgeous Latina and our future valedictorian. You're not some booty call." Hannah was indignant.

"I think I'm going to call things off with him," I sighed. "We just live on different planets."

"No. I have a better idea," she said and her eyebrows arched in victory.

"What?"

"We're going to spy on him."

"No!" I laughed. "No way. I'm not a stalker."

"Please!" she said. "It'll be fun! We're not stalkers. We'll be like investigators. You know where he lives. Tonight is Friday night and we're not doing anything-"

"Because we're lame," I chimed in.

"Because we're lame and our boyfriends hate us," she agreed. "But he'll probably go out tonight and we can follow him. We can determine if he's dating other girls too."

"Wow…I think I'd rather not know."

"No. This is great. I'm picking you up at four. We want to get there early before he leaves his house." I could tell she was gathering steam and I wasn't going to talk her out of this. Besides, I guess this was better than sitting at home on a Friday night?

"He lives in a condo. Not a house."

"Whatever, shut up, people in the city are weird. It'll be fun!"

Hannah Walker's car is as gorgeous as she is but she drives like a woman possessed. I held my breath for a two-mile stretch on Interstate 5 while she battled and cursed at a delivery truck! We missed our exit so she roared to the San Bernadino Freeway at almost a hundred miles per hour to make up the time. Miraculously, a parking spot was available within sight of his building's entrance. I had ten dollars in quarters to feed the meter, which would buy us three hours.

"I wish there was some way to know that he's here," she complained after half an hour of waiting, and she hit the steering wheel in frustration. Her speakers were LOUD and she was alternating between pop and country music. "What if he's out already? Or gone for the weekend?"

"I'll text him!"

"Good idea!"

"But…I don't want to lie. I feel skeezy enough as it is," I said.

"You're not being skeezy, you're just verifying that you've made a good investment of your time. Text him," she ordered.

Hey Tank! Miss you! Hope you have a good Friday night. I've got plans, but I hope to see you soon. Are you doing anything fun?

"Hah! Nice. You're telling him the truth, too!" she said. He didn't reply immediately, which frustrated and saddened me. Chase always texted me back instantly. Well, almost always.

Hannah ordered us sandwiches and mochas and had them delivered directly to our car. I didn't even know you could do that! She paid with her mom's credit card. We ate in silence for the next ten minutes while I enviously wished my mother was rich.

"Hey," I said around a bite of chicken salad sandwich. "Hey! I think that's Natalie North!"

"Who?"

"The actress! I forgot this is her building too. She and Tank both have condos here. Right there!" I pointed with my pinky while holding the coffee. This was REALLY exciting! I loved Natalie North, and she even hugged me once. She and some guy walked into her building with their heads down.

"Oh right. Her. She's not even pretty," Hannah sniffed.

"You're crazy. She's the best. Do you think that's her? She's wearing that hoodie so no one recognizes her, I bet. Who do you think is with her? I can't tell but he's probably famous."

"Who cares," she groaned. "Calm down."

Natalie and the guy quickly disappeared into the building. Ten long minutes later she emerged alone and walked westward. Hannah absolutely forbade me from chasing her down for a picture. She even locked the doors!

I was beginning to get angry when Tank texted.

>>...Nothing fun tonight. Business to take care of. Been in bed sick for about a week. Feeling better. Let's do something fun soon. You pick, my treat.

I showed Hannah the message.

"Aw. That's kind of sweet," she said. "Maybe."

"Right? A little. It's hard to tell. Boys speak in cave-man language, which is hard to decode."

"Business. Business on a Friday night? What's he talking about?" Hannah asked.

"I have no idea. I know very little about him."

We stewed and plotted and giggled for the next thirty minutes, and then Hannah said, "Wait. Is that...isn't that Tank right there?"

"Where??"

She pointed away from the building and towards the traffic light. "There. In the green Hummer. It looks like him. I think."

"It is him! How'd he get past us?"

"I don't know!" She started the car and violently swerved into the street. "Keep an eye on his truck so we don't lose him."

"Of course!" I said. "I know what happened. I bet his building has an underground garage. He didn't exit through the doors, he exited through the garage."

"You're right. You're so right," she said and she gunned the engine to beat a red light.

Tank drove due south through the Fashion District and out of Downtown. Hannah was a pro, tailing him from two or three cars away. He snuck through a few traffic lights but she always caught up. We followed him through Huntington Park and into South Gate. We risked pulling up parallel to him once while I cowered in the passenger seat. Hannah paced him long enough to determine conclusively that he was alone before dropping back to a safe distance again. This was fun!

We left the towers and the money behind, and we entered neighborhoods. The closer we got to Compton the lower the value of the houses and businesses dropped. Gangs of guys lounged on porches or packed themselves around someone's car. The groups were either entirely black or entirely hispanic.

"This place is disgusting," Hannah sneered. She fished in the backseat for hats or something else for us to wear. She thought we looked too good.

"No it's not. It's just different."

"Don't be naive, sweetie. These people are trash."

"They aren't trash," I scolded her. "They just don't have as much as we do. It's not their fault."

"I'm sorry, Katie. I know you're latin american, so you might empathize with them, but these people are nothing like you. They're gross. They just suck up tax money."

Tank's journey started getting exceedingly strange. He would park near a corner and do…nothing. No one came to meet him. He didn't get out of his Hummer. And then he'd drive on. We tailed him from a block behind or from a parallel street, always precisely within our line-of-sight limit. He spent five minutes in one place before moving a mile farther south and did it again. Over and over. He started to zigzag, heading east for several miles, and then back west again. I monitored our progress using the map on my phone as we drove deeper into Compton.

"It's like he's searching for something and wants to cover as much ground as possible," I observed.

"But what's he looking for," Hannah yawned. We'd been on his trail for two hours now, and it was almost nine o'clock. We weren't tired as much as we were bored. Nothing was happening. "I don't think he's cheating on you, babe. I don't know what the guy is doing in this part of town but he didn't drive straight to some girl's house."

"Yeah," I sighed.

"He's got a lot of income property, right? Maybe he's just…checking up on his houses? He told us he needed to take care of business."

"Maybe, but…this feels like a scavenger hunt or a search. Looking for something or someone or…I don't know." I'd said that exact sentence several times during the previous hour. He was parked fifty yards ahead of us near a dimly lit gas station. His brake lights were on and so was his interior dome light. Hannah needed gas but she wasn't about to stop around here. She'd run it down to empty and then have us towed before she got out of the car. "Let's go home."

"Really? You want to?" Hannah asked.

"Yeah. Get us out of here. I'm not convinced he's worth all this work in the first place," I said. It was true; I'd been thinking about Chase half the night.

"You got it. We are gone."

She pulled onto the Harbor Freeway and we left the scary neighborhoods behind, safe in our warm and cozy luxury sports car. I was glad my mother had gone to college and become a teacher. Our neighborhood was much nicer, even if we were the poorest family there. I didn't blame these people for revolting against a new law that would make their lives even more difficult.

"This is ridiculous," Hannah shouted. I shook out of my reverie and looked up. We were deadlocked in a sudden traffic jam. "All these stupid eighteen-wheelers came out of nowhere. We're at the turnoff to 105 and I was going to exit, but ugh. Now we're stuck."

"Must be an accident ahead." Our view was cut off. A giant tractor-trailer sat idling in front of us. Another one was beside us. Both were oil tankers. I could see a city bus parked in the mirror.

"This sucks," Hannah complained and she hit the steering wheel. She did that a lot. "We have like…one gallon of gas left. We're so close to the ramp."

"But look. Interstate 105 is completely gridlocked too. Look at all the stalled cars. Exiting would do us no good."

"Both 110 and 105? Priceless. Just perfect. Exactly what I need."

So we sat. And we sat. Idly I texted Chase but he didn't answer. And then we sat some more.

We were still sitting three hours later. She'd turned the car off to conserve gas and we were cold. We hadn't spoken in forty-five minutes and I detected through minor clues that she blamed me for this. The trip had been her idea, though, so I didn't feel bad. But I was cold and tired.

Pedestrians began streaming by my window a little after midnight. First a handful of people walked past and then more joined. Soon an entire river of humanity flowed by. They seemed…scared.

"What's going on?" I was growing alarmed.

"I don't know," Hannah sighed. She was busy on her phone. "I hate this place so much."

"Hannah," I said urgently. "Hannah look."

A man had approached our car from the rear and now he stood in the brilliant glow of our headlights, examining us. A bandana was tied over his hair. He also wore some sort of mask that covered his mouth…oh gosh. He was dressed in a poor imitation of the Outlaw. That can't be good. Worst of all he carried a pickax! Why did he have a pickax??

"Seriously," Hannah said contemptuously. "This is just ridiculous."

Someone knocked on our window. We both screamed. A man bent down to yell through the window. "He wants you to get out of the car!"

"In his dreams!" Hannah yelled back.

I rolled down the window and asked, "Why?"

"Dunno, lady. But I'd get out if I were you." He indicated the man with his head and then he kept going. The scary man shrugged and walked out of our headlights towards the tanker. He hefted the weapon over his shoulder and swung with all his might. The tool clanged off the curved side of the big oil drum.

"Oh god," Hannah groaned. "What is this idiot doing?"

He swung again, further denting the metal. The next blow pierced the outer shell.

"Hannah, we need to go," I urged.

"No way," she scoffed.

He hit the tank again and again with loud bangs and finally the sharp point buried itself deeply and oil or gas or whatever burst forth. The liquid spray soaked him as he yanked free his pickax from the shower. He turned and calmly walked to the other tanker. The pungent smell of gasoline wafted through the open window.

"Hannah, now!" I yelled. I pushed open the door and climbed out. "This is dangerous, let's go!"

"No!" she shouted. "I'm not leaving my car and walking into Compton! Look at those people!"

"Hannah!" I screamed but the crush of people surged me away from her Audi. "Hannah come on!!" The last time I saw her she was frowning and shaking her head at her phone.

There were other men dressed like the Outlaw ghosting through headlight cones. Their masks were wrong and none of them got the costume exactly correct but their intent was obvious. Dozens of Outlaws were walking through the traffic and directing travelers out of their cars. They had axes and shovels and were punching holes in all the gas tanks. We walked through streams of the gasoline.

We were herded away from the headlights and forced to climb over the interstate's security railing. We stumbled like cattle down a poorly lit grassy hill and into a city intersection. There, however, strangely enough the Outlaw imposters forgot about us. Scary men with flashlights were ordering us down the hill, away from the interstate and into the heart of Compton, but then the crowd was allowed to go where it pleased. Most of my fellow castaways were obviously trying to get through to the police on their phones. It was midnight, the streets were mostly deserted, and we'd been forced to abandon our cars. Couldn't get much worse!

I yanked out my phone as I stumbled along with the crowd flow.

Hannah!! Please! This is scary and they have guns. You're sitting in a RIVER of gas. Come find me! We'll stay together!!

Just then, Chase texted me from an unknown number!

>>Hi Katie! It's your handsomest friend, Chase Jackson! My other phone is broken but you can text me at this number. Hope you had a good Friday!

I dialed the strange number frantically but I got a weird busy signal. I tried again. Still busy.

On the third time he answered. "Hi there! You're up late. How's it going?"

"Chase, I'm in trouble," I said, trying not to cry. I was standing on the sidewalk beside a closed car detail shop. This was the closest spot I could find near the interstate. I could still see Hannah's car on the raised Freeway. "A lot of us are."

"What?" he asked and his voice turned hard, almost scary. "What's wrong?"

"I'm not sure yet, but…" I screamed. Out of nowhere, one of the masked men put a gun to my temple. I tensed and shuddered but he didn't pull the trigger.

"Come with me," he ordered. I didn't argue. He shoved the gun against my head and pushed me into the street. I looked around desperately but a lot of my fellow displaced travelers had guns to their heads too. Twenty of us had apparently not been walking fast enough and we were being pressed into the middle of an intersection towards a waiting city bus. The bus had been parked underneath a blinking yellow traffic light. It was empty until we were forced to climb aboard. This was madness! What was happening?? Why was no one helping us??

A man in a mask with an assault rifle came aboard too. We sat very still in our seats. We were all cold, and wet with gas, and terrified. The bus was dark.

"Stay here," he said. "Don't cause trouble. You won't be hurt." Then he left and forcibly closed the bus doors. Trapped. Someone behind me wailed.

My phone rang. Chase!

"Chase," I cried into the phone. "Chase I'm so scared."

"Tell me exactly where you are," he said.

"I don't know! Not exactly."

"What's happening?"

"Men in Outlaw masks started pulling people out of their cars. Hannah is still in hers," I sniffed.

"Are you in Glendale?"

"No," I laughed bitterly, wiping my nose. "I'm in Compton."

"Compton?!" he shouted. "Why are…never mind. Just tell me where."

"In a bus," I said, trying to think straight. "Where 105 and 110 meet. Harbor Freeway."

"Okay."

"Something big is happening, Chase." Tears poured down my face and I was shivering. "We've been stuck for hours and I haven't seen any police, even though everyone's been calling. And these guys have guns."

"Alright. I'm coming to get you."

"No, don't," I sobbed. My sweet Chase. "Traffic is backed up for miles, Chase, and they put me on a bus. I'm trapped. It's no use trying to get here."

"I'm on the way. I will tear this city apart to find you."

Chapter Twenty-Five
Friday, March 3. 2018

I spent Wednesday and Thursday night in an extravagant hotel room downtown. Natalie paid for it without my knowledge. I passed the hours by watching the news, working out in the hotel gym, and soaking in the giant jacuzzi tub. Not a bad life. Even the disease gave me a vacation; I slept and felt great.

I texted Dad and told him I'd be spending the night with Cory. But if I didn't figure out how to appease Carter soon then I'd need to come up with some other excuse.

On Friday, after Natalie's college classes ended, we went out for dinner. It was the nicest restaurant I'd ever been in; there were white tablecloths and candles! She dressed in disguise and no one noticed her. The diners adjacent to our table were discussing the Outlaw's newspaper interview. To my astonishment, Natalie's fascination with the Outlaw did not slacken as she spent more time with his mild-mannered alter ego, Chase Jackson. She plied me with countless questions about the masked man and his nighttime shenanigans. After she swore to secrecy, I told her about the Infected and the Chemist and PuckDaddy and the FBI and the Sniper. I left out Tank because she knew him.

"This is unbelievable," she said when I was done. Our dinner was finished. "I mean…it's the most incredible story I've ever heard."

"Yeah, it's wild."

"So now you're just waiting around, biding your time until the Chemist starts a big fight?" she asked with a faraway look.

"Basically. Then I'll help Carter deal with him and any Infected we find, and everything will be back to normal."

"You hope," she said.

"I hope."

"It sounds dangerous."

"Yeah," I nodded. "But I'm okay with that. My body is…weird now, and I think it needs action and excitement almost as much as sleep or food. I can't run from it."

"Okay. This is too perfect. My surprise for you is ready. Let's go look," she said with the wild-eyed smile of an excited little girl. We walked back to her building to fetch my motorcycle. "Bikes make me nervous. I'll meet you."

She gave me the address and she set off to walk there. I rode to the location she'd provided, five blocks away It was an enormous Self-Storage warehouse on 6th street.

"You got me a storage unit?" I asked, bemused, when she showed up.

"Yes! Come on!"

She led me deep inside the structure to a rear deluxe unit. She used a key to take off the padlock and I raised the roll-up steel door. The extra large unit had been transformed from a bare industrial concrete bunker to a fully furnished hideout. Carpets had been installed and maps hung on the walls. A made bed was in one far corner and a computer desk in the other. A blue couch faced a flat screen television. Several large lockers and trunks had been pushed against the walls. So had two mini-fridges.

"There's food and water and a place to recharge your bike. And a heater if it gets cold. And extra clothes. And disposable phones and tablets and a laptop and everything!"

"Natalie, what…" I was speechless.

"You need a base here in the city," she explained. "It's dangerous not to. Just don't make too much noise. Technically people aren't allowed to live in storage units."

"This is too much."

"Oh and there's money," she remembered.

"Money?"

She opened a desk drawer *stuffed* with stacks of cash. Each stack was worth five hundred dollars. I didn't know that amount of money *existed* in one place.

"There's twenty-five thousand in cash," she said. "I think. I also put a check card in here for you, which accesses a bank account with five hundred thousand dollars."

"Five hundred thousand…" I repeated but my knees got weak and I sank into the desk chair. "Natalie. You can't."

"Yes I can."

"No. This is far too much."

"Outlaw, I have so much money. I have six million dollars in my checking account. Twice that in a savings account. And it just sits there. This is the most fun I've ever had with it. Additionally, you're a good man and I know you're responsible and this is important. Los Angeles is getting crazy and you're our rallying cry. And after your interview in the newspaper yesterday? You set the whole world on fire and it's going to get even more dangerous."

I didn't know how to respond. What do you say to such blind loyalty?

"Besides," she continued with a coy smile. "Once you realize you're in love with me this can be our love nest."

Natalie had a swanky party to attend. She begged me to accompany her but I declined, pointing out that I might be recognized. Instead, I settled into my new hideout. I plugged in the bike, inventoried the lockers and storage trunks, watched television, and surfed the internet. With the door rolled down, the room was pleasantly warm. I didn't check my email or Twitter or anything else because PuckDaddy would be monitoring their access and could track the log-in information. I wished I could talk with him. Or Samantha Gear. Or Katie. Katie!

I texted her from my disposable phone. It was late. I hoped it wouldn't wake her. She called back instantly.

"Chase," she said. There was a lot of background noise. "I'm in trouble. A lot of us are." Her voice was shaky.

"What? What's wrong?"

She screamed and the line clicked dead. I leapt off the couch and called her back but the call wouldn't go through.

"What's going on," I said out loud, panic rising in my throat. I turned on the television and started scanning for a news channel. "Come on Katie. Answer." I dialed again but the call wouldn't connect. I tried again and again before stumbling across CNN.

Finally the sixth call went through.

"Chase! I'm so scared," she cried.

"Tell me exactly where you are," I demanded. *Compton*. Home of the Chemist. My heart sank. What on earth was she doing there?! CNN came back from a commercial break and immediately put a map of Los Angeles on the screen. Police were reporting a bizarre traffic jam in south LA. All of the freeways surrounding Compton were blocked by stalled vehicles. Videos from phones showed people running down the highways, abandoning cars. It would take days to clear the mess. The city of Compton was neatly boxed in. It had to be the Chemist. This was it. He was making his move.

"I'm coming to get you."

I hit the stopped traffic on Highway 110 three miles north of Katie's location at one in the morning. The Compton congestion was causing snarls everywhere. Most travelers were beginning to abandon their vehicles, fearing reports of masked gunmen ahead. Some still waited in their cars, hopelessly marooned but exhausted. I glared down the jammed highway, furious at this obstacle.

My Outlaw costume was earning startled second glances. Guy next to me rolled down his window and said, "Hey, you the Outlaw?"

I turned on the Outlaw's phone for the first time in several days. **Puck, it's me. Katie's trapped in Compton. I'm going to call you. You better**

freaking answer.

Before I could dial him, he called me. His voice came through my helmet. "There you are! Where have you been, dummy??"

"Hiding. You told me to," I snarled.

"I didn't mean it, jerk. Or, whatever. Don't ever leave again."

"Katie is trapped," I said. I began slowly picking my way through the vehicles at three miles per hour. There were too many pedestrians and too many car doors ajar to open up the throttle. I wanted to scream.

"I know, I just located her phone. She's near one of those big loopy pretzel shaped highway interchanges, about three and a half miles ahead. She's alive, dude. She just texted her mother."

"You think this is the Chemist?"

"No doubt," he replied.

"Where are Shooter and Carter?"

"On their way. East of you, going through the neighborhoods. It's go time, baby!" He sounded giddy.

"Chemist must have hundreds of guys working with him, right? He hijacked twenty miles of interstate."

"Right you are. Carter is shocked. But the plan remains the same. Remove the Chemist, let the rest fall apart."

"Any sign of the target?" I asked.

"Negative. I zeroed in a satellite and I'm running facial recognition programs on all media pumping out of that area. But he's staying in the shadows so far. Hey, Shooter is on my other line. I'm piping her into this call."

"Why not Carter too?"

"He doesn't love technology like the rest of us. Shooter, you hear me?"

"Yeah, I'm here," she said. "En route to the target. Welcome back, Outlaw."

"Samantha," I said. "Katie is in Compton."

"What?!" she shouted in my ear. "Why?"

"I'm not sure."

"Damn it! Damn it damn it damn it!"

"I'm coming to help," I said. "But Katie is my number one priority."

"This is why Carter says not to get attached," she grumbled under her breath. "Now I'm worried about a high school junior. Damn it."

"Are you with Carter?"

"We got separated."

The pedestrians were jumping out of the way as I advanced. Some of them began recognizing me and they waved. First one guy put his hand up for me to High Five. Then another. And another. News of my approach flew down the interstate. Before long I had a corridor lined with smiling faces and cameras.

"My journey is not going unnoticed," I commented inside my helmet.

"Of course it isn't," Samantha sighed. "That's what you do."

"This is ridiculous." The crowds actually cheered. Drivers were backing their cars out of my way, hastening my headlong dive towards Katie. Into the jungle. Into madness.

PuckDaddy said, "You guys want some more fun news?"

"Not really," Samantha replied.

"Our old pal Tank is in Compton too," he said.

"Oh. Great," I said. Shooter and Puck fell quiet. We were all thinking the same thing: *that's* why Katie was in Compton. She was with Tank. Not with me. I burned with embarrassment and jealousy. But why had he taken her there? She hadn't mentioned him on the phone. "What's he doing there? Could Tank be working with the Chemist?"

PuckDaddy responded, "No way. I've been monitoring his texts for weeks. Tank hates the Chemist. Also, Tank is in his car about a mile from Katie. I don't think they drove to Compton together."

"I'm confused. And pissed," I said.

"Wow," Puck said. "Think about this. When you three get there, that'll be the highest concentration of Infected in...what? A hundred years? Seriously. This is awesome! Wooooooooo!!"

"PuckDaddy. Focus," Samantha ordered.

"It's times like this I wish I could walk. I'd jump so high!" PuckDaddy shouted.

"You can't walk?" I asked, stunned.

"Long story," he replied. "I'll fill you in later. I can barely think right now, the disease is so loud in my ears."

"Wait, why can't you walk?"

"Outlaw. Focus," Samantha ordered.

I focused just in time to witness a shift in the crowds. They started screaming and running. That can't be good. They flew past me. I pulled the bike into the shelter behind a car, out of the stampede. Beyond the fleeing mob, in the light of a streetlamp, I caught sight of men in masks. Four of them calmly approached, carrying guns and axes.

"Bingo. Four masked gunmen heading north," I said.

"Don't let them see you."

"Too late," I said and I dove behind a blue Honda Accord. They opened fire with pistols, unloading into the car from a range of fifteen yards. Civilians screamed, cowering anywhere they could.

PuckDaddy asked, "Were those gunshots?"

"Yes!" I shouted. "And they're aiming at me! And I hate it!"

"The war has begun."

"Stop being dramatic! Now what do I do?"

"What do you mean?" PuckDaddy asked. "You're the Outlaw. Kick ass."

"Chase! Stop screwing around and put those guys down," the Shooter yelled.

"This is my first time," I grumbled.

Clunk! Something bounced off the car and hit me in the helmet. A grenade! Where'd they get a *grenade*?! No time to think. I grabbed the explosive and hurled it straight up. I can throw hard. The grenade was a hundred yards in the air when it ignited. The four gunmen were staring up at the fire in the sky when I descended on them. Nothing fancy. I hit them each as hard and as quickly as I could. That worked. "Okay. They're down."

"Identify the explosion I heard," Samantha said.

"Grenade. I think these guys are dressed like me. Or at least they tried."

PuckDaddy mused, "Imitation is the sincerest form of flattery."

"They look stupid," I said. "I hope I don't look stupid."

I took several deep breaths. I needed a weapon. The situation was escalating quickly. Far off to the east, two helicopters were roving southwards, their searchlights stabbing into Compton's fringes. The whole world was converging on this section of greater Los Angeles.

I left my bike. I could move faster on foot and I didn't want to ride into an ambush. I really needed a weapon! Something to throw. I found a box of heavy bullets in an unconscious gunman's pocket. I took the bullets and tossed their weapons off the interstate. Then I pulled off their masks.

I said, "These guys look like they've been snorting something."

Shooter answered, "Chemist's new compound. Probably causes delusions, immunity to pain, aggressiveness, and other fun stuff. Don't get close to them. Put them down."

"Put them down? But they're people. People unfortunate enough to be addicted to a drug."

"Chase!" she shouted. "You're entering enemy territory. Thousands of people, probably tens of thousands of people, have sided with the Chemist. They've put on masks, picked up guns, voluntarily snorted a drug, and now they're hurting innocent people. You want to get Katie out? Worry about morality later. Ten thousand guys with guns stand between you and her. It's you or them. It's her or them. We need to get the Chemist out of there, and that means going through whoever gets in our way. Understand?"

"Yeah," I said. "It's them or Katie. I get it."

I proceeded south steadily but cautiously, peering into cars for possible projectiles while on lookout for Chemist gunmen. Could there really be ten thousand guys waiting for us? That didn't seem possible. Shooter announced that she reached I-105, the northern boundary of Compton. She met enemy resistance in the graveyard of vacated vehicles, all with punctured fuel tanks. Sporadic gunmen were waiting in the cars, but she quickly dispatched them. Still no sign of Carter, although we knew he was nearby.

After half a mile I'd scavenged a pocket full of bullets, two lacrosse balls, five golf balls and a baseball. Better than nothing. I hoped. I could probably take someone's head off with the baseball.

"Be advised," PuckDaddy announced. "Lakewood Police have engaged enemy forces on the southern side of Compton. Seven miles from your position. Sounds like the Police are outgunned. That should wake up the entire world."

"Not our problem," Shooter said. Nothing was my problem until Katie was safe.

Gunfire! I didn't see the guys laying in darkness underneath a semi-truck until they fired. Angry bullets snapped at the cars and ripped through the air. I fell back.

"More contact," I reported. I pulled out a lacrosse ball, crouching in the safety provided by a Toyota's wheel well.

PuckDaddy said, "Lots of guys in masks heading your way, Outlaw, pouring in from the next exit. Dozens. You've been marked. I'm watching them on satellite."

Squeezing the ball, I grinned. "It'll be a bowling alley."

I was already throwing as I rose. The red ball ricocheted hard off a guy's face with a hollow 'Thunk' sound and bounced violently under the trailer. I didn't want to kill anyone, but that ball was screaming.

I jumped over the car and got shot squarely in the chest. Boom! The gunner rose from the top of the trailer at the precise moment of my jump and cleanly picked me off with a heavy semiautomatic pistol. The impact wholly reversed my momentum, tossing me backwards. Before I landed, another shot connected with my helmet, effectively shattering it.

Owww! I gasped and prodded the dent in my kevlar plate. I felt like I'd been sacked on a football field. Shouldn't it hurt more than that?

Maybe not. I'm Infected. The Outlaw.

And I'd stumbled upon another Infected! No one else could've shot me twice that quickly. My helmet was a mess. The interior bluetooth headset was busted. I had another earpiece in my pocket but now wasn't the time to switch. I pulled the helmet off, and then I got lucky. The Infected was a young guy, about my age. Young and stupid. He brazenly walked around the car, confident I was dead. His gun was twirling around his finger.

I didn't have time to be scared and he didn't have time to be surprised. I smashed the helmet shell into his jaw. The pistol clattered to the road and blood spurted out of his mouth. The astonished gunmen behind him opened fire again, firing wildly. I had enough warning to duck behind the car again. He didn't. He caught bullets in the shoulders and in the back of his skull.

He hit the ground already dead. I looked away in horror.

"Oh jeez oh jeez oh jeez," I repeated, trying not to gag at the ruined body.

I'm the worst hero ever.

I jammed the backup bluetooth headset into my ear and called PuckDaddy.

He shouted, "Holy crap, dude. I thought you died!"

"Almost," I said. I was shivering. Gallons of adrenaline were surging through me. "I'll be fine in a minute."

"What happened?"

"Infected shot me. I'm okay. Or I will be in a sec." I ripped open a trembling fistful of granola bars and shoved them all into my mouth.

Shooter asked, "What's the status of the Infected?"

I choked out a muffled, "Dead."

"My man!"

"He was just a kid. So young."

"Outlaw, you gotta move, dummy. Gonna be be swarmed."

"Okay," I said, thinking. "Okay." I didn't want to get off this road. It was the straightest shot to Katie. But what about incoming guys with guns? I could barely think over the roar of the disease.

"Big explosion in south Compton," Puck said. "Don't know what it was."

Just how much adrenaline did I have pumping? Didn't that heighten my strength? Let's test it out.

I squatted and got my fingertips under the Toyota Camry. "One two three," I grunted, shoved my shoes into the ground, straightened my legs, and hauled up on the car as hard as I could. The vehicle flipped, landed on it's side with a tremendous crash, and rolled into the semi-truck ten fifteen feet away. The last I saw of the hidden gunmen they were cowering against the oncoming Toyota that wrecked their hiding spot.

"Fun fact," I said. "I can throw cars."

"This is the best night ever," PuckDaddy hooted.

That took care of a couple of them. Maybe. But dozens more were approaching.

Quickly I scavenged for busted car parts and used them to destroy every streetlamp within a hundred yards. I threw nuts and bolts and scraps of metal in streaks that ripped through the lights in a shower of sparks. My aim was deadly. There were still car headlights, but now I could hide in shadows. The playing field was level.

"Watch your back! Group of ten un-friendlies, just beyond that big truck," Puck warned.

The Outlaw smiled. *The night is mine.*

I fell on them from the sky. The slowly advancing mob of poorly dressed Outlaws didn't know the authentic terror stalked them until it was too late. I knocked them unconscious and kicked them down and jumped away from their bullets and landed on them from above and threw their own guns into their faces until it was over. They were destroyed. I crouched in a starburst of prone, immobile, wheezing, weaponless drug addicts.

I took a deep breath and said, "That might have been the best sixty seconds of my life".

"Hundreds more, heading your way," Puck reported. "Wow, where'd he find all these guys?"

Hundreds?!

I went hunting, stalking them like a bad dream. The Outlaw impostors watched their friends disappear with helpless inevitability, the shadows moving faster than they could aim. I landed on them, slid under cars in ambush, incapacitated them with flying debris, ran through clusters like a fiery bowling ball, and tossed them over the highway's guard rails. They shot at nothing. They shot each other. Their bullets whined by, not even close to me. I was impervious within the night's cloak.

Despite my impressive trail of destruction, I was losing the battle. More kept coming, a never-ending waterfall of evil. Eventually I'd be unable to swim upstream through the dark tide any longer.

"Okay," I panted behind a school bus, momentarily alone. "There's too many."

"Outlaw," Puck said. "I was watching. That was…indescribable. I have no words. You're a wizard."

"Counter productive," I said, hands on knees, trying to catch my breath. "There's always more. Violence isn't the answer here."

"Abandon the road," Puck suggested. "Head east. It'll take you longer but you'll get there eventually. Puck's your eye in the sky, Outlaw. Puck will guide you."

It had been almost two hours since Katie's phone call! I was furious and frustrated. I lowered the mask to my chin and shouted in anger. *Really* shouted! I roared. The sound rattled the bus windows and hurt my ears. I could hear it echoing for miles.

PuckDaddy called me. I answered and he said, "I think you shouted so loudly the phone disconnected."

"That was you?" Shooter asked. "Shouting? I heard it way over here."

"Where are you?" I grumbled.

"Deep in Compton. Roving. Looking for the serpent's head." Her voice was hushed.

"I guess I'll have to abandon the interstate," I sighed. "It's too popular right now."

But I heard the helicopter before I moved. The beat of blades pulsed on my ear drums. Emergency medical and news aircraft were hovering far up in the sky, but this helicopter was close. There! It was skimming the interstate, maybe fifty feet in the air.

"That chopper is heading due south," I said. Into the storm. Towards Katie. "And I'm hitching a ride."

Chapter Twenty-Six
Friday, March 3. 2018

Katie

I knew nothing about the Chemist. I hadn't listened to Lee's rants and I didn't watch the news. But I knew him when I saw him.

A caravan of SUVs came rumbling out of the gloom. The pack of trucks drove with their lights off, presumably so they could travel in stealth. But what caught my attention was the man *standing* on the foremost Toyota Sequoia. The vehicle was traveling around twenty-five miles an hour but he stood rock solid on top, feet shoulder-width apart, holding a staff that was braced against the roof. He was tall and thin and he wore an old-fashioned trench coat. His long white hair was tied in a ponytail and at second glance he looked shockingly old. At least his face looked old. He appeared to be eighty? Eighty-five? WAY too old to be standing on the roof of an SUV. But when the caravan stopped near our bus he gracefully walked down the roof and jumped off, as a teenager would. He moved like a gymnast. Everyone on my bus was staring at him. His staff was apparently made of metal, because it sparked occasionally on the sidewalk.

We had pushed open a few of the windows to circulate air through the bus, having been imprisoned in it for over ninety minutes. One of my fellow captives was on a continuous call with a 911 operator, relaying everything we saw and heard but it had been an uneventful hour and a half.

Hannah texted me every twenty minutes to tell me how bored she was. I stopped replying.

I surfed the news on my phone. This act of terrorism had gotten worldwide attention. It isn't easy to take a small city like Compton hostage. The police made several attempts at entry but they'd been rebuffed. There were *thousands* of guys with guns waiting for them. I saw our bus once from a helicopter's point of view.

The old man with the staff approached a committee emerging from a nearby building to receive him. But he wasn't an old man! Was he? He looked lithe and alert.

"Everything is ready," the man said. It wasn't a question. His assistants assured him that all was prepared. We pressed our ears against the window openings to listen. "Good. Alert the Sheriff. Inform him I will call an hour from now."

He had a multi-racial retinue that jumped whenever he spoke. He sent them on errands to fetch spotlights and food and water and other things I couldn't hear.

Three other individuals had arrived in the caravan but they were different. These three were unquestionably subordinate to him but they didn't jump at his every word. They lounged against their truck instead of trailing him. Two girls and a guy. They looked young and fearless and...sinister. Instead of goofy masks, they wore battle fatigues. They were tall and strong and well-armed and one of the girls was absently juggling knives without looking. They terrified me. I started to tremble again.

"Walter," the man with the staff said. One of the sinister three, a young black man wearing stylish sunglasses in the middle of the night, pushed off the SUV. "Arm yourself with the launcher. I anticipate requiring several rounds." Walter nodded and walked to the rear of his vehicle. "Carla, take up position on the roof. Stay hidden. Carter is near. I want to know where. And I want to know who he brought with him." Carla, an attractive black girl with braided hair, nodded and jumped onto the roof of a mini-market. *Jumped!* Our bus filled with gasps.

"The Outlaw was right," I whispered, my breath fogging the glass. "There are others like him."

The white-haired man with the staff walked back to his perch atop the Sequoia. Only now did I notice that a girl was sitting in the passenger seat. She looked my age, and she hadn't moved. The man with the staff said, "Turn on the news. I am anxious to know if our masked friend The Outlaw has made an appearance yet! Him I'm eager to meet." The girl inside clicked on the radio. Walter, now carrying heavy hardware, and the other sinister girl settled by the open window to listen.

Uh oh. Oh no. Was this just a trap for the Outlaw?? And who was Carter?

After that, nothing happened for ten minutes. The old man sat crosslegged on the Toyota, his staff across his lap, and he stared into the sky. That was all. Everyone around him looked anxious but he appeared to be enjoying the helicopter movements above. He was a very handsome man, for his age.

After a while the man glanced sharply to his left, peering down the road at something we couldn't see. Twenty seconds later the rest of his posse looked in that direction too. A car was approaching. Fast! I could hear the engine roar.

"Don't shoot," the man said and he stood up. "It's the ogre. We want him alive."

A green Hummer charged into the intersection and rammed the old man's SUV, completely t-boning it! The collision was earth shaking, metal and glass erupting like a volcano. The white-haired man calmly hopped off the Sequoia just before impact and landed deftly nearby. Both trucks threatened to flip over but managed to stay upright.

As the vehicles resettled, hissing air and spraying liquids, the old man raised his staff and whipped it down on the Hummer's crunched windshield. Again and again, and the noise was awful. A huge man bailed out of the driver's seat just before the glass fully shattered.

I couldn't believe my eyes! It was Tank!

The old man hopped easily onto the Hummer and smiled. "Hello, Tank," he said. Behind him, Walter and the other sinister girl were helping free the passenger from the destroyed Sequoia. She was a thin and shockingly beautiful girl, maybe my age. And furious.

"Got a bone to pick with you, Chemist," Tank said darkly, getting to his feet and dusting himself off.

The Chemist! The old man *was* the Chemist. I knew it! And then I knew with certainty that I was going to die.

"You wear gloves," the Chemist noticed. "Just like Carter. How tawdry. Now listen, young man. Without a doubt, you are owed an apology. I attacked you mistakenly several weeks ago. I presumed you were the Outlaw. I apologize," he said politely. "But to be fair and honest, had I known about your condition I would have ordered you *executed* instead of kidnapped."

"You tried. Didn't work," Tank growled. Someone tried to *kill* Tank? That's terrible!!

"It was not me that tried to execute you. Most likely Carter," the Chemist mused. "I cannot blame him. You're a wild bull." Without warning, the white haired man struck with his staff. He was fast but so was Tank. Tank caught the staff in his fist and yanked it. Instead of letting go, the man jumped over Tank's shoulder and landed on his feet, still holding the staff. The Chemist's skin was saran-wrapper tight, exposing all of his wiry muscles and tendons when he moved. Tank looked unnerved. This had clearly been a bad idea. One of the sinister girls had an assault rifle trained on Tank. "Remarkable. You are stronger than I assumed. Melissa, shoot him. I want to see what happens."

"NO!" I screamed. I startled everyone on the bus, and I even gained the attention of sinister Melissa, the Chemist, and Tank. The bus windows weren't tinted and Tank immediately recognized me.

"Katie? Wait," Tank ordered. "Stop. Why do you have her?"

"You know this young lady?" the Chemist asked, indicating me with his finger. I shivered when our eyes met.

"Yeah, and she doesn't belong here. Let her go."

"Why would I do that?" the Chemist smiled.

"Let her go and I won't beat you to death. Maybe."

"I believe, my monumental friend, that a twist of fortune brought her here. I didn't seek her out. It must be fate."

"It's not fate!" Tank said, his voice rising to a full-throated bellow. He stalked towards the Chemist. "Release her! Now!"

But it was too late. Melissa, one of the three scary henchmen, steadied herself and shot Tank in the head. "No no!" I cried. Tank staggered to the side…but…he was alive! I forgot to breathe. Tank shook his head and remained on his feet. My mind was spinning. Who ARE these people?? Is Tank one of them? How is he still alive?

"Dear ogre, you are in full bloom," the Chemist laughed quietly. "I believe I'll keep you." Before Tank could recover, the Chemist was behind him with the staff pulled tightly against his neck. Tank couldn't breathe! I screamed again and hit my hand against the window, but I was as powerless as Tank. He jumped and shook and crushed the Chemist against the ruined cars, but it was no use. Watching was torture. Soon he quit struggling and fell forward. I cried noisily and freely. "Melissa, administer the tranquilizers, please. He is a handful. Use the vapor; you'll never get a needle through that thick hide." The girl bent over Tank's inert body and sprayed something up his nose. Tank was out, and the Chemist left him and looked up at the sky. "Where oh where are you, Carter," the man said softly to himself. "And why didn't you try to use this one? He's the strongest in decades. Melissa, stow him in your vehicle, please. Mine has been ruined."

"Yes sir."

"Situation report," he said to nobody in particular.

"You've made a mess. And nearly killed me," snapped the beautiful thin girl, being lowered into a chair by Walter. She was gorgeous but appeared feeble. Her voice cut like a whip.

"Yes, well…" he waved her off. "Sacrifices."

Two of the Chemist's drones presented themselves. "We think the police have temporarily discontinued their efforts to penetrate our forces," one of the men said. The Chemist listened as he stepped on to the roof of a different vehicle. These men were normal, not scary. One had a tablet in one hand and the other held a phone to his ear. "Appears to be a cease fire as they wait on your phone call."

"No sign of Carter," The Chemist stated.

"No sir."

"No sign of the Outlaw."

"Mr. Troy reported spotting the Outlaw north on the interstate," the man said. "He ordered reinforcements. But we cannot confirm the sighting."

"Splendid. I hope Troy is correct. Let's ring the Sheriff," the Chemist smiled. "And let caution be damned."

"Yes sir. Calling now."

I texted my mother that I loved her again. She was in hysterics. This was the second time in five months I'd been kidnapped, and the strain might kill her. If I survived, I would NEVER be let out of the house again. I also texted Chase and told him that I love him. The people around me were on phones speaking with their loved ones but I didn't feel like talking. I kept staring at poor Tank being manhandled into the back of an SUV. It was beyond belief that little Melissa could heft Tank's body.

The man with the phone walked back into the light from the streetlamp and reported, "Sir, the Sheriff is unable to take your call for the next ten minutes. Are you willing to communicate with an intermediary until that point?"

"Common negotiation tactics," the Chemist smiled. "I will not bow. Tell the Sheriff to watch his television screen and witness his punishment."

"Yes sir," the man said and walked off again.

"Light the southern flare. And then light the southern bus," the Chemist ordered. Several of his goons jumped to obey. "Then prepare this one."

We couldn't see what happened but we could guess. In the reflection of SUV windows we saw a red flare arc into the sky. And then we felt and heard a distant explosion. A bus had been detonated.

The passengers aboard my bus wailed with grief, and the screams only strengthened as the scary girl called Melissa walked up and punched a hole in the bus's gas tank. Thick liquid splashed on the ground and we smelled gasoline. That scent was getting old fast.

I was sitting near the front. Through my tears, I noticed something I should have seen before. The keys were still in the ignition. Could I drive this thing? I stole forward and sat in the driver's seat.

"Sir, Sheriff is on the phone," I heard through the window.

"Good evening, Sheriff Scott. I trust I've gained your attention. The bus I just detonated was empty, vacated hours ago. The next bus will not be. I will only spend lives when I must to gain your cooperation. I know you have questions but simply listen, for the moment. The Outlaw was correct; there *are* several of us monsters living among you, and we've decided to live in Compton for the near future and for a variety of reasons I won't bore you with. Tonight I established a perimeter that you will not cross. I will light the perimeter on fire soon, so there is no mistake. It is our Sanctuary. Leave us unmolested and in return we won't stay very long. Perhaps a few months, only. We will require your assistance with several matters but, actually, no, let's discuss those later. All innocents inside Compton are now hostages but will be treated humanely. Anyone leaving Compton will be shot, no questions asked. Anyone entering without permission will be shot, no questions asked. Now, I grant you three minutes to ask questions. Am I not generous? You may begin now. ...I'm sorry, Sheriff. Poor decision. I have no time for your petty posturing. You lost your chance. Next time, remember your manners."

He hung up. All was quiet. For several minutes we all waited to see what he'd do next but he simply sat. Gasoline was still dripping out of the bus's tank.

"Our work tonight is done," he said at length. For the first time I noticed the crowd surrounding us had swelled. Masked gunmen with nothing else to do encircled us. They wore a mixture of expressions, from anger to apathy to sleepiness. Bored drug addicts with guns. Great recipe. The Chemist addressed them and said, "Tonight is a success. You've done well. Tomorrow will be a new challenge!"

"What about Carter?" the girl named Melissa asked. She looked fidgety, like pent up energy.

"Yes, Carter," he breathed out. "He's near. I can smell him. I would rest easier with that issue resolved. But he's out of time. We'll keep the hostages. Light the cars and pack up."

Light the cars??

Get out of there, Hannah!! NOW!!

Melissa shoved off from her car and walked purposefully towards the bridge. Rivers of gasoline had streamed down the grassy hill and through the overpass's gutters. She was going to set twenty miles of cars on fire from the pool gathered there. In desperation I started the bus. Maybe I could run her over. The engine rumbled to life but no one heard it. Nobody paid the bus any attention. The Chemist and his retinue were all gazing up at the sky.

Someone had shouted in the distance. I heard the echoes over the soft engine drone. The shout was impossibly loud.

"What was that?"

"That," the Chemist said, "is the sound of one of us."

"Carter?" Walter asked.

"Someone else."

"The Outlaw?"

The white-haired man stared feverishly in the direction of the noise, and he didn't answer.

A helicopter was approaching, fast and close to the ground. Maybe the bus explosion had spooked the police and this helicopter was here to shoot first and ask questions later?

"It's him," he whispered. I barely heard. "He has arrived."

The helicopter looked odd. Something was dangling underneath. Something...or someone?

"He comes riding the wind, like thunder," the Chemist said. Mania clouded his eyes. "He comes to destroy us all."

The Outlaw was coming! He was soaring in at over a hundred miles an hour, riding a steel bird of prey.

Walter raised his rocket launcher.

"No, Walter!" the Chemist screamed, but he was too late. Walter fired. The weapon erupted in fire and noise and the streaking projectile moved like lightning. The helicopter had no chance; it shattered in midair.

It's bizarre. I didn't know what happened to the helicopter wreckage until later, after the nightmare ended and I saw the news. The aircraft somersaulted into the ground several blocks away, destroyed in a grisly billow of flames and smoke. I never saw that. Like everyone else I only had eyes for the Outlaw, who landed like a movie action hero in the middle of the Chemist's forces and sent them scattering.

Chapter Twenty-Seven
Friday, March 3. 2018

Katie

Both Melissa and one of the drugged gunmen opened fire. The Outlaw *dodged* the bullets. He simply...moved. He was too fast and the bullets couldn't catch him. One of the Outlaw imposters was inadvertently shot in the leg. The gunman sprayed our bus by accident. We screamed and the glass blew inwards.

The Chemist pulled out a pistol from his cloak. He shot Melissa in the head and he was about to shoot the wildly firing gunman but he was too late. The Outlaw threw a ball that connected like a hammer and the gunman collapsed. The Chemist shrugged and put the gun away.

I couldn't take much more of this. It was overwhelming. I was sick from crying and my nerves were raw. All the bus prisoners, including myself, were staring ravenously at the Outlaw, our only source of hope.

The Outlaw indicated Melissa's body and said, "The Evil Henchmen Union isn't going to be happy with you."

"I'm so pleased to see you've ditched the motorcycle helmet," the Chemist said, walking boldly towards the Outlaw. His staff sparked each time the tip connected with the road, and the sparks fell dangerously close to the gasoline. "It was impersonal. The helmet distanced your audience from you. Your face and your persona are what drew the crowds to begin with, and, as they say, you should dance with the one that brought you."

"I think the whole outfit's pretentious," Walter said. He was puffed up in the presence of the Outlaw, like a peacock. The Outlaw paid him no attention.

"That's because you're jealous, Walter," the Chemist said. "Don't be blinded by envy. This costume is bold, simple, and memorable. For a young adult such as the Outlaw, it's almost elegant. Except for the helmet."

"One of your Infected shot the helmet off," the Outlaw responded. He and the Chemist stood five feet apart.

"That would be Troy."

"He's dead."

The Chemist said simply, "Is he."

"He is."

Walter glanced uneasily at the beautiful girl sitting in a chair. They were clearly shaken by the news.

"Then I've lost two tonight," the Chemist sighed, looking at the limp body of Melissa. "Perhaps I acted rashly."

"How many Infected are with you?"

"Don't ask infantile questions, young man. Walter, fetch us two chairs please."

The man in the mask asked, "You want to sit down and chat?"

"I do. Unless you prefer my team open fire."

I tore my eyes from the surreal parlay. A growing number of the Chemist's army was arriving. Maybe seventy were here now? The Outlaw was entirely surrounded. But I knew they weren't the real danger. The real danger was Walter and Carla, who was still on the roof. And the Chemist himself.

While Water was bringing the chairs, the Outlaw turned in a circle and scanned his surroundings. He zeroed in on the bus and then he found me. My heart skipped a beat. Our eyes locked. His face whitened but his gaze intensified, almost a physical force. I swear he was radiating heat. He appeared scared and furious. He was hopelessly outnumbered, just him and this mad funhouse.

"Where is Carter?" the Chemist asked and he sat in the canvas camping chair Walter brought. The Outlaw sat in the other.

"Don't ask infantile questions, Chemist."

"So you've met him."

"I have," the Outlaw nodded.

"And?"

"I like him just barely more than I like you."

The Chemist threw his head back and laughed richly, genuinely. "I don't blame you. We are cut from the same cloth, he and I. And I'm sorry to reveal that you probably are too."

"I know about the disease."

"Of course you do. But you are a special case. Like the mighty Carter was, many years ago. And like me."

"And like Tank?"

"No no," he waved the question away with his hand. "Not like the ogre at all. The ogre has sprouted. We know what he is. He's muscle."

"A lot of it," the Outlaw nodded. How did the Outlaw know Tank? My head was spinning.

"The disease manifests itself differently in different bodies. Did you know this? I imagine you've met Carter's hired gun, the mercenary sharpshooter. I believe it's a woman, though I haven't had the pleasure of meeting her. She's a shooter, like Walter here. Like Troy used to be."

"What about the rest of your hit squad?"

"Well. Let's not spoil all the surprises. I'm not sure they even know themselves, yet."

"Contact!" Carla yelled from her perch above the market building. I was so entranced by the conversation that I jumped. "Movement on the roofs."

"Monitor and report," the Chemist replied. "Probably one of Carter's Chosen, but not the man himself. Carter would never be spotted on a roof top."

"Chosen?" the Outlaw asked.

"Carter calls us the Infected. An unhappy term. I prefer Chosen."

"What are you doing here, Chemist? Why do you need an army? Why do you need hostages?"

"I need hostages because of you, to put it bluntly," the Chemist smiled. "Your newspaper stunt has turned everything upside down. Not that I mind. In fact I thrive on chaos."

"Carter said you're building an army."

At the Outlaw's statement, there were murmurs of agreement within the ranks of onlookers. Someone fired a fully automatic weapon into a wall and they all cheered. Walter silenced them with a glare.

"Of course Carter said that," the old man said. "Don't be simple. He wants you...on his team."

"You are obviously building an army, Chemist."

"Don't be certain about things you do not know," he snapped in reply. "You know nothing. You are an infant, yet."

"I know you should leave these people in peace."

"Peace," he shook his head grimly. "You've obviously never walked this part of the city if you think they live in peace."

More shouting, more cheers, more gunfire. The crowd was growing restless.

"Doesn't matter, Chemist. You're not helping them."

"I'm not here to help."

"Then enlighten me," the Outlaw suggested and he spread his arms expansively. "Why all this?"

"Teach a newborn how to dance? Explain calculus to a toddler? I think not. Have you controlled your headaches?"

"I think so," the Outlaw shrugged.

"How?"

"I found peace. In a person and in a place."

"You found love," the Chemist nodded. "Love is the only hope for broken minds. The human psyche was designed to be loved and only then are we whole. And love will protect you from the coming insanity. Carter refuses to teach that to his spawn."

"Is that what you're doing in Compton? Spreading love and joy?"

"I'm here on a mission, boy. I bring with me purpose and community and I give it to those who have nothing. I don't offer my followers love, but I do offer them identity. Which is the next best thing."

The Outlaw asked, "What mission?"

"I will *teach* you that and many other things. You belong here."

"Teach me?" the Outlaw cracked. "How? You want me to move into your hovel and start snorting coke with the rest of your drug addicts?"

"The drugs would not work on you, Outlaw. Nor do they work on Walter. He tried. You would know this, if you had a guide."

"I don't need a guide."

"No one on earth needs a guide more than you," the Chemist pointed a finger wavering with emotion. "You're just now realizing that you've stumbled into a larger story but it's even bigger than you think. Trust me, Outlaw. You've stepped into a minefield and Carter will not help."

"Tell me why you're in Los Angeles."

"I'm here for the same reason Carter is," the Chemist replied.

"Which is?"

"We're here to harvest, Outlaw."

"Harvest what?"

"You haven't told him," the Chemist said quietly. "Have you, Carter?"

A new voice, one directly above our bus, barked, "Of course not. Don't be stupid, Martin."

"You are here to keep an eye on your protege?" the Chemist smiled. His name was Martin?

"He's not my protege," said the voice above. It was a gravely and sharp voice. "Kid's a damn nuisance, actually."

"You're still smoking," the Chemist said. "The habit of fools. I could smell your foul reek a mile away."

"Weird looking team you've assembled," the man on the roof said. "Buncha kids that can barely walk, thinking they can hide in shadows."

The Outlaw asked, "Why don't you two grumpy old men just kill each other?"

"I've tried," the man above said.

"We were imprisoned together in Turkey for several years," the Chemist sighed. "When we were younger. The Turks kept us weak through starvation, too weak to escape, too weak to kill each other, too weak to kill ourselves. Have you told him he's special, Carter?"

"He's not special. Neither are you. Neither am I."

"And how do you plan on killing me this time?" The Chemist seemed genuinely bemused and interested, like he was enjoying this. No one paid attention to the helicopters circling helplessly far above.

"I'm going to give drowning a try."

"This boy of yours seems authentically unspoiled. Perhaps we should leave him in peace?" the Chemist suggested.

"That's funny."

"I'm not joking," he said.

The man called Carter said, "It's funny because you don't know him. Kid's got a noble streak. He'd chase you around the globe. He'd never leave *you* in peace."

"Oh, very well. Tell him why we're both here, Carter."

"Yes," the Outlaw chimed in. "Please. This is crazy boring."

Carter jumped off the bus, which rocked gently, and landed near the Outlaw. The Chemist stood up cautiously. The audience of faux Outlaws hooted and raged, but Carter ignored them.

"I'd just as soon drag you to the ocean now, Martin," Carter said. He was a tall man. Completely bald, dressed similarly to Walter. Walter had a fresh rocket trained on him. "And tie you to a submarine."

"We're here for the Chosen that are emerging," the Chemist told the Outlaw. Carter had rattled the Chemist's dignity. His cool demeanor was tinged with anger and tension. I wanted to scream. Nothing made sense. "We're here for you. And for those like you."

"Where are these Infected coming from?" the Outlaw asked. He'd risen too, forming a triangle with the other two men. He kept glancing towards the bus, towards me. "Why am I Infected?"

The Chemist grinned triumphantly. "Your first good question of the night."

"Martin," Carter warned him. His voice was low and menacing.

The Chemist brought the staff down hard and sparks flew. He said loudly,

"You have changed, Carter. For the worse. You can't save him and you can't save the rest. And since when do you even care?"

"Perhaps I'm having second thoughts."

"Unlike you, I have resilience," Martin said. Several other faces were beginning to materialize out of the darkness above the mini-market. They weren't masked and they were sinister. They had the arrogant aggressiveness of Walter and Carla in their features. The good guys were wildly outnumbered. Assuming Carter was a good guy. "I have fortitude. I can finish what we started."

"*What* did you start?" the Outlaw asked in exasperation.

The Chemist looked at the Outlaw and said, "You're here because Carter *infected* you intentionally. At birth."

The Outlaw was visibly shocked.

"He's insane, hero," Carter said. "Our insanity grows as we age. Don't listen to him. Let's just take him now."

The Chemist spat, "*You're* delusional, Carter. You still think the boy is on your side."

The awful tension was briefly abated by a muffled roar, and then Tank burst through the side of the SUV! He pushed through the screaming metal but he was clearly woozy and unable to stand up.

"Outlaw," Tank growled, on all fours. The man in the mask was stunned. The audience laughed and mocked and fired celebratory rounds into the air.

"Carla," the Chemist called. "Hit the ogre with a lethal dose of the tranquilizers, please. It may kill him but at least it'll shut him up. And remind me to alter the troops' formula. We want our soldiers to have better control over their...animal instincts."

"Outlaw," Tank coughed, trying to fend off Carla. "Katie. On the bus. Get her out."

"He's still trying to save the girl," the Chemist howled in wicked pleasure and he brought the staff around in a singing slice that showered sparks into the gasoline. "Let's light the world on fire!"

"The girl?" Carter asked, and he whirled and stared at the bus, at me. Then his eyes went to the Outlaw. "You're here for *her*," he breathed.

Time started moving in awful split-second eternal frames.

Walter fired.

He missed; Carter was fast beyond belief. The rocket tore through our bus and detonated as it punched cleanly through the other side. The sound was deafening. Fire spilled onto the pavement and some of the smaller gasoline pools lit up.

Carter and the Chemist met in midair. Their elegance and civil words disintegrated into hate and they hammered each other savagely in a blur too fast for comprehension. It was ugly and horrible.

The Outlaw tried to reach the bus but Walter and Carla overwhelmed him. They both had knives and they pinned him down. The surrounding crowd of gunmen shrieked in tribal pleasure. More bullets hit our bus. A war was raging above the mini-market, silhouettes thrashing in the dark.

Chaos! Madness, pure and terrible.

"Katie MOVE!" the Outlaw screamed at me from underneath writhing bodies. The gasoline under the bus finally ignited, like a lake of fire. I stomped on the gas pedal and we lumbered forward.

I didn't see what happened but Carla cried out and was propelled fifteen feet into the air. Her arms rotated wildly to gain balance and she landed on the remaining shreds of our bus's roof. A passenger behind me screamed in terror and Carla laughed. Carla wasn't scared; she was mentally unhinged, drunk with excitement. Before she could move, a gunshot louder than all the others crushed her, flinging her from the roof. She landed in the fire but quickly rolled out, holding a bleeding shoulder. Who shot her??

I swung the HUGE bus through the intersection, away from the gunmen, and cried, "Everyone out!" I jammed buttons until the hydraulic doors protested and crashed open.

>>What are you people DOING down there??!

Dying, Hannah. We're dying. I rammed the bus against the overpass's support post, directly under the bridge. "Hannah!" I screamed. "Jump onto the bus! The gas is going to catch fire!"

Carter lost the fight. The Chemist had Carter by the throat with a gun pointed directly into his ear. They both had blood spilling out of their eyes and noses. The rest of the fighting stopped, which was good for Walter. He'd lost the fight too. The Outlaw let him go and he collapsed. No sign of the injured Carla.

"One final offer, Outlaw," the Chemist panted haggardly. With his chin he indicated the complete circle of guns surrounding the Outlaw. "But you'll have to ask politely."

"So if I want to live," the Outlaw said, "I have to beg?"

"More or less. Your place is here. With me."

The Outlaw raised his arms to the sides, like he was about to surrender. "No deal. Remember this, Chemist. Los Angeles is mine. And I'm coming for you." The night seemed drawn towards him, as though he held darkness like a blanket in his fist. He made phony guns with his thumbs and fingers, pointed them at the idiots in the masks, and said, "Bang!"

"No!" the Chemist cried.

The Outlaw jumped and disappeared into the night as a hundred guns erupted. I couldn't even watch. It was horrendous. The exhausted drug addicts tore into each other, mowing down the other side of the circle. It was meaningless carnage. The sound alone almost caused me to vomit. Blood and screaming everywhere.

The Outlaw landed silently on the bus's roof. I muffled a startled cry. He hurled something at the Chemist. I never saw what it was, just a blur. The Chemist's head snapped back from the impact, allowing Carter to stagger free. Before the white-haired man could recover, a phantom detached from the roof of the mini-market and collided with him. The phantom was a man dressed in black, like a shadow. The Chemist fought like a man possessed. More and more fighters were pouring into our intersection, fueling the fire. In confusion they were even fighting each other.

The Outlaw dropped next to me and said, "Time to go. This place is about to be overrun."

"What about Tank? He'll be killed," I said weakly, trying not to cry again.

"Who cares about Tank," he answered.

"I do."

He looked at me a long time while the war raged but at last he said, "For you, Katie, anything."

He turned to fetch Tank but…Tank was gone. He'd vanished. What…?!

"A fortunate turn of events," the Outlaw remarked. "I'd have surely died fetching that overgrown moron."

"Outlaw!" someone yelled from a nearby roof. "Move! Now!"

"We're out of here," he said, almost cheerfully.

"No wait!"

"Now what?" he sighed but I thought he was smiling. How could he be enjoying this?

"There's a girl named Hannah. She's stuck up on the bridge in her car."

"She can walk home. Actually that'd be really good for her," he laughed. "Besides, half a dozen police helicopters are about to show up."

"But she's stuck in a lake of gasoline."

"Oh."

I'll remember what happened next for the rest of my life. I saw it over his shoulder. The Chemist threw off the attacking shadow and started deflecting gunfire with his remarkable staff. He could actually move fast enough to block bullets!

Sparks flew from the staff. The sparks landed on gasoline, which ignited with a WHUMP! The trail of fire flew up the grassy hill towards the abandoned cars. Twenty miles of interstate were about to blow.

The Outlaw saw flames on the hill. I barely had time to scream before he pulled me onto his back and jumped.

My ability to focus was exhausted. Time lost all meaning. Only my throbbing heart marked it's passage.

We were in the air. Over the bridge. The fire was roaring, moving quicker than us. We reached Hannah's car. The vehicles began erupting, jumping in succession as flames hit punctured gas tanks. The Outlaw shattered the windshield with his fist. Where had Hannah gone? The flames were right behind us. Hannah was at the side of the bridge, one leg over the guard rail, six feet away. The flames were under us.

The Outlaw leapt for her. The tanker beside Hannah's car ignited like a bomb going off. The blast of unbearable heat flung everything into the air, including us. The Outlaw and I separated like rag dolls.

"Katie!" he yelled.

I looked down. Hannah was gone. Nothing but fire. Fire and falling cars everywhere. The bridge began collapsing.

I was falling through the sky above the intersection from hell. It was lit with fire and spotlights, like a demonic ceremony.

Then the Outlaw had me wrapped in a tight embrace. "Gotcha!" Something snapped and we jerked. A small parachute above us. I closed my eyes and kept them that way. The parachute worked well enough to pull us away from the fire but we hit the earth hard. My ankle popped.

Briefly, all was quiet. He simply held me. We were lying in thick grass. The distant sounds of war were muted by my ringing ears. Our enemies still fought each other.

Someone was coming. I didn't care. My thoughts were no longer lucid. I was being carried. Strange voices.

"Is she okay?"

"I think so."

"What's wrong?"

"…Hannah…she was on the bridge."

"The cheerleader? Oh no…"

"I couldn't get to her."

Silence.

"Okay, we have to go," he said.

"We're moving, Puck."

"Any sign of Carter?"

"None."

"Are you hurt?"

"Everything hurts. You?"

"All over. But Katie is safe. Other than what appears to be a broken ankle. And being blown up. And almost killed half a dozen times."

"Can't believe it. You got her out. Well done."

"We didn't get the Chemist."

"Not tonight."

"Until we do, no one in Los Angeles is safe."

"We?"

"Of course, we."

"Carter is going to have very mixed emotions about this."

I could no longer listen. Exhaustion took over.

Chapter Twenty-Eight
Wednesday, March 8. 2018

"Is he really dead?" Carter asked.

I was sitting on my front porch in the sunshine, reading a newspaper. I usually didn't read papers, but I figured I owed the LA Times after all the free publicity they granted me. The front page headline was **OUTLAW ASSUMED DEAD.** The helicopter cameras had lost track of the masked man after the big explosion. Complete incineration was the likely cause of death.

"I'm not sure yet," I grinned. "The Outlaw's a lot of trouble but I kind of like the guy."

"He was growing on me. Despite the stupid newspaper stunt," Carter said and he sat down beside me. "I hope he sticks around."

"I have to ask. Why do you always wear gloves? Tank does too. I can't figure it out."

Carter said, "Simple," and tugged off a glove. His hand was misshaped. Or...something. The fingers were blocky, and the bones looked like they were about to push out when he made a fist. "The virus causes it. Bones grow too big. Same with toes. The rest of the body hides the abnormal growth, but no such luck with finger and toes."

"Tank has it too?"

"Assume so. Kid's got some big bones. Doesn't happen to many of us. Virus affects us all differently. You just get back from the girl's funeral?" he asked, indicating my shirt and tie.

I nodded. Hannah Walker's funeral had been brutal. No body had been left to bury. Her mother could barely function. Our whole school had shown up, looking for ways to make sense of the nonsensical. How are people supposed to process video of a genuine superhuman battle? It was beyond belief but a large section of our city was being held hostage by a criminal mastermind with…super powers. The police had besieged his kingdom but could now only guess how to deal with him. This was both impossible to believe and also just fifteen miles down the road. I'd been there and I still couldn't fathom it. Like everyone else, I was walking around numb. A lot of people had died. One of them had been the most popular kid at our school. The secret of our breakup died with her. I cried my eyes out while everyone watched and I hadn't been pretending.

"This is probably a sore subject, but…" I said. "How did the Chemist get you in that headlock? I thought you had him."

"Bah," he growled. "That stupid stick of his. He's had it for years and I don't even know what it's made of. Hurts like hell, though," he said, rubbing the side of his head in memory.

"I saw him block gunshots with it," I shook my head. It had been a haunting sight. "How do you fight *that*?"

"He was showing off, mate. When you're as old as Martin you can *hear* the bullets coming and step around them."

"How many Infected you figure he had?" I asked.

"Seven, at the beginning. I think. He kept three with him at all times. Puck told me you killed one, that makes four. Shooter says there were three others on surrounding rooftops. And there was a pretty girl watching from a chair I can't figure out, so maybe eight."

"Troy died. And Martin shot one of his girls. So it's down to five. Did Samantha or your shadow kill any of them?"

"My shadow?" he grunted.

"Well, what the heck do you want us to call him? I won't pretend I didn't see your body guard."

"Shadow works," he sighed. "And Samantha thinks they got two."

"So he has three Infected left, maybe four."

"That we know of."

I said, "We got lucky. We didn't lose any."

"Not luck. Martin's recruits were young and inexperienced. Not ready yet."

"What a mess."

"I owe you an explanation," he said. "After what Martin told you."

"About time.

He lit a cigarette and smoked it silently for several minutes. I didn't mind. I had nothing to do. After the funeral Katie had gone to the hospital to visit Tank, who still hadn't woken from a coma.

Gosh I hate that guy.

Tank's involvement had been recorded by helicopter cameras, and by all appearances he *looked* like he was trying to save the hostages trapped in the bus, not just on a personal vendetta against the Chemist. The video showed him getting shot, but since he survived everyone assumed it was a wax bullet and the shooter was the infamous Sniper. Tank was being hailed as a hero, especially after his relationship with Katie Lopez became public knowledge. News channels were reporting on his condition hourly and his awakening would be a celebrated event in an otherwise depressed and shell-shocked city.

GOSH I hate that guy.

"Martin was telling the truth," he said finally. "You were intentionally infected with the disease at birth. So were a lot of other newborns during a sixty-day span at Glendale Memorial."

"That's why so many have suddenly been popping up," I observed. "And why they're all my age."

"Yes," he nodded. Smoke was leaking out of his nostrils as he stared off into the past. "Most of the kids died around puberty. A lot of them moved away, so we might potentially hear rumors of them around the globe soon. But the rest are here."

"Which is why the Chemist is here. He's collecting them."

"Yes. He's collecting them. We both are. It was a mistake and I regret it, and I'm fixing it the only way I know how. We thought it was too much work to track all the children growing up, but in retrospect we should have. Now we're just…looking for clues."

"Mathematically not many should survive, right?" I asked.

"He's figured out a way to preserve their sanity. He is using powerful medicine to keep them comatose for months at a time. Somewhere in Compton. That should increase his numbers. Might double the survival rate," he chuckled without humor. "Clever bastard."

"Great," I groaned. "What will he do with his growing squad of physical freaks?"

"Martin is arrogant. He creates chaos and draws power from it. He was the ruler of a small country in northeast Europe in the 50's. Arranged for his own assassination, and threw the entire country into chaos. Not sure it even exists anymore, now that I think about it. I'd forgotten about that debacle," he smiled as if in fond memory. "He's here for the attention and the chaos and the power. He doesn't have too much longer to live before his organs give out, so I bet he has something big planned. Whatever it is, we'll have to stop him."

"Did *you* infect me in the hospital when I was born?" I asked. "Like, stuck a needle in me?"

"One of us did, Martin or me. We're both licensed to practice medicine in all fifty states, so it was easy."

"You once told me you didn't know many medical terms," I remembered.

"I lied."

"I didn't think the disease was contagious," I frowned. "How'd you do it?"

"The virus is only communicable under the right circumstances."

"What are those circumstances?"

"I'll explain that," he said. His voice was fierce and earnest. I never saw him look worried before. "Soon. I promise. The only thing you need to know at the moment is that Martin will achieve those circumstances *again* in the near future. Unless we stop it."

"He'll be able to infect other children soon?"

"Correct."

"Carter. You suck. For a lot of reasons. Seriously. You should be in jail."

He nodded and said, "I'm making penance for past sins, kid."

"Sounds to me like all of Los Angeles could pay for them."

"Which is why I want the Outlaw to stick around," he said in a cloud of smoke.

"I will not be one of your stooges, Carter. You've strong-armed good people like Samantha and Puck into being your puppets. Not me."

"I'll call in some additional reinforcements." He ignored me, his white pointy teeth flashing. "And we could use Tank's help too."

"What?! Tank hates me. He hates you too!"

"Not as much as he hates the Chemist. We'll handle him with care."

"If he ever wakes up," I noted wryly.

"He'll wake up. I'm his doctor," he chuckled. "Best chance his brain has is to stay under a while longer."

"You're his doctor??"

"I didn't drag him out of there just to let him die, mate. When he's fully developed he'll be a big bomb to throw at Martin."

"Carter, you're the worst. Some of my friends will be here soon and I want you gone."

"Keep something in mind. I've got a short temper," he said and he stood up. He threw his cigarette butt into my lawn. "And I'll throw your dead body into the ocean if you cross me."

"I destroyed the listening devices you planted in my room," I growled at him.

"I always protect my investments," he shrugged. "I'll put more in soon. I don't want to be your adversary, Outlaw. Remember that. We're on the same side."

"Then act like it."

"Martin told you that you're special," he said as he started walking away.

"I remember."

"That's bad news for you."

"Why?"

"It means he wants you for his protege. Wants to be your mentor, a father figure, pass everything to you. And he'll stop at nothing. I'll explain more later."

"I don't care," I called. A black SUV pulled up. Carter got into the passenger side and it roared away. "But I am hungry," I said to myself. "For some chocolate."

My phone rang. Or, the Outlaw's phone rang.

"Yeah?" I answered it.

"Carter's driving away," PuckDaddy said. "What'd he say? Both Shooter and I are listening."

"Carter is the worst," I said.

"Yeah we know. What'd he say?"

"He wants the Outlaw's help."

"Woohoo!" PuckDaddy shouted. "I knew it! We're joining forces with the Outlaw!"

"Weren't we already on the same team?"

"Yeah but now it's official. Makes us cooler by association, dummy. Plus, he told us it was 50/50 whether he would kill you or not."

Samantha asked, "Is Katie coming over?"

"Yes," I said.

"Are you going to tell her that you're the Outlaw? That you're in love with her?"

"No way. Not while she's waiting for Prince Charming to wake up." I wanted to tell Katie so badly, but as usual Tank screwed it up. One of these days she'd see through his disguise. I hope.

She asked, "Are Cory and Lee coming over too?"

"Yeah, they're coming too."

"I'll be there in fifteen minutes."

"Great!" I said.

PuckDaddy said, "Leave your phone on! Puck wants to listen. Our lives are SO much more fun now."

"You people are weird," I smiled. "Puck you should come over too."

"I don't live near you, stupid."

"Oh yeah."

"But you're the first person that's invited me to hang out in ten years. This is a weird feeling," he said.

"I have to go. Here comes Katie. She's early," I said. She was limping down the street in a soft ankle cast. She looked so pretty I thought my heart would break.

"Of course she's early," Samantha Gear laughed. "She's in love with you."

The End

Epilogue
Excerpt from Katie Lopez's Journal

October 28th

Mami and I are wondering if we should pack up and move. The Outlaw recommended downtown Los Angeles be evacuated, and the city is now taking him seriously. Thousands of people are streaming east on the interstate. Probably more like tens of thousands. We live less than ten miles from downtown.

The Chemist seems unstoppable. I know the military is considering carpet bombing large portions of southern Los Angeles. The stories coming out of the Chemist's territory are hard to fathom. Wild men running like animals in the buildings. Cannibalism. Rampant drug use.

I think about my encounter with the Chemist often. I know I'm lucky to be alive.

What I remember most about that night is the Outlaw, especially our retreat. As we fled that intersection I heard two voices. The Outlaw's voice and a girl's voice.

One thought keeps surfacing. How did they know Hannah was a cheerleader?...

The story continues in…

The Sanctuary

Book Three of the Outlaw Series

Available Now!

Alan Janney…

-is married to a beautiful girl

-has two handsome boys

-used to teach high school English (brilliantly so)

-leads Young Life

-invites you to consider John 10:10 "I have come that they may have life, and have it to the full."

70429946R00146

Made in the USA
Middletown, DE
26 September 2019